I0673175

Larrikin Gene

B. R. Snow

A Damaged Po$$e Novel

This book is a work of fiction. Names, characters, places and events are either used fictitiously or are the product of the author's imagination. All right reserved, including the right to reproduce this book, or portions thereof, in any form. No part of this text may be reproduced, transmitted, downloaded, decompiled, or stored in or introduced into any information storage and retrieval system, in any form by any means, whether electronic or mechanical without the express written consent of the author. The scanning, uploading, and distribution of this book via the Internet or any other means without the permission of the publisher is illegal and punishable by law.

Copyright © 2013 B.R. Snow

ISBN-10: 0984967591

ISBN-13: 978-0-9849675-9-9

http://www.brsnow.net/

To Brian and Amanda

Thanks for the pig story. I hope I did it justice.

Larrikin

Australian - A boisterous, often badly behaved young man with an apparent disregard for convention. (1)

Gene

A portion of a DNA molecule that serves as the basic unit of heredity. (2)

1) Oxford Dictionary © 2012 Oxford University Press

2) The American Heritage® New Dictionary of Cultural Literacy © 2005 Houghton Mifflin

**

"Where do I stand on the question of nature versus nurture? Well, I have a science background, so I understand the powerful impact that genetics have on shaping a person's motivations and choices. On the other hand, when I fuck up, it's always easier just to blame my parents."

Merlin

Chapter One

I stared into the mirror at the man in the dark blue suit. It could have been any man, any suit. Unfortunately, for him, it just happened to be this man, that suit. And after three and a half martinis, the man's mood matched the suit's color. I studied him as he stood, removed and folded his jacket, and draped it over an empty barstool. He checked his hair in the mirror, brushed some stray hairs back in place, and sucked in his stomach. He cast a slow furtive look around the bar then sat back down.

I almost felt sorry for the man in the blue suit. I often manage to find some degree of sympathy for men like him. At first glance, that might appear to be one of my better traits. Actually, it's just me looking for my good side.

Soon the man in the blue suit would firmly believe fate had brought me to this bar, at this time. In fact, not only would he believe it, he would tell me so. Somewhere into his next martini, he would turn his head towards me, touch my arm, and speak in hushed tones in an attempt to display confidentiality and a sense of intimacy. But I would know that the softness of his voice was designed to conceal weakness. And fear.

He would profess genuine gratitude and pronounce eternal friendship in the manner that only sad drunks have truly mastered. He would be verbose, then morose. Charming, then sullen. One minute, a playful young boy. And then he'd dissolve into a world-weary old man. And at the exact moment when he truly believed I was the best friend a man like him could have, I would order another round and make my move.

For I was far from becoming this man's best friend. The savior role he had in mind for me, even at this early point in our *friendship*, was misplaced. But misguided men, driven by ego and a misplaced sense of their own destiny, make bad decisions all the time.

Perhaps when surrounded by bank statements or the comforts of their chosen profession, they feel less vulnerable.

Perhaps when surrounded by others of their own ilk, they feel more protected.

Perhaps others surrounding them simply don't notice. Mirror images offer true reflection only to those searching for it.

Perhaps.

I finished the last of my martini, sucked the pimento from the olive, and ordered two more with a casual wave. The man in the blue suit slumped forward and ran a hand through his dwindling hair. The creative comb over on display earlier had disappeared and two large bald spots threatening a merger shined under a bank of overhead lights. He wiped his hands with a napkin and sipped from his fresh martini before it even had time to get comfortable on the bar.

I lifted mine by the stem and savored the frigid stream that trickled down my throat. The first taste of frostbitten Grey Goose, like one's initial encounter with any fresh object of desire, was always the most satisfying. No matter how much pleasure one took from the overall experience, after the initial sensory overload, everything was pretty much downhill from that point forward. I carefully returned my glass to its place of honor on the bar and swiveled ninety degrees.

**

"I know, John." I nodded in sad agreement. "I know exactly what you're talking about."

John forced a smile and refocused on his drink.

"Most people would spend all night debating that."

He glanced over at me. "Debating what?"

I nodded at his drink. "Whether your glass is half full or half empty."

"I always thought that it was a good question. Which is it for you?"

I smiled as he bit the hook. I decided to let him run and tire himself out before reeling him in.

"For me, John, that question has always been irrelevant. The real issue is about control. Most people go through life debating half-empty, half-full with pop culture concepts they've picked up from self-help books. And if you get advice from a book someone else has written, that's not self-help, that's help."

"That's good."

"I was quoting George Carlin."

"I love Carlin. I saw him at the MGM in Vegas one time and he did this bit about-"

"Yes, I know, John." I placed a hand on his forearm. "But I want you to stay with me. Okay?"

"I'm *with* you, buddy. I'm with *you*."

"Good. As I was saying, most people don't get what I'm about to tell you. Whatever amount is in the glass is completely under your control. Too much in the glass? Pound that baby back. Drain it dry. Not enough in it? Order a fresh one."

"Just like that?"

"Just like that."

"Are you telling me it's my round?"

"No, John." I laughed and squeezed his forearm. "What I'm telling you is that you control everything. You have the power to control how much is in your glass. Except, of course, with one very big exception."

He looked up at the ceiling then glanced back at me and held my stare. "Love?"

"Precisely. Love. In the end, it's the only thing that really matters to people of substance. Sweet, but evasive.

Tender, but heartbreaking. The eternal quest beaten back by the demands of daily life."

"Amen."

"Yes. Amen, my brother. But even prayer has failed you on your quest for love. Hasn't it, John?"

"Yes," he whispered. He drained his glass and waved a finger in the direction of the bartender.

I looked away as he dabbed a napkin at the corner of one eye. This close to closing the deal, I didn't want him embarrassed. I needed him strong and decisive. Let him feel weak and powerless on his own dime.

I waited until the fresh martinis arrived then recaptured his stare in the mirror. "And when everything including prayer fails, you're forced under cover of darkness to confront the question all of us face at one time or another."

He turned his head towards me and waited.

I took a slow sip of frostbite.

"What's the question?"

"Is this all there is?"

"Yes." He nodded and exhaled. "Yes, that is the question isn't it?"

"And it's at that precise moment, in that perfect moment of clarity, when the question of whether the glass is half-full or half-empty becomes meaningless. If you've got the wrong glass, John, why would you care how much is in it?"

"That's so true."

"I know you, John. I meet men like you all the time. It's my business to meet men like you. And when I meet them, do you know what I do?"

"No," he said, raising an eyebrow.

"I help them, John. I help them."

"That's very nice of you."

"Well, thank you, John. That's nice of you to say. Would you mind if I told you a little bit about yourself."

"I wish somebody would."

4

I slowly began to reel him in. I tested the hook. Secure. He wasn't going anywhere. "Right now, you're at a point in your life where you should be jumping out of bed at the crack of dawn every day."

"But I do," he said. "Well, actually I don't jump. Lately, it's been more of a crawl."

"That's precisely my point, John. You should be on top of the world but you feel like life has nothing to offer. Despite your success, you feel like you're wasting away. You're getting up at five because you feel you have to, not because you can't wait to see what the day will bring."

"How do you know that?"

"Like I said, John. It's my business to know. You're in your thirties. You've killed yourself getting to this point. And now the people in your firm believe that even if you don't walk on water, you at least know where all the rocks are. You've got a nice place on the Westside worth in the neighborhood of three million. You've got the Jag or the 740 for work, and the SUV for weekends just to show everyone you're still a regular guy. You go to Vegas and stay at the Bellagio because they make you feel like a high roller. You usually take along some fresh wannabe starlet with juices sweet enough to put in your coffee. But in the back of your mind, you know she's only there because it's a free weekend and maybe, just maybe, you'll spring for a new boob job. And after giving her a couple grand to gamble, then dinner and a show, she fulfills the unspoken demands from her side of the deal."

"And cocktails."

"What?"

"Don't forget all the cocktails."

"Well, sure. That goes without saying. Try to stay with me here, John."

"I'm *with* you. I'm with *you*."

"Finally you're there. And it's fresh and new. But mid-stroke, you're either trying to convince yourself she's

5

worth the effort or you're fantasizing about Peggy Sue from high school who took your cherry in the backseat of your father's Ford."

"Chevy."

"What?"

"It was a Chevy. Dad worked for GM."

"Chevy. Got it. Stay with me here, John. So while you're sipping your nightcap in solitary because she just had to have a shower, you smile to yourself and say *at least she's not a hooker*. Because you've convinced yourself that you've never paid for it before in your life. Haven't you, John?"

"Yes," he said, nodding. "I've never paid for it."

I smiled and sipped my drink. It was deteriorating rapidly. I motioned to the bartender.

"Can you please shake what's left with fresh ice?"

The bartender nodded and left with my glass. Moments later he returned with a fresh glass of frostbite. I took a sip, found it lacking and turned back to my new friend. He, too, was in desperate need of fresh ice.

"Every one of those weekends, unless you get lucky at the tables, costs you around ten large. Maybe more depending on how much shopping you let her do. In a year those weekends, plus the other trips to Europe and Hawaii, end up costing you, what, maybe a hundred grand? I hate to say this, John. But you've been paying for it for a long time. "

I fell silent and went back to my drink. Through the mirror I watched him chew on his lower lip.

"But what you crave is one woman," I whispered. "One woman you could be sure loved you. Someone you'd be happy to spend all your money on and spoil rotten."

"Yes. I do."

"I do." I smiled. "Your deepest desire is to be able to repeat that phrase in the most traditional of settings. To find a woman who's beautiful and smart. A woman you can

6

have an intelligent conversation with. A woman successful in her own field. Not a wannabe, but an already is. Someone mature. Someone who can captivate a room full of heavyweights over dinner then take you home and fuck you like a whore. Someone who wants you inside her, not out of obligation, but just because she loves it. Needs it. That's what you crave, John. That's what you need. That's what all of us need, John. And all you have to do is have the courage to change the glass."

"Change the glass."

"I have that glass, John."

He suddenly turned all business and swirled his glass in front of him. I waited patiently. I was about to pull him into the boat and didn't want any extreme movements that might snap the line or let him wriggle away. I sipped my drink and waited out the silence.

"I don't know," he said. "Twenty-five thousand is a lot of money."

"Yes, it is." I placed a hand on his shoulder. "But tell me, John. How much money have you spent the past five years looking for the right woman?"

"Probably half a million," he whispered. "Maybe more."

I whistled softly. The bartender glanced up from his magazine and caught my eye. I shook my head and he disappeared back into the World's 50 Most Beautiful People.

"Half a million? Jesus Christ, John. If you're looking for a way to blow your money on cheap thrills, cocaine's cheaper."

"So, if I sign up what guarantee do I get?"

"You get a guarantee that I will personally identify three extraordinarily successful and beautiful women who fit your personality and lifestyle perfectly. You will mutually decide what type of first date the two of you would prefer and, once I am satisfied that the logistics are finalized to both parties satisfaction, you're on your own."

"That's it?"

"That's it? Let me ask you, John. How many women like the type I just described have you met, let alone gone out with the past year?"

"I meet successful and beautiful women all the time."

"Let me rephrase it. How many have you met that are not only available, but are looking for exactly the same thing you are at this precise moment in time?"

"None."

"None." I drained my martini. "Change the glass, John. It's time to change the glass."

Chapter Two

Merlin stared up at the night sky wishing he could be out there somewhere in the universe hanging around with Summerman and Murray. Or even downstairs amid the endless clanging of slot machines.

Anywhere but here.

Hedaya, the octogenarian casino owner Merlin and Doc were ostensibly working for at the moment, shook his head in Doc's direction then glared at the diminutive man sitting to his right.

"Are you listening to me, Merlin?"

"Well, I'm certainly hearing you, Hedaya. But I don't have much of a choice about that, do I?"

"Hearing, listening. You make a distinction between the two?"

"Certainly. Listening implies intent to understand." Merlin sipped vodka and smiled at the old man. "But yeah, I hear you, Hedaya."

Normally slow to anger, Hedaya flushed red and grabbed a cigarette from Doc's pack. He blew smoke skyward, dropped both elbows on the table and leaned forward. "I really don't like you."

"Get in line." Merlin drained his glass and waved it at a nearby waiter.

Doc motioned for another drink and lit a cigarette. Worn down by another day of the two men's ongoing battle, he rubbed his forehead.

"So what do you have to say for yourself, Merlin?"

"I'm going to need a little clarification here, Hedaya." Merlin accepted a fresh drink from the waiter and took a sip. He stared back up at the night sky and sighed.

Hedaya shook his head and took a long drag on his cigarette. "Doc, help me out here."

"What am I supposed to do, Hedaya? You two have been going back and forth about this for weeks."

9

"But he's wrong," Hedaya said. "He's totally wrong and he knows it. But he's too goddamned stubborn to admit it."

"I'm rarely wrong, Hedaya. Misguided at times, but rarely wrong." He flashed a smile and drained half his drink. "Besides, you should have thought about this sort of thing happening before you started skimming millions for your democratic China wild goose chase."

"Goose chase? Look you little bastard. How many times do I have to explain it to you? It's not skimming. It's an investment."

"Tomato, tom*ah*to, Hedaya. Frankly, I don't give a shit why you're doing it. You can open a chain of Chinese restaurants with it for all I care."

"And stay out of my personal business." Hedaya turned to Doc. "He's been hacking my personal emails."

Doc beat back a smile. If Hedaya had a clue about what else Merlin hacked into on a regular basis, he wouldn't be worrying about his email. "Merlin, have you been hacking Hedaya's email account?"

"No, I haven't been hacking," Merlin said, fixated on a shooting star. "They were simply...redirected."

"Bastard." Hedaya crushed out his cigarette and sat back with his arms folded across his chest.

"She must be good, Hedaya."

"Merlin-" Doc said.

"A little risky just for some horizontal mambo, but you're old and rich so why not, huh? It's probably as good an investment as your skimming operation."

Hedaya slowly rose to his feet. "She's just a friend...who also happens to work for me. Now you listen to me, I want you out of here. Tonight. You're fired."

"Nothing would make me happier, Hedaya," Merlin said. "Just clear it with Samuels and I'll be out of here faster than I can change your password."

Hedaya took a deep breath and exhaled. The mention of Samuels took away most of his steam. Hedaya knew Merlin and Doc weren't going anywhere until Samuel's objectives had been met. And that meant another four or five months with Merlin as his Chief Information Officer. Hedaya then did something he'd never done before. He snapped at his good friend Doc.

"This was your idea. So fix it. Either get control of this little prick or I will."

Doc glanced up at Hedaya and nodded. "Okay, Hedaya. I'll do my best."

"You'll do better than that, Doc. I said fix it. Good night, gentlemen." Hedaya wheeled and strode towards the elevator that led from his private rooftop garden to the casino below.

"I thought he'd never leave," Merlin said, extracting a small glass bottle from his shirt pocket. Doc watched as he meticulously wiped down a small section of the glass table with a sanitized wet wipe and dried it with a clean napkin. Merlin chopped and drew out two large lines of coke and devoured them. He returned the bottle to his pocket, sniffed twice, and took a large sip of vodka. He leaned back in his chair and stared up at the stars. "Much better."

"Merlin, you gotta lighten up with Hedaya."

"Yeah, I know. But he loves to push my buttons and I can't help pushing back."

"We've got a long way to go and I'd like to enjoy it."

"I'm sorry, Doc."

"So you've been reading his email."

"Yeah. I still don't know how he figured it out. I must be slipping." Merlin cocked his head in Doc's direction. "Don't you want to know who he's doing on the side?"

Doc thought for a moment then nodded. "Yeah, actually I do."

"Your little FBI friend who works for him."

"Grace? You're kidding me."

"No. It started about a month ago. She caught him at a weak moment one night and since then they've been hooking up a couple times a week."

"Unbelievable. Her fiancé doesn't know, does he?"

"I doubt it. She seems to be the type who doesn't kiss and tell. And as we both know, Gentry's pretty clueless."

"Hedaya and Grace," Doc said, sipping his drink. "I wonder what his motives are."

"From what I can tell from the emails, his are strictly prurient. But he's pretty conflicted about sleeping with an FBI agent, especially one who seems to love poking into other people's business."

"He put that in an email?"

"No, I've got his therapist's office bugged."

Doc shook his head and sighed. "You're a piece of work. But what the hell, more power to him. Hedaya's in his eighties and he's sleeping with her? We should all be that lucky when we're his age."

"You should be that lucky at yours."

"I was. Well, one time. I have to admit I'd love a return visit."

"They're spicing up their sessions with a couple bottles of Perrier-Jouet, opium and Viagra." Merlin chopped two more lines then looked up at Doc. "Of course, she probably adds something to the mix as well."

"Well, sure," Doc said, flashing back to his lone session with Grace. "That goes without saying."

Chapter Three

My suite at the Pasadena Ritz Carlton was immaculate. Whatever training programs the hotel used to maintain that standard, while making guests believe they were doing the hotel a favor, not the other way around, should be bottled and sold. If there is one thing I understand is what constitutes good service. And what makes customers keep coming back. Despite whatever judgments you make of me as we move forward, one of my strongest proficiencies rests squarely in my understanding of the black and white of human behavior.

My choice to work and live in the gray zone is another matter altogether.

My current business, like most others, can be boiled down to two seemingly simple, yet increasingly complex concepts; understanding human behavior, and having a solid grasp of how to make the numbers work. It doesn't matter to me if it's perfume or dog food. Just convince me the numbers work and turn me loose to influence or cajole, chastise or praise, make laugh or cry, or exude sorrow or joy.

Of course, that's assuming I would ever work on behalf of a perfumed dog food pusher. And if you've been paying attention up to this point, I think the answer to that question is pretty obvious.

Tonight, I'm tired. The grind of the past fourteen months has finally overtaken my physical and mental capacities. My attention span has dwindled, my patience shot. Fortunately, a lengthy vacation looms on the horizon and it beckons, offering sun hot enough to melt your skin and beer cold enough to crystallize your tonsils. Australia awaits my return, and I'm increasingly forced to tell her to be patient. I'm on my way, Oz. It won't be long. Keep a cold one handy.

Los Angeles is my last stop on this bizarre and lucrative leg of my current odyssey. I have other tasks before I can enjoy the delights that only Oz offers, but the end is squarely in my sights. The City of Angels-and I can't help but wonder what those who bestowed that moniker would call their beloved city today-is the thirteenth and final leg of what I've cynically dubbed the Sleeping Sheep Tour.

After an initial stop in New York that lasted six weeks due to startup issues, I've spent a month in twelve other cities. Tour stops have included Boston, Chicago, Atlanta, Miami, Austin, St. Louis, Seattle, Las Vegas, San Diego, San Francisco, and San Jose. Each city was full of wonderful people and offered countless local diversions, but I was unable to enjoy any of them. Someday I hope to revisit many of these cities on different terms for different reasons and I hope to discover what makes millions of people consider them worthy of permanent residence.

Twelve hours a day, six days a week. An impressive output even by the most demanding of corporate expectations. Monday through Saturday I worked the phones, did advance work for upcoming tour stops, worked the numbers, and drank martinis with men virtually identical to the man in the blue suit. And then on Sunday, I only did what we agreed to do, which was usually nothing. For Sunday was ours alone. In the not too distant future, I'm hoping it will be Sunday every day.

Chapter Four

Doc ended the call and leaned back in his lounge chair. Merlin took a final look at the report he was reviewing and tossed it into his work bag. He waved at a waitress and looked at Doc who was staring off into the distance.

"Who was on the phone?"

"Samuels." Doc grabbed a towel and wiped sweat off his face.

"I hope you sent him my best."

Doc smiled. Merlin and Samuel's enmity was deep and shared.

"Actually, he's very happy with the progress on the replacement system."

"He oughta be happy," Merlin said, accepting his drink from the waitress. He signed the tab and dismissed her with a quick wave. "Between keeping Hedaya's systems humming and managing the project team at Langley, I'm working around the clock."

"And yet here you are sipping cocktails."

"Well, maybe around the clock is a relative term."

"Samuels wants us to be ready to move as soon as we're done here. You still think the new system will be ready to go sometime in May?"

Hedaya's long-term plan to fund a democratic uprising in China had included getting his hands on a bootleg copy of the Company's extremely secure software application called Run Rabbit Run. Doc and Merlin had uncovered the software along with the rest of Hedaya's plan several months ago. And to avoid both public embarrassment for the Company and keep an eye on Hedaya's activities, Doc had devised a way for he and Merlin to remain in Vegas until Merlin and his project team could build a replacement system. Merlin had also reluctantly agreed to serve as Hedaya's interim CIO until it was complete. Merlin hated the job, but it was the perfect cover. Doc was here to keep an eye on the overall operation as well as keep Hedaya and Merlin from killing each other.

"You still here?"

"What?" Doc said.

"You drifted off. The voice talking to you?"

Doc chuckled. "No, he's still being quiet. I was just thinking."

"I said that May is still looking good. I can't wait to get out of here."

"Yeah, I know. Me too."

"Any ideas about how we're going to get at Whitley?"

"Not yet. It won't be easy. Especially since both you and I know him."

"What about Summerman?"

Doc considered the possibility of using their new business partner, a part-timer who lived in the spirit world nine months out of the year but returned as human during the period of the summer solstice. Both Doc and Merlin were still trying to get their head around the strangeness of that, but they'd both been convinced during Summerman's visit the previous summer. Before he'd departed for the other side, Merlin, Doc, and the part-timer had joined forces in a still fledgling operation. And the prospect of getting out of Vegas meant that they could finally get started on what promised to be an interesting, and highly lucrative, operation.

"I'm sure we can use Summerman in a lot of areas. But we can't run the risk of using him as the front guy in case we run out of time and he crosses back over."

"So we need to find a fourth posse member?"

"Yeah, that's what I've been thinking."

"We'll need to find somebody very comfortable working outside the rules."

"Yeah."

"And it'll have to be someone we can trust."

"Probably."

16

"You know any criminals you trust?"

Doc laughed. "None come to mind. But if we can't find someone we can trust, at a minimum, we'll need someone we're able to control."

"Makes sense. Someone with a lot to lose."

"Exactly. An accomplished crook looking at some serious time in prison would be perfect."

"Maybe Gentry could give us some leads," Merlin said, laughing.

Doc laughed along. "You know, that's not a bad idea. Let's keep our eyes open and see whose life he's trying to make miserable these days."

"You think we might find somebody right here in Vegas?"

"An accomplished crook with a lot to lose hanging around Vegas? You gotta like those odds, Merlin."

Chapter Five

I selected my current business after being surrounded by malcontents on a daily basis. Incredibly prosperous people who should have been glowing were miserable. I got up in the morning and saw them on the TV. Every time I turned around, I saw them on the news. I heard them on the radio. I saw them in the grocery store. I watched them in restaurants and bars, at weddings and funerals, at the beach and in the mountains. Then I coined the phrase that best described it for me.

The urban malaise of the corporate captive.

Several years back I first noticed it posed as a question. *Is this all there is?*

From that question it transitioned into a defiant statement of self-identity and self-worth.

I want something more.

Eventually, the media caught up and turned it into a societal phenomenon with the marquee; *America's Growing Discontent.*

Then it turned into a whine.

And when the well-to-do started whining, I knew I was on to something.

I started working the numbers. And the numbers worked so well I originally thought I had missed something. But the numbers spoke for themselves. There were hundreds of thousands of single men who fit the profile. All I needed was a screening tool, now refined to a simple twenty-one question survey that took two minutes to complete, some readily available background information, and my ability to understand the black and white. And it certainly didn't hurt that working in the gray had become second nature.

As well as my preference.

Out of the hundreds of thousands of men who fit my target market, I only needed a hundred and four. Eight men per city. Twenty-five grand each. Roughly two and half million over the year. After advertising and living-well expenses, I was sitting on just over two million net. Even tax-free it isn't rock star money, but it sure beats what the Vice President of West Coast Marketing for Eau de Fido makes.

And has to do.

By now, you're probably wondering about the women on the other side of the transaction. The ones paired with the men on these arranged, high-end first encounters. Quality women looking for a spark or the jolt of joy that could end their own malaise. The ones searching for, if not their one true love, at least a partner worthy of spending the balance of their lives with. You're probably asking yourself where the women who participate are.

That's a very good question.

And you're not alone. I've been asking that question all evening.

Because she's late.

**

The knock woke me from my unscheduled nap. I looked down at the can of Diet Coke still resting in my hands and wondered how long I'd been out. I opened the door and yawned hello to the bell captain. I watched him organize three suitcases and hang two garment bags in the closet. I handed him a twenty that generated a smile and he backed towards the door, cart in tow.

"She said to tell you she'd be right up. She's downstairs reading."

"Reading?"

He shrugged and stuffed the twenty in his pocket.

"Okay. Thanks." I waved and closed the door.

Wanting to help, yet cognizant of her privacy, I ignored the suitcases and proceeded to clear some closet space. I sat down and reviewed this month's schedule. I tossed it aside moments later when I heard the door open.

She stepped inside the suite and closed the door without looking up from her reading. She smiled down at the page then at me and waved casually. She shrugged her shoulder bag down her arm, caught it with one hand, and tossed it into the corner, her eyes never leaving the page. More intrigued than jealous, I watched as she worked her way across the room and sat on the edge of the couch. I studied her face for movements that revealed emotion. Delight appeared prominent, but intermittent flashes of confusion and concern flashed through her eyes as her forehead wrinkled, then relaxed.

"Oh my," she said, folding the letter and slipping it into the back pocket of her jeans. "What a sweet letter."

"More fan mail?" I stared at the television.

"Does my baby want some attention? Is that the problem? Have I've been ignoring you?"

She laughed as she approached from behind and nuzzled the back of my neck. Her arms draped my shoulders and she gently scraped her fingers across my chest. I pulled her petite frame to one side of the chair then deposited her in my lap and kissed her.

"I missed you," she mumbled through the kiss.

"Me too. You're late."

She settled into my lap and helped herself to my Diet Coke.

"Yeah, I know. Dinner ran late last night and I missed the red eye. So I slept in then did some shopping."

"What happened at dinner?" I said, trying to remember who'd been scheduled.

"The architect." She rolled her eyes. "You remember him?"

"The one from Oakland?"

"Yeah, Mister Self Important. I swear this guy has the same five stories he must tell on every date."

I remembered the bald, lumpy forty-two year old with the Napoleon complex.

"He's got one story about his dog to let you know he understands unconditional love. He's got another one about his ex-wife to let you know that he's not afraid of commitment. Two more stories about his house and cars to let you know he's got money. And like every other man on the planet, he got the other story."

"The one about his mother."

"Of course. She must be a piece of work. This guy's convinced he's God's gift."

"Despite what you see in the mirror, Wilbur, you're a six foot stud."

She laughed and nuzzled my neck. "I went as the redhead just to torture him."

"That was cruel. Poor bastard."

"Yeah, I know. But he's a total shit. I wore that slinky black cocktail number with the spaghetti straps and topped it off with a temporary tattoo of a snake above my left breast. Whenever I leaned forward, the snake's head would poke out. It drove him nuts, but at least it saved me from listening to any more of his nonsense that I had to."

"Another satisfied customer."

"I guess," she said, getting up to grab two beers from the minibar. "He was all over me at the table so I kept ordering drinks. For a little guy he handles his booze pretty well, but around eleven he went face down into his tiramisu. I faked indignant and caught a cab back to the hotel."

I laughed and took a sip of beer. "I wish I could tell you that this month's crop was any better."

"Not tonight, baby," she said, yawning. "I'm tired and officially off the clock. And tomorrow's Sunday. And you know what I always get on Sunday, don't you?"

"Anything you want."

"Anything I want."

"I've created a monster."

21

"Yes." Tears welled up in her eyes.

"What's wrong, baby?"

"It's nothing. Take me to bed."

**

There are many wondrous ways to begin a day. And many glorious sights to see in the early morning light so powerful, that no matter what ill winds blow throughout the remaining hours, a day of greatness has been secured. I have seen sunrises around the globe with colors pulled from a palette I didn't know existed. I have stood awestruck on mountain tops overwhelmed by my own special place in the universe, yet simultaneously dwarfed into insignificance. I have walked magnificent, desolate stretches of beach one minute calm, the next windswept by forces unseen and unimaginable.

All these magnificent things and more remain forever burned into memories, yet nothing compares to waking next to the naked form sleeping beside me. I slowly pulled back the sheet and, again, fully understood the success of our current venture.

Our success comes from our client's desire to experience the same feelings and range of emotions I have developed for her over the past year, feelings captured eloquently in song and verse for centuries. But it doesn't come from any physical intimacy our clients have enjoyed with her.

At least none that I'm aware of.

I caught myself staring at the long lines of her back that curve into round firmness and eventually recede into taut upper thigh. She stirred from the chill of the air conditioning and I returned the sheet.

After a long shower I pulled on the plush terrycloth robe that will serve as my wardrobe for the day. I grabbed the Sunday paper from the hallway outside the suite. I returned

22

to the bedroom and found her naked staring out the window.

"You look beautiful."

She beamed and kissed me softly on her way to the bathroom. I heard the shower hiss and took my cue to order breakfast. It arrived twenty minutes later and we spent the next hour nibbling and reading in silence.

"Only four weeks to go," I said, peering around the sports section.

"Shhh. It's Sunday."

"I'm aware of that. But-"

"I know. We have a lot to talk about," she said, selecting another section of the paper. "And we will. But for now, I don't want to talk about anything."

I leaned forward to pick up the business section, but paused when I saw the photo staring back at me.

"He looks familiar."

She didn't move, but I sensed her discomfort. She put the paper on her lap. "It's James Whitley. He was one of the New York group."

I rolled the name around in my head and tried to remember. But New York had been a year ago and my memory failed. "No, I got nothing. I remember the face though."

"He was the guy trying to take his company public. He's in high tech."

"Yeah, now I remember. He makes guidance systems for missiles." I sipped my coffee. "You said you liked him. I thought he was a total asshole."

"Yes, I know you did. He's a nice guy. Actually, I'm amazed he slipped through your screening."

"My screening tool is never wrong. And the next time you see the latest collection of innocent bystanders bombed into oblivion, try to remember how this guy makes his money. Trust me, he's an asshole."

"I guess it takes one to know one."

"What?"

"Assholes," she said, reaching for her bagel. "Sometimes you're a big one."

"Well, sure. That goes without saying." I scanned the article. "It looks like he's hit the big time. A billion and a half. That's a big number."

"Yes," she said. "It is."

"All he needs now is the right woman, huh?"

"Yes, so he keeps telling me." She put the paper down and got up from her chair. "I think you should take me back to bed."

**

Normally, I would enjoy the irony of the moment when a self-proclaimed expert in human behavior is caught totally unprepared to deal with an unexpected turn of events. Except when that self-proclaimed expert happens to be me.

I'm sure there's plenty of irony to go around right now and, at some point in the future, I'll probably find it. Perhaps I'll even enjoy it. At the moment, however, I'm stunned and more than just a little pissed off.

"Don't yell at me."

"You can't be serious." I sat down on the edge of the bed. "Why?"

"You know the answer," she said, staring out the window.

I sat searching for whatever answer she obviously believed I already knew. Several possibilities raced through my mind and were all quickly discarded. Even if I did have the answer, I was not in the mood to help prove her point. I focused on what I did understand and stared at her robe and tried to visualize the curves tucked safely inside.

"It's just a job," she said, tugging at the terrycloth belt. "I'm just going to work for him."

"Don't bullshit me, Emily," I whispered. "That's the one thing we agreed we would never do to each other."

"Okay." She turned away from the window. "I'm sorry. But it's partially true. Technically, I will be working for him."

"He hired you on some phony consulting gig just so he can keep an eye on you before you marry him."

"Phony? I do have the MBA from Wharton or have you forgotten that?"

"No, I remember. It's just that if it wasn't for me, you'd still be hustling pool for fifty bucks a game."

Her eyes flared. She then relaxed and smiled as she leaned against the wall enjoying a memory.

"Whatever happened to the woman who said she could never go the corporate route no matter how much they paid her?"

"She's still here. And I'm not going the corporate route."

"No, I guess you're not. But corporate *wife* is a pretty close second wouldn't you say?"

"You're such a prick sometimes," she said, gnawing a slice of melon from the rapidly deteriorating fruit salad. "This needs fresh ice."

"Don't we all?"

"Look, I have no idea what's going to happen. But if I do ending up settling down with him, so what?"

"Settling." I spit the word out. "An interesting turn of phrase. I thought settling was what you did when you accepted less than what you wanted."

"Gene. Please stop."

"But I guess that's a tough call when the guy is worth a couple billion."

"It's more about lifestyle than the money and you know it."

"Yeah," I said, spreading my arms out to take in our surroundings. "You really need to do something about improving your lifestyle. A person could really waste away living like this."

"Yes, one could waste away," she said. "In a jail cell."

"That's what this is about? You're worried about going to jail?"

"The thought has crossed my mind, Gene."

"We haven't broken any laws," I said, shrugging my shoulders. "We've delivered everything we promised these guys."

"Jesus Christ," she said, shaking her head. "You really believe that don't you?"

"Of course I do."

"Twenty five grand for three dates with the same woman, Gene? Is the word fraud even in your vocabulary?"

"A minor detail," I said. "Besides, these guys are never going to admit they used our service. That would be too much of a hit to their ego if it got out. Nah, that doesn't fit the profile."

"The profile?" she asked. "Screw your profile, Gene."

"It worked pretty well for you didn't it? It got you your Magic Man."

"I'm done with this conversation."

I stretched out on the bed and stared at the ceiling. "I guess if you kiss enough frogs, eventually one of them is bound to turn into a husband."

Chapter Six

James Whitley grew up poor and chunky with a devout interest in science and engineering. Poor and chunky were more than enough to doom him socially, but it was his devotion to expressing how much smarter he was than everyone else that guaranteed the daily ass kicking he received from an equally devoted group of jocks. And the occasional misguided physics teacher.

Desperate for any human contact that didn't include clenched fists and steel-toed boots, James joined a college fraternity of like-minded geeks and nerds. Giving himself the nickname, Straight A. Whitley, his self-aggrandizing nature left even his most socially challenged fraternity brothers running from the library. Straight A soon became known around campus as Straight A-Hole Whitley. This was later shortened to A-Hole Whitley. Clarity and brevity were finally achieved when James became known across campus as A-Hole.

But it was his organization of a 1950's style panty raid that forever doomed A-Hole to fringe dweller status in college. Noticing what he believed to be several pairs of female panties hanging in the bedroom windows of the off-campus apartment next door, A-Hole led a group of six timid members of Sigma Phi Delta on a late night mission. The men's swim team was, at first, bewildered by the sight of the geeks from next door wearing their Speedos on their heads, but they quickly recovered. And the subsequent ass kicking delivered by members of the 1,000 meter relay team remains legendary.

Social acceptance arrived slowly and was directly correlated with the arrival of his first million. A-Hole soon discovered that people tended to avoid attacking if there was a good chance you'd be picking up the check.

Now, moments away from the one signature that would catapult him into the economic stratosphere, A-Hole

Whitley's lifelong dream of money and a woman to share it with had come to fruition.

Chunky, however, remained an on-going challenge.

**

Summerman and Murray drifted down and came to a stop outside the 58th floor. They hovered, then glided forward towards the window and peered inside at the two men sitting on either side of the massive desk. Murray looked at Summerman who nodded. They passed through the window and hovered about five feet over the desk.

Sir Bentley Carruthers shivered and looked across the desk at Whitley. "Do you feel a draft? The temperature just dropped about ten degrees."

Whitley stopped staring at the pen in Sir Bentley's hand long enough to glance around the office. "I think you're right. That's odd."

"Damn maintenance people." Sir Bentley picked up the phone and barked. "Shirley, tell those people downstairs that if my office temperature isn't back to seventy-three in five minutes they can all go home and not bother to come back." He rolled the gold pen back and forth in his fingers and smiled at Whitley. "I love moments like these."

"Making someone's dream come true?"

"No, making people like you wait until you start worrying that I might have changed my mind." Sir Bentley gave Whitley a blank stare then laughed. "I'm just kidding. Relax. You look like you're going to explode."

"It's a lot of money," James said.

"Of course it's a lot of money. I don't do small deals."

**

"Well, now we know where Sir Bentley is getting his missile guidance technology from."

28

"Yeah, I guess if you can't make it or steal it, you're left with having to buy it."

"You make a good point, Murray."

Yeah, I know. It is odd isn't it? When we're on this side, Murray and I are able to talk to with each other. I'm still not sure if it's a human language we speak over here.

Maybe, by design, spirits all speak the same language.

Maybe it's a telepathic thing.

Maybe I've just learned to speak dog.

**

Whitley continued staring at the pen twirling in Sir Bentley's hand. He leaned forward and glanced back and forth between the pen and the man about to give him over a billion dollars. He licked at a trace of spittle forming on the corner of his mouth.

"You look like my Springer Spaniel waiting for me to throw her tennis ball," Sir Bentley said, his hand inching towards the contract sitting on the desk. "Well, let's get this over with." His pen hovered over the signature line. "Oh, yes. I almost forgot to ask you."

"Yes?" James stared at the pen again twirling back and forth in Bentley's fingers.

"Your upcoming nuptials."

"What about them?"

"It's the real deal, right? I won't tolerate any sham marriages in my executive ranks."

"Oh, it's real, sir. But I'm still not clear why my being married had to be part of the deal."

"Let's just say I'm a bit of a traditionalist."

"But you're divorced, sir."

"That's a vicious rumor. I'm not divorced…I'm separated. There's a big difference." Sir Bentley placed the pen back in his pocket and leaned back in his chair.

"Hedaya was right. This guy Bentley is a total prick."

"You think Doc and Merlin are onto this guy Whitley?"

"Well, I'm sure Hedaya has been following the deal. And assuming he and Merlin are speaking to each other, I'd bet they're starting to take a look at him."

Murray started scratching and I shook my head as his image turned into a vapor whirl then reemerged when his fruitless efforts at finding the imaginary itch stopped.

"Murray, why do you even bother with that over here?"

"Force of habit. Damn, I can't wait to cross back over. I miss scratching."

"And Guinness."

"Well, sure. That goes without saying."

**

"Yes, I understand, Sir Bentley. A temporary separation brought on the demands and pressure of work." Whitley stared longingly at the pen. "I'm sorry. And I'm sure the two of you will work things out soon."

"Hmmmm." Sir Bentley stared out the window and put his hands behind his head.

"And I'm sure the problem is with your wife."

"Well, certainly. That goes without saying." Sir Bentley placed his elbows on the desk and leaned forward. "So what's she like?"

"Who?"

"Your fiancé. Who the hell do you think I'm talking about?"

"Oh, she's…nice. Smart and quite funny. Not as funny as me, but I think one cut up in the family is plenty. And funny is highly overrated."

"Yes, I can see that," Sir Bentley said. "How are her other talents?"

"Other talents?" Whitley's forehead wrinkled as he considered the question. "Well, I know she cooks a little…her meatloaf is quite good. She's got an MBA and I think she plays piano."

Sir Bentley rolled his eyes. "I was referring to how she is in the sack."

"The sack? Oh, that. Well, up to this point, I'd have to say she's pretty well covered."

"Got all the bases covered, does she? Good for you."

"No, actually I meant literally. She's well covered. Head to toe."

"Really? You mean the two of you haven't…?"

"Had intercourse?"

"Had intercourse? You're a real romantic, Whitley."

"I'm a bit inexperienced in that area, sir."

"I see. And what about her?"

"What? Her level of experience in the bedroom?"

"No, her position on IMF policy. Jesus, Whitley. I thought you were supposed to be an expert in…*missile guidance.*"

Sir Bentley waited for a laugh but received a blank stare.

"To be honest, sir. I can't speak with authority about her experience with intercourse."

"I see. So you're saying she's a bit of a traditionalist as well?"

"One would hope, sir."

Sir Bentley shrugged, removed the pen from his pocket and leaned forward. "Let's get this over with." He scribbled his signature, put the pen back in his pocket, and shook his hand. "Welcome aboard, Whitley. I hope you've got an airtight pre-nup."

"I don't believe in those, sir."

"Neither did I."

"You being a traditionalist and all?"

Sir Bentley frowned. "Yeah. Something like that."

31

"Can we go now?"

"What's your hurry?"

"I want to head back to Cannes. There's a French poodle that's been coming on to me."

"She hasn't been coming on to you, Murray. She's scratching the back of her head."

"Yeah, but every time she scratches and reemerges, she's flashing me. Trust me. She knows what she's doing."

I laughed. Although on this side it was hard to tell since laughter gets muffled and lost.

"Cannes, huh? What the hell, I guess I wouldn't mind spending a few days hovering around the beaches."

"Good. You want to race?"

"No, a leisurely hover is more my style."

"You're getting old, Summerman."

"You're one to talk."

Murray cocked his head. "This Sir Bentley is the sneaker guy, right?"

"That's him."

"I've never liked his stuff."

"What? His sneakers?"

"Yeah. They always leave a funny taste in my mouth."

Chapter Seven

Merlin rubbed a piece of romaine between his thumb and forefinger and studied the waiter standing next to the room service cart.

"Lettuce double rinsed?"

"That's what they told me in the kitchen, sir."

"You can't believe anything those people say." Merlin turned his attention to the chicken. He tore off an end piece and nibbled.

"Chicken cooked to 175 degrees?"

"Yes. But Chef Louie wasn't happy about doing it. He says anything over 160 ruins it." The waiter glanced at his watch.

"Does he now? Well, Chef Louie can eat his chicken right out of the fridge for all I care. No raw egg in the dressing?"

"No, sir. No raw egg. Will that be all?"

Merlin took one more look at his plate then glanced at Doc who was already halfway through his club sandwich. "You got any questions, Doc?"

Doc continued chewing as he shook his head and waved goodbye to the waiter.

"Thank you, sir." The waiter nodded at Doc and made a beeline for the door.

Doc grabbed a piece of bacon that had fallen onto the floor and gulped it down. "I'm surprised they still deliver to you."

Merlin stared wild-eyed at Doc's bacon rescue. He refocused on his salad. "They don't have a choice. Delivering food to people like me is what Hedaya pays them to do."

"There are no other people like you, Merlin.

"I'll take that as a compliment."

"I'd be shocked if you didn't," Doc said, taking another bite of his sandwich. "Of course, if he was that mad at me,

I'd be worried that Hedaya might also be paying them to spit on my food."

Merlin poked his way through his salad with a fork and scanned the Romaine for signs of foreign objects. He shrugged and took another bite of chicken.

"If people paid more attention to what they put in their bodies, this country would be a lot healthier."

"Maybe they could start by putting the nutritional value of cocaine on baggies."

"You're pretty funny for a burned out spy." Merlin started working on his salad.

"What did you find out about Whitley?"

Merlin slid a folder across the table. Doc flipped it open and began reading.

"I already know he's selling his company."

"Keep reading," Merlin said, wiping imaginary remnants away from his mouth with a fresh napkin.

"A billion five…the buyer is some conglomerate based in Italy. Growing at thirty percent a year the last three years." Doc glanced up. "Merlin, this was all in the newspaper."

"Jesus, Doc. Just keep reading will you? You're worse than a little kid sometimes."

Doc refocused on the folder and fell silent. Merlin chewed salad and stared out the window as he waited.

"Son of a bitch," Doc said.

"Indeed."

"How did you find this?"

Merlin stopped chewing and gave Doc a blank stare.

"Never mind. Forget I asked," Doc said, refocusing on the document. "Sir Bentley Carruthers owns the Italian weapons company that's buying Whitley's company?"

"Yup."

"Are you sure it's the same one?"

Merlin drew out two large lines and Doc watched them disappear. Merlin sniffed twice and wiped his nose. "How many Sir Bentley Carruthers do you think there are, Doc?"

"But what the hell does he think he's doing? He's been on Samuels' shit list forever. Five years ago, Bentley was lucky to get out alive.

"I know. I remember Samuels telling him to stick to making sneakers."

"Samuels is going to go ballistic when he finds out," Doc said. "You haven't told him yet, have you?"

"Giving Samuels bad news is your job."

"So Sir Bentley is acquiring missile guidance technology."

"Yeah. And two questions come to mind." Merlin poured two vodkas over ice and handed one to Doc.

"What sort of weapons is he planning to use it on?"

"Very good," Merlin said, sipping his drink.

"And, more importantly, who's he planning on selling them to?"

"You are on your game today."

"I have my moments." Doc closed the folder and slid it back across the table.

Merlin glanced at it then back up at Doc. "You got mayo all over it."

"I'll get you a new one." Doc swirled the ice in his glass with his finger. He caught Merlin's look of disbelief and chuckled. "So how was the chicken?"

"Actually, it was a little dry."

Chapter Eight

The back of the limo was dark and silent. In the past, we would have taken full advantage of the luxury and privacy the vehicle provided and the parking lot the 101 had become would have been seen as a blessing. Not cruel and unusual punishment.

"You didn't have to take me to the airport."

"I have an appointment at nine so I'll just take the limo from there to the restaurant."

"That should impress him."

"Yeah." She fell silent and stared out the window.

I looked at her and did my best not to marvel at her beauty. For her date with the Man in the Blue Suit she'd selected what I had dubbed her South American look. The jet-black wig cascaded over her shoulders and didn't stop until it reached her waist. Her eyes, now emerald green, sparkled despite the darkness of the limo. A tiny beauty mole highlighted one corner of her mouth. Her skin was golden brown from the tanning lotion I'd watched her apply for the last time a few hours earlier, all the while fighting the urge to grab her naked, lithe body and pull her into bed. Borderline-tart eyelashes completed her transformation and, despite my sadness, I smiled. Even after all these months, I was still amazed by her ability to become someone else.

"Have you slept with him yet?"

"No." She sighed and looked up at the sky through the open moon roof. "Well, just a little."

"Just a little? What the hell does that mean? Does his guidance system have a problem with early launches?"

"Very funny." She glanced at me then back up at the evening sky. "Don't be mean."

"Sorry. Just curious." I chewed on my bottom lip. "But you're going to? More than just a little."

"Yes."

36

I nodded, more to myself than her. I felt the limo surge forward, then stop.

"Thanks for finishing up here. I appreciate it."

"There's only three scheduled. If I double up a few days, I can finish in a week."

I pondered how casually we had both agreed to wrap up our work. A year ago, the concept of leaving over a hundred thousand dollars on the table would have been inconceivable. Now it seemed like chump change. Amazing how one year can simultaneously change a person's life for the better and worse.

"How long are you going to be in Vegas?"

"Not long," I said. "Probably no more than a week."

"What about Christmas?"

"I'm going home to see my father. I exchanged our tickets to Hawaii this morning."

Even through the darkness I could see her tears welling. I choked out my next question.

"What about you? Where's the Magic Man taking you?"

"We're still talking about it. He wants to go to Maui, but that's not going to happen."

"Don't worry, you'll get there someday," I said. "Maybe he'll end up buying it for you."

"Gene," she whispered. "Please. Don't."

"Okay." I sunk deeper into the thick back seat. "I transferred the rest of your money into your account this morning."

She looked at me and smiled. "I still can't believe this actually worked. Who'd have thought, huh?"

"Me," I said. "That's who."

The limo started moving and was soon traveling at a speed I knew would end our trip far too soon. I looked at my black haired beauty and felt another wave of emotion.

"I could stop," I said. "You know that don't you?"

"When?"

"Two, maybe three years tops."

She slumped back in the seat. "Wrong answer, Gene."

"I just need a few more years," I said. "That's all."

"I can't do it. I mean, I've done it and have to live with that. But I just can't do it anymore."

"Is that fear I'm hearing," I said, smiling. "Or just a guilty conscience?"

She smiled back, the smile she saved just for me, the smile I would miss the most.

"Probably both," she said, crossing her legs. "But just in case you're wondering, forget it. I'm keeping the money."

I laughed and touched her hand across the divide. "I'd be very disappointed if you didn't."

"I love you, Gene."

"I know. But don't worry, you'll get over it."

Chapter Nine

"No. I need an 800 number account. Not eight hundred individual phone numbers."

I switched the phone to my other ear and motioned to the bikinied waitress working the pool. Vegas was going through an unseasonably hot December and all the non-gamblers were taking full advantage.

"So I can do this over the phone? That's great." Back on hold, I grabbed my wallet from my bag and looked up at the waitress who stood over me blocking the sun.

"You're burning," she said, balancing a full tray of drinks. "You should put some lotion on."

"Good advice. But I already have plenty of that. What I need is another Bloody Mary. Thanks."

"Breakfast of champions, huh? I hope you're not planning on driving later."

"Only an inner tube."

"Promise to stay in the slow lane?" she said, laughing.

"Yes, Mom."

"Call me, Grace."

"As in state of?"

"So they tell me."

I dismissed her with a crisp twenty. Despite my current pledge of being sworn to heartbreak-induced celibacy, I caught myself staring at her sway as she walked off.

"Yes," I said. "That's me. Yes, that's correct. Good. Yes, just charge the card. What's that? Three days? Really? No, that's not a problem. It just seems like an odd policy. Thanks. You too."

I tossed the phone into my bag. "Background check," I said, shaking my head. "Knock yourself out, guys."

The waitress reappeared and handed me my fresh drink. I savored the initial sip then slid it under my lounge chair.

"Are you having any luck at the tables?"

"I don't gamble," I said.

"You don't gamble? Why on earth would you come to this ungodly place if you don't gamble?"

"Work."

"Do you mind if I ask what you do?"

"At the moment, I'm in telecommunications."

"Yeah, sure you are," she said, one hand on her hip. "And I'm a struggling neurosurgeon."

I stared up at her. In another time, another place, I could have made her a very rich woman. Unfortunately, for her, the timing was wrong and the game had changed.

"You're funny. I like that."

"That's not all you'd like." She wheeled on her platforms and strolled off.

I took a long sip from my drink, returned it to the shade then dove into the pool. I crossed the width of the pool underwater in one breath, surfaced, and repeated the process. I spread my arms on the edge of the pool for balance. I put my sunglasses back on and realized my drink was out of reach. Enjoying the water more than the alcohol, I stayed in the pool and rested my chin on the edge.

"Gene? I'll be damned. I thought that was you."

I craned my neck up at the sound of my name and recognized the man standing directly above me.

"Roger Gentry." I climbed out of the pool to shake hands. "Jesus, what's it been? Ten years?"

"At least," he said. "What are you doing in Vegas?"

"What do you think?" I said, laughing.

"Yeah, I get it," he said, nodding at the pool filled with partying women. "I guess some things never change."

We sat down in adjacent lounge chairs and sized each other up.

"You just come from the golf course?"

"No, I'm working today," he said.

"I should probably apologize for not knowing. Who do you work for?"

"The FBI."

40

I blinked and hoped he didn't notice. "Good choice. I hear crime is a growth industry." I managed a small laugh. "Not the way I would have gone."

"No, I imagine you wouldn't, Gene." He flashed a fake smile. "What are you up to these days?"

"Not much really. I just can't seem to find myself. You know?"

"No. I don't."

Same old Roger. Mr. Personality: If any of you have lost a large stick, I have a good idea where it might be.

"So you're assigned here?"

"Yeah, the Bureau believes in going where the scumbags are," he said, ignoring three scantily clad women brushing past our chairs. "Are you going to make it home for Christmas this year?"

"As I matter of fact I am."

"That's good. Me too." The sun's glare was only partially blocked by his shoulder and I caught myself squinting.

"Let's try and get together for a beer."

"I'd like that," I said. "Are you staying with your folks?"

"Yeah. Give me a call. And be sure to say hi to your Dad for me. I was sorry to hear about your Mom. She was a saint."

"Thanks. I appreciate that. Maybe I'll see you over the holidays."

"Oh, I'm sure I'll be seeing you soon, Gene. You take care."

I accepted his outstretched hand and watched him stroll towards the casino. I tried to categorize my encounter with my childhood acquaintance turned FBI agent as pure chance, but it nagged like a toothache. I reached under my chair, drained my Bloody Mary and tried to catch my breath.

Chapter Ten

"Jerome?"

"Yeah. Who's this?"

"It's the Owl."

"The Owl? No shit?"

"No shit."

"Wow. Cool. Can't believe I'm actually talking to the Owl."

"Just don't spread it around, okay?"

"Sure. No problem. What's up?"

"How you'd like to be on TV?"

"Huh?"

"Television. A commercial."

"You're joking, right?"

"I never joke, Jerome."

"Sure. I can understand that. What's the commercial about?"

"It's about my betting system. I'm doing a big push before the Super Bowl. And I've got a new book coming out so I'm doing some marketing before it gets published. I'm personally calling some of my best clients and asking them if they'd mind doing a short testimonial about how they've done using my service."

"How they've done? Man, I've won seventeen weeks in a row. I'm looking at buying a new house after the Super Bowl. Of course I'll do it. I'd love to be in a commercial."

"That's great, Jerome. Thanks for that. I'll need you to be in New York on Monday."

"New York? Yeah, I can do that. It's not far from here."

"Great. I'll send you the all the information along with the check."

"Check?"

"Yes, the check for doing the commercial. Is five grand okay?"

"Five grand? Just for the chance to be on TV? You bet it's okay. It's way more than okay."

"You've earned it, Jerome."

"Me. I ain't done anything. All I do is read your emails and make the bets. So I'm finally going to meet the Owl, huh?"

"No, Jerome. I'm afraid I'll be tied up." I was convinced that, if I ever got caught running this betting scam, any jury would acquit me just to reward me for the scam's brilliance and elegant simplicity. But I wasn't going to push my luck by putting my face on it. "Plus, I try to keep my public appearances to an absolute minimum."

"Sure. I get that. The mob, right?"

"Yes. And a potentially unruly one at that."

"What?"

"Nothing. Make sure you smile for the camera, Jerome."

"Will do. So who do you like in the playoffs this week?"

"Just wait for the email, Jerome."

"Got it. And thanks again."

"No thanks necessary, Jerome. I couldn't have done it without you."

I put my phone away and headed downstairs. The unusual weather was holding and it was still hot. On my way to the pool, I walked through the casino and studied the crowd. I leaned against a wall that provided a view of the sports book. It was broadcasting a handful of meaningless bowl games, plus horse racing out of Florida and California. Even with these low marquee events, the room was full and loud. Every bit of action seemed to make half the room happy and I shook my head at the idea of wagering one's hard earned money on a group of young kids and horses of indeterminate age.

I took a seat at one of the bars that ringed the casino floor and waited for the bartender. Eventually, I caught his eye and he strolled over.

"Morning. Bloody Mary, please."

"You got it," he said, grabbing a large glass. "You drink for free if you play." He nodded at the video poker games built into the bar. "Are you going to be playing?"

"No, just drinking," I said, reaching for my wallet.

"Then that'll be four fifty."

Finding only a stack of hundreds, I handed him one which he unceremoniously accepted. He made change and strolled to the other end of the bar. I sipped my drink and swiveled in my chair.

"I thought that was you." A middle-aged man sitting with a young attractive blonde at a nearby table was pointing in my direction.

I tried to put a name to the face. He got up and walked towards me leaving the blonde by herself. She seemed grateful for the break.

"It's Jerry," he said, shaking my hand. "Jerry Goldsmith from Boston."

"Jerry," I said, chastising myself for presuming I'd have anonymity in Vegas. "How have you been?"

"Great. Just great." He nodded his head in the direction of his table.

"She's gorgeous," I said, accepting his cue.

"Yeah," he whispered. "She's been a little standoffish, but I think I'm wearing her down."

"Well, you did impress me as a man who doesn't take no easily."

"You got that right," he said, waving to the blonde. "I never got a chance to thank you."

"Thank me? For what?"

"For setting me up with those three women. Man, you were right. They were incredible." His eyes sparkled from the memory. "Of course, I never got past dinner with any of them. But that was okay. Man, I would have killed to get that redhead naked but what are you going to do?"

"So you didn't get anywhere with any of them and you're still thanking me?"

"Of course." He sat down on the stool next to me and snapped his fingers at the bartender. "Grey Goose martini. Very dry."

Out of the corner of my eye, I caught the bartender's expression. I smiled and sipped my drink. Moments later, the bartender, his face more frozen than the martini, placed the drink in front of Jerry Goldsmith from Boston.

"I've got that one," I said.

Jerry Goldsmith from Boston picked up his martini and sipped it slowly. He sighed with delight and put the glass back down on the bar.

"Now that brings back some good memories. Do you remember that night in Boston? I got hammered on these."

"That was a good night," I said.

After seven martinis, he had grabbed our waitress's ass, punched a bartender, and almost got arrested. That was the moment when Jerry Goldsmith from Boston had decided it was time for him to settle down. I'd put him in a taxi and left with his check for twenty five thousand in my pocket.

"I learned a lot from those three dates."

"Really?" I was surprised to find myself genuinely interested. "How so?"

"Those three were simply out of my class. Now don't get me wrong. You delivered everything you promised and more. But a man has to know his limitations. And having a woman like any of those three on a permanent basis would be a lot of work. Know what I mean?"

"More than you'll ever know."

"What?"

"Nothing."

"They were all so goddamned *smart*. I'd never be able to get anything past them."

"You mean like lying and cheating on them?" I said, laughing.

"Exactly." He downed his martini and clapped his hands together. "This one's really hot," he said, nodding in the

45

direction of the blonde. "But I think she might be a little dumb for me."

Jerry," I said. "She's dating you. How dumb can she be?"

"Yeah." Jerry Goldsmith from Boston pondered my question. "You're absolutely right. Well, I better get back? Nice seeing you, Gene. Merry Christmas."

"Merry Christmas, Jerry."

"Who was that?" The bartender grabbed the empty glass and wiped away all signs of the previous occupant.

"That was Jerry Goldsmith from Boston."

"Friend of yours?"

"No."

"Lucky you. What an asshole. Man, I swear, there are thousands just like him everywhere you look."

"Fortunately," I said, draining my Bloody Mary.

I watched Jerry Goldsmith from Boston whisper in the blonde's ear. She took a deep breath, forced a smile, and trudged out of the bar allowing herself to be towed by one hand. I adjusted my hat, put my sunglasses on and headed for the pool.

Chapter Eleven

Hedaya, looking very much like the contented billionaire he was, leaned back in his chair and put his feet up on the ottoman next to his desk. Rose fluttered her eyes at Merlin and rubbed her foot against his calf. Merlin inched his way down the couch and stared out the window. Satisfied that everyone was in their usual place, Doc took a sip of vodka and lit a cigarette. He shook his head at Merlin's ability to remain doggedly asexual in the midst of Rose's constant affections and called their standing weekly status meeting to order.

"Okay, Merlin," Doc said. "What have you got to report on the Casino side?"

"Nothing." Merlin continued to stare out the window.

"Nothing?" Hedaya said.

"What can I say, Hedaya? From a technology perspective, this place is humming. Thanks to me, I might add."

Hedaya exhaled loudly and stared up at the ceiling.

"Merlin is doing a wonderful job, Uncle," Rose said. "He's a gem. Don't you agree?"

"Yes, my dear…a real gem." Hedaya poured himself a glass of wine. "Or an unformed lump of coal I'd like to squeeze the shit out of."

"I heard that," Merlin said.

"Guys, please. Not today," Doc said. "On that happy note, let's move on to an update on the new system for the Company. Where are we at, Merlin?"

"We're about two weeks ahead of schedule. That's great news if we can maintain that pace. I'll be able to get out of here that much sooner."

"Maybe there is a God." Hedaya stared at the ceiling and stretched out in his chair.

"Stop it," Rose said. "Let's not talk about anyone leaving, okay?"

Doc exhaled cigarette smoke and waited.

"Go ahead, Doc," Hedaya said. "I'll try to restrain myself."

Doc took a sip of vodka and opened the folder Merlin had provided.

"What do you know about James Whitley?"

"The guy selling his company to Sir Bentley Carruthers? Not much. If you like, I can have my people take a look."

"Don't bother, Hedaya," Merlin said. "I've already done it."

"Of course you have," Hedaya said. "By all means, enlighten me."

"There's not much there. He's your basic asshole who got lucky. Now that he's bought the company, Sir Bentley is going to put Whitley in a box and do whatever he wants with the technology."

"What he wants is to sell miniaturized shoulder-fired weapons to the Chinese government they can use in their outer provinces on anybody they feel isn't toeing the party line. And with the addition of Whitley's guidance system, they will be incredibly accurate. You two need to stop him."

"Just like that?" Empty glass in hand, Merlin laughed on his way to the bar.

"Yes, Merlin," Hedaya said, "Just like that. Isn't that your job?"

"Actually, Hedaya, it's only one of several I have at the moment. But if I didn't have to spend so much time dealing with your shit, maybe I would have some bandwidth to save the planet from itself."

"Merlin, knock it off," Doc said. "Hedaya, it's only been three days since we found out that Sir Bentley even owned the weapons company. And it was Merlin who figured it out."

"A simple thank you would suffice," Merlin said.

Hedaya glared at Merlin, but remained silent.

"We're thinking that infiltration of Sir Bentley's operations might be a possibility," Doc said. "But we're going to need to recruit a new person."

"I see," Hedaya said, propping his elbows on his desk. "Can't you do it?"

"No, I'll be playing a different role if our plan comes together."

"What about one of your previous colleagues from the Company?"

"We thought about it, but Samuels is against it. And I agree with him. Our new operation-"

"Your posse?"

"Yes. Our posse's approach is to work outside authorized channels. While we're happy to help and take their money, we don't want any...interference."

"What skill set are you looking for?"

"I'm thinking we need someone with a...flexible moral compass. Someone comfortable living and working in the grey space."

"You're looking for a crook," Hedaya said, laughing. "Well, I'm sure I can help you out with that."

"Too late," Merlin said, tossing a folder on Doc's lap. "I've already found him. Gentlemen, meet Gene Wagner."

Doc and Hedaya stared at Merlin, who shrugged his shoulders.

"It was easy."

"I told you he was a gem," Rose said, squeezing Merlin's thigh.

Merlin squirmed away to the end of the couch. Doc perused the folder and raised an eyebrow in Merlin's direction.

"How the hell did you find all this?"

"You asked me to look into who Gentry, our friend from the FBI, was focused on. Well, now you know."

"But this says the Feebs are looking at him for a land scam he was involved with in Florida years ago."

Merlin shrugged. "So the Feds are a bit behind what he's up to these days. What else is new?"

Hedaya leaned over Doc's shoulder and read from the file. "I've seen this betting website advertised. The Owl." Hedaya laughed. "Some people will believe anything. Even that they can make money betting football."

"The Owl website?" Rose said. "He's so cute. I just love him."

Doc and Merlin stared blankly at each other.

"It's the cartoon character featured on the website," Hedaya said.

"I know," Merlin said. "I've seen it. And I have to say it's a pretty cool scam. He's impressed me. And you all know how hard that is to do."

"Yes, we know, Merlin," Hedaya said.

"How's he working it?" Doc said.

"He started off with a couple hundred thousand people at the start of the football season. He's down to only a handful of people who are still standing."

"The half-life scam?" Doc said.

"Yeah. And he's worked it to perfection."

"Half-life scam?" Rose said.

"He selects one game a week and sends half the people an email about why Team A will cover the spread. Then he sends a different email to the other half about why Team B can't lose," Doc said.

"And each week, the total number of people who continue to win gets cut in half," Merlin said. "By the end of the season, the people left standing have won seventeen weeks in a row."

"And the odds of that actually happening are astronomical," Hedaya said. "Is he making any money on it?"

"Yeah, twenty-five bucks a call."

"Not a fortune. But still major fraud if he gets caught," Hedaya said.

50

"Maybe, maybe not," Merlin said. "It looks like he's only charging people when they win. Technically, I'm not sure he has actually committed fraud. Apart from the fact that the thing is a total scam." Merlin chuckled and selected an olive from a dish on the coffee table. He examined it closely before putting it in his mouth.

"I think this could be our guy," Doc said.

"Oh, he's our guy. No doubt about it. But if the Feds make their case about the real estate deal in Florida, he's looking at time in Federal prison."

"Maybe, maybe not." Doc lit a cigarette. "If we need it, we'll see if Samuels can earn some of his money."

"But the really interesting thing this guy has done recently is a high-end dating service scam. I'm not sure how he worked it yet, but he pulled down a couple million this year. But he only seems to have kept half of it."

"He's got a partner?" Doc said.

"That would be my guess," Merlin said. "But, so far, I'm coming up empty."

"How do you do this, Merlin? Where on earth do you find this stuff?"

Merlin smiled at Hedaya. "It's what I do, Hedaya. At some point, I'll share some secrets with you."

"Will you now?"

"Sure, Hedaya. But I'm not sure when I'll get around to it so, if I were you, I'd just do what I do."

"What's that?"

"Keep checking your email."

Rose's giggle was cut short by Hedaya's glare. Merlin examined another olive and took a small bite.

"I guess we better have a word with him then," Doc said.

"We better hurry," Merlin said. "Right after the Super Bowl he's headed to Australia. He booked two first class seats about a month ago."

"A woman going with him?" Doc said.

51

"No, he's taking his father."

Doc sipped his drink, deep in thought. "Maybe the old man is his partner."

"His partner in a dating scam? Really, Doc?"

Doc glared at Merlin, but said nothing.

"That's a nice thing to do," Hedaya said. "You know, take his father on a trip like that."

"Maybe," Merlin said.

"How so?"

"Our Mr. Wagner spent some time down under a few years ago."

"And?" Doc said.

"He was…dabbling," Merlin said.

"Dabbling?" Hedaya said. "He was involved in another scam?"

"Well, he certainly wasn't spending all his time surfing."

Doc exhaled and shook his head at Merlin. "Did you get up on the wrong side of the planet this morning? Jesus, Merlin, knock it off."

Merlin nodded and sipped his drink. "His old man once did time. But he went straight several years ago. Now that he's widowed, maybe he wants to get back in the game."

"When did the wife die?" Doc said.

"A couple years ago at least," Merlin said. "I can't remember exactly. But it's in the file."

"Interesting. I guess it's a possibility," Doc said. "Like father, like son."

"Nature vs. nurture," Rose said. I've often wondered about that question." She arched her back which threatened to destroy the buttons on her silk blouse. Doc snuck a peek at the stretched fabric. Merlin, bored, stared out the window.

"I'm definitely the genetic offspring of my uncle." She winked at Hedaya. "But surely the environment you've provided has had a major impact on me."

"My dear, you would be successful regardless of environment," Hedaya said.

"That's because I have your genes."

"That's true," Hedaya said, laughing. "How about you, Merlin?"

"Where do I stand on the question of nature versus nurture?" Merlin sipped his drink, deep in thought. "Well, I have a science background, so I understand the powerful impact that genetics have on shaping a person's motivations and choices. On the other hand, when I fuck up, it's always easier just to blame my parents."

Chapter Twelve

"Back so soon? People will talk."

My favorite waitress was back, sassy as ever.

"Bloody Mary?"

"Yes, please." I peered over the top of my newspaper then put it down when I caught sight of the hotel's Saturday uniform. "They don't actually let you swim in that thing do they?"

The hand went back on her hip and she smiled in mock indignation. "And what's wrong with this outfit may I ask?"

"Not a thing," I said, now having full permission to conduct a more comprehensive inspection. My eyes lingered then met hers. I was greeted by an expression I recognized immediately. "You look great."

"Good answer." She laughed and strolled off.

My phone rang and I reached into my bag while still enjoying the view. I found it on the fifth ring.

"Hello. Hey, Dad. I'm glad you called. Say, what's the statute of limitations on starting to date again after a breakup?"

"That depends," he said. "Do you want be seen as one of those sensitive types, or do you just want to get laid?"

I laughed into the phone. "So, how are you doing?"

"I'm good, but bored shitless. If this town gets any deader, we're going to have to dig a big hole and start tossing dirt."

I sat up in the lounge chair. "Are you behaving yourself?"

"Yes, I'm behaving myself. You sound just like your mother." His voice softened. "Rest her soul. So what happened with Emily?"

"She couldn't take it, Dad."

"Well, you'll have to tell me all about it when you get in." I recognized his subtle warning of *not on the phone* and nodded.

"I will," I said. "I'll call you from the road."

"Okay, son. Can't wait to see you. I love you."

"Love you too, Dad."

I tossed the phone back into my bag. When I looked up an outstretched hand was holding a Bloody Mary.

"Here you go," she said. "Sorry to eavesdrop, but did I hear you're leaving soon?"

"Tomorrow morning. Christmas with Dad. You know the drill."

"That's nice."

"But I'll be back next month for the Super Bowl."

"Will you be staying here?"

"Actually, no. I'll be at Mandalay Bay."

"That's good." She scribbled on a coaster.

"Why is that good?"

"Because the staff isn't allowed to date guests."

I accepted the coaster and glanced at the name and phone number.

"Call me when you get back," she said, shifting the tray to her other arm.

"I will."

"And just so you won't have to worry about it, I eat everything."

"That's good to know," I said. "Merry Christmas, Grace."

"Merry Christmas. And I'm sure it will be a very happy new year. For both of us."

She smiled, flipped her sun bleached hair away from her face, and strolled off. I watched her go then reached into my bag and placed the coaster in a safe place. I sipped my drink, slid it under my chair, and jumped in the pool. As soon as I surfaced, I heard my phone ringing again. I climbed out and dripped water into my bag as I searched for the phone.

"Hello," I said, slightly out of breath.

"Hi."

I paused to let the voice work its way through me. I grabbed a towel and wiped my face and sat down. "How are you?"

"Not great," she whispered. "But okay."

"Where are you?"

"We're in Vail."

I tried to ignore the fact she already seemed comfortable using the language of couples. I looked for safer ground. "How's the ski trip?"

"Great. Got eight inches last night."

"Any fresh snow?" I said, immediately hating myself for the crack.

"Funny," she said, not laughing.

"Sorry."

"Forget it. It doesn't matter. How's Vegas?"

"It's done. I'm heading home tomorrow."

"I would have liked to have met your father."

"I guess you can't have everything."

"No, I guess you can't. Well, I just called to make sure you were okay."

"I'm fine. Really."

"Okay." She paused. I forced myself to wait out the silence. Finally, she spoke. "I should go I guess."

"Time to hit the slopes?"

"Yeah. Take care of yourself."

"You too. Bye."

"Merry Christmas."

"Same to you." I hung up and tossed the phone back into my bag. I drained my Bloody Mary and scanned the pool area searching for signs of Grace.

Chapter Thirteen

Unable to sleep, I got in my car at 4AM and headed north on Route 95. I soon found myself away from the concrete of Vegas in the middle of desert scrub. My plan was to average seventy and make it home in time for dinner.

Fighting boredom and highway hypnosis, I reviewed the gifts I'd gotten for my father. One in particular I knew would thrill him. I then remembered the gift I'd bought for her and made a mental note to return it after Christmas. Anything I gave her would pale in comparison to what her new Santa would be offering. A diamond ring, regardless of size, didn't stand a chance against a diamond mine.

I headed west on Route 80, worked my way around Reno and then picked up 395 North. From there, Route 89 took me past Mount Shasta to Interstate 5 and I headed north towards home. At one point, I noticed a black Taurus in my rear view mirror for several miles but then it disappeared. Chastising myself for excessive paranoia, I put the possibility of being followed out of my mind.

About an hour from home, I saw the sign, slowed and pulled into the parking lot. I turned the car off but continued to sit behind the wheel and let the memories of the last time I'd been here wash over me. A mere eighteen months had passed since I'd walked inside and had my life rearranged. The million bucks notwithstanding, I was forced to consider the possibility that it hadn't changed for the better.

**

I locked the car and glanced up at the sign precariously attached to the roof of the derelict building. Several neon letters of *The Barbarian* needed replacing and the sign had lost its battle to be seen against the night sky.

I entered and waited for my eyes to adjust. As always, guitar rock blared, but the handful of patrons scattered around the bar continued their conversations unabated. I waved to the bartender who, judging by the finger she was shaking at a pair of glassy eyes, was vigorously defending a strongly held opinion. Either that or the drunk had broken her golden rule; admire, but don't touch.

Approaching sixty, she still maintained a youthful appearance and a no-nonsense environment in the bar. She finished scolding the drunk and caught my eye. She stared at me with a small smile then wandered down the bar.

"What the hell are you doing here on your night off?"

"I was bored sitting at home."

"And you think this place is gonna help?"

I laughed. She slid a bottle of beer in my direction and leaned forward. Deep cleavage foretold the possibility of escape.

"What do you think?"

"Are those new?"

"Best money can buy," she said, gently squeezing her breasts. "I had them done last week. They're still a bit tender, but I couldn't wait to take them for a test drive."

"Nice."

"You want to touch them?"

"No, that's okay. I'm trying to cut back."

She laughed and poured herself a shot of bourbon. "Your loss, sugar."

I glanced around the sparse crowd. "Since I'm here, do you need any help?"

"Handling this lot? No, I'm good. But if you're looking for some action, you might want to check out the pool room."

Immediately intrigued, I glanced towards the back of the bar. "What's going on?"

"There's a new kid in tonight. She shoots a mean game of nine-ball but nothing you can't handle. I think she's working something, but nobody's talking. I imagine they're all embarrassed about getting beat by a woman."

"I don't know, Sadie. I haven't been playing much lately."

"Oh, come on. A couple of games and you'll get it back. Besides I'd love to see somebody take her money. I don't like her. Even in her current condition."

"Well, I guess it couldn't hurt." I sipped my beer.

"Say, how's your Dad doing?"

"He's bored too."

"Must run in the family."

I took another sip. "That must be it. He's still missing my Mom, but he's doing okay."

"Yeah, we all miss her. Tell him I said hi." She winked. "And be sure to tell him about my new tits. That'll drive him crazy."

**

"Hundred a game okay with you?"

"Fine by me," I said, chalking my cue stick. "For starters."

Despite the long stringy hair and nose ring, the blonde was stunning. She smiled as she stared at the fresh rack. Well into her third trimester, she was having difficulty getting close to the table. But as she hammered the break, sinking the nine in the process, it obviously wasn't affecting her game. I tossed a hundred on the table and racked the balls again.

"Nice shot," I said. "When are you due?"

"Seven weeks," she said, hammering the fresh rack.

I watched the balls scatter around the table. I surveyed the table, made the first two then missed an easy shot on the three ball. Silently cursing myself, I stepped back from the table and watched as she waddled back and forth surveying the table.

"Tough way to make a buck, huh?"

She stood up from her shot, surprised by my comment. "What's that?"

"I mean this," I said, gesturing around the room. "I would think that a woman in your condition would be home getting spoiled by her husband."

"Husband?" she said. "Is that what you call somebody who runs off and leaves a woman with three kids and another on the way?"

I nodded and leaned against the wall directly behind her. She leaned forward onto the table and I studied her baggy jeans and oversized hooded sweatshirt. I then looked at her boots. They were expensive. Too expensive.

"Can you believe he would do that?" She hammered the three ball into a side pocket. "I mean, how can you do something like that and still call yourself a man?"

"Especially with Christmas just around the corner." I continued studying her.

"Exactly." The four, five, and six disappeared. "And here's Mom out shooting pool just to make sure there's a few presents under the tree."

She grunted and groaned as she leaned forward on the table to get at the seven ball. I caught a glimpse of what should have been another layer of clothing underneath the sweatshirt creeping up her back. She stretched further and the unmistakable sight of a thong appeared. It was the first time I had ever admired the ass of a seven-month pregnant woman. The seven disappeared. Soon the eight and nine followed. I tossed another hundred on the table and racked the balls again.

"You know," she said, chalking her cue. "It's not like I miss him. It's just that kids need a father. The son of a bitch probably won't even call on Christmas. What do you think?"

"I think we should make it two hundred a game."

"Your funeral."

60

I rediscovered my stroke and began winning. As my game improved, she increased the frequency of her tales of woe. After sinking the nine on the break, I learned that one of her children had been born with one arm. After winning three in a row, I discovered that her oldest, the seven-year old, had just been diagnosed with a rare kidney disease. By the time we were playing for three hundred a game, I was up seventeen hundred and she'd run out of maladies.

"Let me see if I've got this straight. Your oldest is actually the son of your father's friend who raped you when you were thirteen?"

"Yeah," she said, sweat beading on her forehead. "But since my family is so religious, they decided I had to keep the baby."

"Well, that's certainly understandable. But given the fact that your Dad is a housebound cripple, he's kind of like a built in babysitter." I slowly rolled the nine the length of the table. We watched the ball hug the rail then drop out of sight.

"Fuck," she whispered, dropping three hundred in twenties on the table. "Let's go again." She racked and stood waiting impatiently. She tapped the bottom of her cue on the cement floor and brushed greasy hair away from her face. "C'mon, let's go. I could go into labor waiting for you to break."

"Man," I said, chalking my cue stick. "You sure have been through a lot for someone who's only twenty years old."

"Twenty two." Her face flushed and the tapping stopped. "No, you're right. Silly me. I'm twenty."

"So you told me," I said, hammering the cue ball into the new rack. We both watched the six ball fall. I chalked and stalked the table. "You know, with just a little more attention to detail, you could pull this off."

"What are you talking about?" she said, striking a defiant pose.

"You need to study," I said, shaking my head. The one ball disappeared, quickly followed by the two. "Learn about what being pregnant is really like. If you're going to name drop a bunch of childhood illnesses on a mark, at least know what you're talking about." I made short work of the next four balls. "And when you're trying to generate sympathy, you might at least try being a little sympathetic." I banked the seven then rolled the eight the length of the table. "Drop the biker chick image. Lose the fake nose ring and wash your hair. Clean yourself up. Do you think anybody is going to believe that a woman who doesn't take care of herself is actually taking good care of her kids?"

"What makes you the expert?"

"I'm just saying if you're going to run this scam, don't be an amateur. At least do your best to try and get it right. Have some pride. Be a pro."

She pushed her hair behind her ears and glared at me. "You don't know shit."

I rolled the nine into a side pocket. "I know I just took two grand off you. How long are you going to survive at that rate?"

"Don't worry about me. I'll survive."

"Survival's easy. And survival is for schmucks."

"You have something better to offer than survival?"

"How about prosperity?"

"You? You're going to explain prosperity to me?"

"What have you got to lose?"

She placed her cue on the table and considered the question. "Okay, enlighten me."

"What's your definition of prosperity?"

Her response was immediate. "At least a million a year." She dragged her fingers through her hair in an attempt to improve her appearance. It didn't work.

"A million a year?" I placed the cue stick on the table and was again struck by how beautiful she was, even through the grease and grime. "We could do that."

She laughed, but stopped when she saw my expression. "Okay, Goober. I'm sure you're totally full of shit, but go ahead. Explain how I can make a million bucks in a year."

"Why don't you lose that fake pillow and sit down? I'll get us a couple of drinks."

"If I take the pillow off, I'm afraid my pants will fall down."

"I could live with that."

Chapter Fourteen

Deciding the last thing I needed were more memories, I passed on my Barbarian reunion, exited the parking lot, and headed for home. I crossed the Oregon border and it started raining.

"Now there's a surprise." I flipped the wipers on and turned the radio off. I slowed, located my phone, and called my father. Four rings in, he answered.

"Hey, it's me."

"It's about time," he said, yawning. "Where are you?"

"I'm close. Did I wake you up?"

"It's okay," he said. "I didn't get much sleep last night."

"Get your rest because I'm taking you out for dinner and drinks tonight."

"Sounds good. I'll make the reservation. You good with McCauley's?"

"You read my mind. I'll see you soon."

"Drive slow. It's supposed to rain later."

"It's already later, Dad."

I worked my way west towards the coast through a forest of Douglas Fir and pine. In the rear view mirror, I caught my third glimpse of the black Taurus. I sped up around a curve and navigated the wet road at eighty for about three miles. I spotted a dirt access road, backed in and parked facing out. I left the car and wipers on and waited. The Taurus soon cruised by and behind the wheel I saw my old acquaintance, and apparent new nemesis, Roger Gentry. I waited a few minutes then pulled out onto the highway.

I remembered he'd said he was going home for the holidays. Perhaps he preferred not to fly. Perhaps he enjoyed the peacefulness of driving through desert and forest. Perhaps he had needed to make a stop along the way. Perhaps he was just another son heading home to spend Christmas with his parents.

Perhaps.

He was obviously monitoring my movements and I needed to find out if he was carrying out an official investigation or merely using his power of position to fuck with me as payback for stealing his lunch money in third grade.

I pulled up directly behind the black Taurus at a traffic light and watched Roger as he scanned the cars in front of him. He then glanced in his rear view mirror and I caught his look of surprise. I smiled and waved. He gave me a small wave then gunned his car through the green light. I slowly worked my through town, my recently rediscovered festive spirit dampened.

I entered the warm, comfortable house I'd bought for him and was impressed with his decorating efforts. I stepped outside onto the deck overlooking the Pacific and immediately felt its calming effect. Even if the FBI was on my tail, it wasn't going to ruin Christmas. I sat down, got swallowed by an Adirondack chair, and waited for him to finish making martinis.

He appeared holding a large metal shaker in one hand and two glasses in the other. He paused to take in the view, closed his eyes, and ingested the wet, salty air with a deep breath. I smiled as I watched what I knew had become a ritual and waited for him to finish on his own time. He sat down in one of the chairs and poured.

"What shall we drink to?" I said.

"To staying one step ahead."

We touched glasses and I savored the first sip. "One step ahead. Are you sure you're okay?"

"Jesus Christ," he said. "All these years you've been badgering me about losing weight and taking better care of myself. I finally lose a few pounds and you're all over me about being too thin. Make up your mind."

"Have you been to the doctor lately?"

"Doctor, schmocthor." He sipped his martini. "I'm fine. I feel great."

I had to agree that he did look good, but the amount of weight he'd lost since I had last seen him seemed unusual.

"I've been walking every day and I cut out desserts." He stared out at the ocean. "It's so beautiful out here."

"Yes. It certainly is."

He continued to stare out at the ocean as he rested his hand on mine.

"Thank you, Gene."

I choked back the lump forming in my throat and eventually managed, "My pleasure."

"Your mother would have loved this place."

"I know. Someday you'll get to tell her all about it."

"Fat chance of that, huh?"

I looked at him and watched the wind whip his remaining hairs. He gulped the rest of the martini and burped loudly. "Fat chance of that."

**

"Now if this isn't the biggest pair of reprobates I've ever seen, I don't know who they'd be."

"Just give us a table for two and be quick about it." My father hugged the woman and held on. "And not one by the kitchen either."

"How are you Mrs. McCauley? Merry Christmas."

"Merry Christmas, Gene. It's good to see you. What have you been up to?"

"Oh, you know," I said. "A little of this and that."

She pulled me close and whispered into my ear. "The house was a magnificent gesture. He's been a different man since then." She led us to our table and headed off towards the kitchen.

"Good table," he said, scanning the menu. "Hmmmm. Let's see. Soft shells to start. Then a New York with baked potato and spinach salad."

"Sure. Sounds good." I closed my menu and glanced through the wine list. "Got a wine preference?"

"Hmmmm. Let's see. The Pinot would be great with the soft shells but I think we should wash down the steak with a nice Cab."

"You got it."

I caught our waiter's eye who took our order and departed. I looked around the elegant dining room. I remembered the rare occasions when our family had been able to afford eating here. As a child, the restaurant had provided my first glimpse into what extraordinary pleasures life offered if one could afford them. Now I was often struck by how casually I dined in the most luxurious of establishments.

Of late, restaurants had lost their luster. I had nibbled at hundred dollar sushi while longing for my mother's meatloaf. I'd eaten exotic wild game covered in every brandied cream sauce ever invented while pining for a cheeseburger with fries. Restaurants had become a nagging reminder of my complete lack of a home life, but elegant food and drink used to loosen tongues and wallets were a necessity in my profession.

My profession.

Could what I did so effortlessly with a clear conscience accurately be described as a profession? Or was it merely a lifestyle? A lifestyle that had taken me so far from normalcy, if pressed, I wouldn't have even been able to recall the last time I'd eaten a home cooked meal.

I watched my father gnaw on an herb-stuffed soft shell crab topped with a yellow pepper and garlic aioli. I drained my martini and had a sudden craving for a peanut butter sandwich.

After dinner and well over the legal limit, we walked to a nearby bar and switched to beer.

"Do you always drink like this?" I said.

"Funny, I was just about to ask you the same thing."

"Usually, I only drink when I'm working."

"Earlier you said you've been working non-stop for the past year."

"Well," I said, taking a swallow of beer, "I guess that answers your question."

He leaned across the table and whispered, "I can't believe you made over a million bucks this year."

"Don't tell anyone," I said, glancing around the room. "It'll be our little secret. By the way, how's your money holding out?"

He waved me away. "Ah, I'm fine. I got plenty." He turned serious. "But this new scam you're running in Vegas worries me. Don't get me wrong. It's a beautiful play, but don't get greedy. Get in…and get out. The technology today is amazing but don't forget *they've* got some pretty amazing technology of their own."

"I know, Dad. In and out. One step ahead."

"Exactly."

The waitress arrived with a fresh pitcher of beer. I tossed a ten on her tray and waved off her half-hearted attempt at making change. I waited until she was out of earshot and was about to resume our conversation when I spotted two men staggering in our direction.

"Shit."

"What?" he said, following my stare. "Shit. Keep your head down. Maybe they won't see us."

"Well, look who's here. Hey, Rog. Get a look at this pair."

The old man staggered to the table and plopped down in the booth next to me. He was hammered and smelled like low tide. I slid over to the edge of the booth as his son sat down next to my father.

"When did you get out of the joint?"

My father let the familiar jab wash over him and he forced a smile at the old drunk. "Twenty seven years ago next month, Sam. Thanks for the reminder."

"Glad I ran into you. Saves me from having to send a card."

"Still an asshole, huh? How you doing, Roger?"

"I'm good, sir. Sorry about this. He always hits it pretty hard around the holidays."

"Yeah, I know. I ran into him on Flag Day."

"Dad, just let it go," I said.

"It was a dark and stormy night...September of...some fucking year." He chortled and slapped the table. "This guy comes strolling out of the back of the art gallery thinking he's going to fence a bunch of paintings. Well, I put a quick stop to that one, didn't I? Up against the wall, scumbag."

Several customers turned towards the loud voice and stared at the outstretched hand simulating a pistol.

"Dad. Stop it," Roger said, pushing his father's hand down under the table.

"Yeah, Sam. You were a regular Barney Fife."

"Put your ass in jail, didn't I?"

"Well, isn't this nice?" I said, glancing around the table. "It's always good to get together with old friends during the holidays and reminisce."

"I need a drink," Sam said, searching for the waitress.

I looked at Roger and felt a touch of sympathy. Gone was the cocky, self-importance of the FBI agent. It had been replaced by the embarrassed, self-consciousness of the adult son of a public drunk. He stared across the table at his father who was having a difficult time unzipping his coat. He shook his head but waved at the waitress who was obviously reluctant to approach. My father got up and headed towards the men's room. Roger leaned forward.

"What a night," he whispered. "My mom kicked him out of the house earlier for about the thousandth time. Jesus Christ. What a fucking mess."

"Sorry, Roger."

"I should have stayed in Vegas," he said, removing a twenty from his wallet. "Here you go," he said to the waitress who was keeping a close eye on Sam. "Bring a round for these two and keep the change. Thanks."

"When are you heading back up?"

"Around New Year's probably."

"Let me know." I forced a smile. "Maybe we can caravan back."

He tried a laugh that didn't work. "Ah, I was just screwing with you. By the way, how did you end up behind me?"

"Trade secret, Roger."

"So you're heading back up to Vegas?"

"Yeah, I've got an offer up there that I don't think I can refuse."

"Is she cute?"

"Gorgeous."

"Do you get up there much?"

"Yeah, sometimes. I like it in short bursts."

"Which hotels have you stayed in?"

"Let's see…Bellagio, Caesars and, of course, last week I stayed at Hedaya's."

"Well, you'll love Mandalay Bay." He shrieked. "Dad, for chrissakes, you're spilling it all over yourself."

The hairs on the back of my neck stood up. Perhaps he had gone over his drink limit. Perhaps he was offering some form of warning. Perhaps he was simply unable to stop screwing with me. Regardless, I knew that I had told only one person where I was staying when I came back to Vegas. And either the FBI was monitoring the hotel reservation systems throughout Vegas or my waitress was holding down more than one job. I sipped my beer and watched Roger's frenzied attempt to wipe his father dry.

Chapter Fifteen

Christmas morning I sat on the deck and watched the most beautiful rainstorm drench everything in its path. Safely cocooned from the onslaught, I sipped coffee and marveled at nature's power and her ability to appear out of nowhere and take complete command of any situation. I barely heard the phone ringing above the storm.

"Hello."

"Mr. Wagner?"

"No, this is his son. Can I help you?"

"This is St. Marks. I'm so sorry to call you on Christmas, but your father hasn't returned our call to confirm his appointment on Tuesday."

"Okay," I said, scribbling the information down on a pad next to the phone.

"We'll see him then," she said, preparing to hang up.

"Uh, if you don't mind," I said. "What exactly is the appointment for?"

"His next round of chemotherapy."

"Oh, that's right," I said. "I thought he wasn't scheduled until after the New Year."

"No, it's Tuesday. Have a Merry Christmas."

I hung up the phone as my father trudged out of his bedroom still half-asleep. He nodded. "Merry Christmas." He headed directly for the coffee and returned with a full cup.

"Who was on the phone?"

"St. Marks."

"Shit," he said, avoiding eye contact.

"Chemotherapy? What's going on, Dad?"

"Guess I'm busted, huh?"

"What have you got?"

I sat down on the couch and waited. Eventually, he sat down in a chair across from me. The weight loss, the gauntness of his features now made sense and I felt self-loathing work its way into my system.

"It's colon cancer. I've been in treatment the past four months."

"Four months?" Anger joined forces with the self-loathing and I found myself debating whether father or son was more deserving of my rising fury. "When were you planning on telling me about this?"

"Soon." He winked and sipped. "Good coffee."

I stared, bewildered by his casualness. "Okay, let's start over."

"Sure." He crossed his legs and continued to sip his coffee.

"How advanced is it?"

"It's at the point where it's considered somewhat dangerous."

"Somewhat dangerous? What the hell am I supposed to do with that?" Does your doctor think it's working so far?"

"Yeah, he's pretty optimistic about killing it off. The odds are no worse than fifty-fifty."

"And what if it the chemo doesn't work?"

"Then I die."

"That's it? There must be other treatments. What about surgery?"

"That's not going to happen, Gene."

"What are you talking about? It's not going to happen. If it's an option that might work, then that's what we'll do."

"No, we won't."

"Jesus Christ, Dad."

"No. My buddy Johnny Clement got colon cancer three years ago. They cut about a foot out of his intestines in one surgery, then another foot and a half in another. He ended up weighing eighty pounds and spent his last year shitting into a bag. I won't go through that, Gene."

I returned his stare then nodded. "Okay, Dad. If that's what you think you want to do."

"No, that's what I'm going to do. I want us to be very clear on that point."

"We're clear."

"Good boy." He stood and placed a hand on my shoulder. "Now, I'm going to go shower and change my clothes then we're going to open presents.

"We're not through talking about this, Dad."

"Oh, I know," he said, strolling down the hall whistling an off-key version of Jingle Bells.

**

I opened the large box and removed the garment bag. I examined it closely and held it up to my face and smelled fresh leather.

"Your bag was looking pretty ratty. Do you like it?"

"I love it."

"I figured you could use it for your trip to Australia."

My smile caught him by surprise.

"What are you grinning at?"

"Nothing," I handed him a large envelope wrapped in colored paper. "Here you go."

He removed the wrapping, realized what it was and beamed.

"Now don't start packing yet. We'll need to talk to your doctor and get his clearance before you go."

"Ah, Gene," he whispered. "I've always wanted to go to Australia."

"I know. But before we go, you've got to promise to do everything your doctor tells you."

"For this, I'll detail his fucking car. But why would we fly out of Vancouver?"

I had already prepared my lie and delivered it without ceremony. "It's just a scheduling thing."

"First class?"

"You got a problem with first class?"

"No, this is almost perfect."

"What's not perfect about it?"

"No, that's not what I meant. This is a wonderful gift. It's just that…"

"What?"

"Well, ever since you started…following in my footsteps, I'd always hoped that we'd be able to work together at least once."

"And?"

"And hearing you talk about the past year and the thing you're working in Vegas got my juices flowing again."

"Dad, we are not going to be working together. Australia is a vacation. I'm offering you the chance to drink cold beer all day and ogle half naked women on the beach."

"I'm tired of sitting on my ass. I've been doing that longer than I care to even think about."

"Why on earth would you want to get involved in something like that at your age? In your condition?"

"Think of it as my last wish," he said, waving the airline ticket in front of my face. "What kind of son would deny his dying father's last wish?"

"Who do you think I am? The Make a Wish Foundation? And you're not dying."

"C'mon son, just think about all the fun we could have pulling off some great scam. What a story it would make. What a memory."

"I wouldn't have a clue what we could do down there."

"So we play tourist until we come up with something. C'mon, Gene. Why not?"

"Why not? I can give you a hundred reasons why not."

"I'm wasting away here, Gene. I want to get back in the game. Just one more time. And I need your help."

I studied my father's expression. Despite having everything I thought someone of his age wanted, he still needed something more. And so it transpired on a rainy

Christmas morning, I reluctantly ended up giving him the one present he truly wanted.

Chapter Sixteen

I flew back into Vegas on the Monday before the Super Bowl carrying my new leather garment bag and good news about my father's condition. Even though, as his doctor kept reminding us, the cancer could return at any time, it had been beaten back into submission.

Convinced I was being watched, I'd decided that all business calls would be done from a pay phone until I got a new cellphone. I called my service from the airport and discovered I had over 10,000 subscribers, each one forking over $25 bucks for my Super Bowl prediction. Ignoring the voice in my head telling me to walk away, I enjoyed the adrenaline rush and took a limo to Mandalay Bay.

I checked in and ordered room service. As I waited for my food, my thoughts returned to my waitress. My prurient desires, while still strong, had been tempered by the need to know what she knew. And didn't know. Over the past several years, I believed that I had become an expert at covering my tracks. I was fairly certain that the dating service wasn't on the FBI's radar screen. My current Super Bowl scam was also an unlikely target. It was simply too new and any complaints would only come after the game, if at all. Any remaining concerns I had about my current operations disappeared.

I decided that their interest in me was based on something historical, from a time when I had been less careful, less proficient. I reflected back on some of my riskier, less elegant scams and decided that any of several could be the basis for their investigation. If that were the case, I knew I was probably home free since I would have already been arrested by now if they had hard evidence. But I also knew that the FBI didn't assign two agents to the same person unless they were looking hard. Despite feeling more confident, I decided to keep that fact in mind during the upcoming week.

I also decided to launch my own investigation of sorts. Although I do my best to avoid behaving like a pig when it comes to women, I couldn't help but smile at the prospect of doing to an FBI agent the same thing they'd been doing to others for a very long time. I called her and made dinner plans for Tuesday night.

**

"Oh, I agree," she said, nibbling her way through a slice of chocolate cake. "Absolutely."

Normally, I would be delighted to spend an evening with a woman who agreed with everything I suggested. But tonight I found it annoying. Hiding my contempt and trying to bear in mind that the gorgeous woman's long-term objective was to put me behind bars, I smiled and let her eat cake.

"Of course, it seems like the country has an attention disorder, or maybe it's a case of amnesia."

"How so?" she said, wiping her mouth, chewing, and talking at the same time.

The third glass of wine had done the trick. Her urban sophisticate façade cracked under the weight of the alcohol and revealed small town. After spending the past two hours with her, I longed for the sassy waitress hustling tips. Once again, the first sip was the most satisfying.

"Well, for one thing, a lot of the people today decrying drug use were the same ones who did everything except drink the bong water when they were young. Then they went corporate."

"If you can't beat them, join them?"

"Probably," I said, signing the check. "But I'm more interested in the movement of the society as a whole rather than any specific behavior. It just strikes me as funny that millions of people, who supported Kennedy and marched for civil rights, now listen to Limbaugh."

"That's funny. You're funny. I like funny."

I looked at her eyes sparkling from the overhead light and saw the real woman emerge for the first time all evening. Blood was leaving my brain and I hoped I had enough supply to stay mentally sharp.

"How's work going?" I said, sipping coffee.

"Oh, I forgot to tell you. I got fired. They said that with the amount of skin I was showing, I should have been moving a lot more drinks."

"That's too bad."

"No, actually that's good. I was getting tired of it. I've been thinking about getting in real estate. The condo market is pretty hot here right now. Ever done anything like that? I mean, I could use all the advice I can get."

I smiled at her mistake. The transition was too abrupt.

"As a matter of fact, I do have some experience in real estate. And all of it bad." I laughed and waited for her next move.

"Well, are you going to tell me all about it?" She gently scratched the inside of my forearm with fire-red fingernails. "Or am I going to have to force it out of you?"

I found her choice of overt sexuality interesting. Perhaps she'd been told that her next promotion was directly tied to the discovery of damaging information about me. Perhaps she considered guilt-free sex with criminals one of the perks of the job. Perhaps she planned on testing out an age-old intelligence gathering technique that the FBI had approved for use.

Perhaps.

Or maybe she just enjoyed doing the horizontal mambo.

Knowing there was only one way to discover her real motives, I talked.

"I sold condos for a couple of months several years ago in Florida. Actually, tried to sell condos is more accurate."

This was true. I had.

"Florida," she said, slowly nodding her head. "I've never been there."

"Hot. Bugs the size of baseballs. Overly developed. And the part that isn't developed is swampland, or as we used to call it, Waiting for Condo. I hate the place."

This was also true. I do.

"But then I found out the guy I was working for was a total scam artist."

This was true. He was.

"How so?" she said, *almost* suppressing her excitement.

"Well, somehow he had managed to get hired as the maintenance manager for three new high-end condo complexes. Most of the condos weren't even finished, but that was perfect for what he was doing."

"What was he doing?"

"He was reselling them." I laughed; something I did every time I told the story. "The corporate owners were off planning their next project and weren't around. He had the keys to the entire complex. So he set up a real estate office and resold condos that were already sold."

This was true. And it was brilliant.

"Unbelievable," she said.

"The actual owners couldn't move in until construction was complete so, for about two months, I had a dozen showings a day. The schedule was brutal."

This was true. It was. Add in the heat and the bugs.

"How did it work?"

"For him, very well," I said, laughing at the memory. "The condo market was on fire and these were high end and being sold…resold at an amazing price. Anyway, my boss figured that he had a three month window before the owners got back in town so he priced the condos to move and let word of mouth drive the whole thing. We had a close rate of fifty percent and people were writing checks for ten percent on the spot as down payments."

"Good scam," she said, nodding. "How did you find out?"

"I took a weekend off and went to Miami and just happened to meet one of the owners in a bar. We started talking, and before you know it, we both figured out what was going on."

This was a lie. I avoided Miami like the plague.

"Did you end up seeing any money?"

"Are you kidding? As soon as I found out what was going on I headed west and didn't stop until I got home to Oregon with my tail between my legs."

"What ever happened to the guy? Did he get ever get caught?"

"I wouldn't have a clue. After I left, I never heard another word."

This was one part lie, one part truth. I knew that he was living somewhere in South America enjoying the million bucks he'd made from the down payments. Since he had absconded with my share of a hundred thousand, I also knew that I would probably never be hearing from him again.

"I ended up losing all my commissions, but I learned some very valuable lessons about people."

This was true. I was still using a lot of it today.

"So you just found yourself caught in the wrong situation," she said, more as a statement than a question. Her face softened. Instead of the look of disappointment I expected, I was pleasantly surprised by her reaction.

"Let's go back to your room."

I returned her stare and considered the ramifications of getting involved any further with this woman. We had both spent our entire time together, however brief, lying to each other. Should I let the fact that I was simply better at it than her ruin the rest of the evening?

Perhaps the rest of the night would have played out differently if she hadn't been willing to concede the possibility I was innocent.

Perhaps she was only capable of sleeping with someone when her conscience was clear.

Perhaps she would have slept with me regardless.

Perhaps.

But I did end up learning one more valuable piece of information that evening.

She sure loved to mambo.

**

The rest of the week was routine. Using a different cellphone every day, I started each morning by checking my total subscribers. Adrenaline surged each time I heard the automated voice announce the number, but a trace of fear crept in as the week progressed. I considered this normal. Like the athletes preparing to do battle on Sunday, the stakes were high and a loss could be devastating.

I would then turn my attention to the final details for my trip. Although I had no idea what my father and I might become involved in, I knew that an Australian corporation would be central to any plan. I completed the paperwork and contacted a bank in Sydney to open a business account and wire transferred a million dollars Australian. I had no plans to spend these hard earned dollars but they would certainly come in handy as collateral for any loans I might require.

And since there was no way I'd be traveling under my real name, I'd been in contact with a colleague who was an expert in creating false identities. On Thursday, I received a package containing everything my father and I would need.

After finishing my work, I would order room service lunch and take an afternoon nap. Then I would either swim or go to the gym, then shower and get ready for another evening with Grace. While we were certainly enjoying each other's company, our nightly encounters seemed cloaked with an unspoken reality that we were merely keeping an eye on each other. Maybe she was merely waiting to be assigned a new case. Or perhaps she'd been told by her superiors to keep pumping me for information. Whatever the reason, I was delighted to spend each evening with her. I indulged her desire to sample some of Vegas's best restaurants and we caught a couple of good shows. We would then retire to my suite where she spent the rest of the night wearing me out.

Around three in the morning, she would get dressed and leave to return to the other side of her own life. And I would lay awake and wonder why I wasn't capable of shaking my relentless restlessness. One early morning I pondered the possibility of trying to make it work with Grace. And then I had the best laugh I'd had in weeks. As my father had often told me, when it comes to this line of work, mixed marriages are doomed.

All in all, the week was idyllic. But by the time Sunday morning finally rolled around, I had to admit I was bored shitless.

As far as the Super Bowl went, it was pretty clear who'd won.

Me.

And I'd won big.

Chapter Seventeen

"I think I used to be an accountant. No, a lawyer."

He whispered this while flipping through his passport repeating the process that, in addition to the poke in the ribs I received every time he changed former occupations, had kept me awake for the past two hours. I had eaten twice, drank, read every magazine, watched a movie and listened to him select, discuss and discard occupations as often as college freshmen change majors. Somewhere far out in the Pacific, seven miles above the water traveling six hundred miles an hour, I had officially run out of things to do. And hit empty on my listening gauge. Unfortunately, his excitement gauge still had a full tank. Since we'd taken off, he'd been through a series of ten-minute careers in occupations ranging from carpenter to carpet cleaner, electrician to electrical engineer, and obstetrician to undertaker.

"Maybe I should stay with something in the medical area." He turned his head to make sure I was listening. "I've got it," he said, snapping his fingers. "Gynecologist." He thought some more. "Nah, I'm too out of practice."

"Why not proctologist?" I looked at him through half-open eyes. "Your qualifications seem impeccable."

"Am I annoying you?"

"Bingo. That's the one. Clairvoyant." I closed my eyes.

"Well, if you don't want to help me…fine."

"Dad," I whispered. "Look, it doesn't really matter. Whatever you pick is probably going to change as soon as we decide what we're going to do down there."

"Excuse me for paying attention to the details."

"Why don't you just try to get some sleep?"

"Are you kidding? I haven't been this awake in years."

I shook my head and longed for a nap. Any concerns about my father's health had disappeared as soon as I had seen him at the airport in Vancouver. He was in the bar entertaining a group of travelers with card tricks and taking twenty dollars bills from several in the process. I watched from a distance and felt a surge of pride when I saw the sparkle in his eyes that had been absent far too long.

"So what do we do first?"

"What's that?" I said.

"When we get to Sydney. What do we do first?"

"Well, after we recover from the flight, I thought we'd spend a few days sightseeing."

"Sounds great."

"We'll tour the Opera House and the Botanical Gardens. Do a pub tour in the Rocks. Maybe go to the zoo. After Sydney, we'll drive up the coast. I got some friends up there I haven't seen for ages."

"When do we start trying to figure out what we're going to do?"

"As soon as we land, Dad," I said, closing my eyes. "As soon as we land."

**

"Welcome to the Four Seasons, gentlemen." The concierge flashed a welcoming smile. "Checking in today?"

"We are."

"Very good, sir." He gestured to a bellman who approached the limo and filled a cart with our bags.

The concierge turned back to me and my father. "I'm assuming that you won't need parking."

"No. We decided to leave our car back in the States."

"Very funny, sir. Very good indeed," the concierge said, forcing a smile.

"I thought you said Australians had a sense of humor," my father whispered.

"He's British, Dad," I said, stifling a yawn. "Plus, it wasn't funny."

I handed the limo driver a bright yellow Australian fifty and watched as he drove off.

"My name is Roger, sir. If there is anything you need during your stay, don't hesitate to call me."

"Thank you, Roger," I said, handing over another yellow fifty.

"Thank you, sir." He gestured for us to follow the luggage cart into the hotel where we checked in and headed for the elevators.

"We're on the top floor?"

"We are," I said.

My father nodded and leaned against the elevator wall. I followed him down the hall and waited as he slipped the card key into the slot. I stepped inside and noticed that the curtains were drawn. I approached the window in the main living area and waited.

"Look at this place," he said, rapidly exploring the suite. "Son, this is a five star hotel."

"I know, Dad."

"Of course," he said, rummaging through the minibar. "I'm worth it."

"Come over here, Dad," I said, preparing to open the curtains. "Are you ready?"

"Ready for what?"

"This."

I opened the curtains and watched his reaction.

"Holy shit," he whispered. "Look at that Harbor."

I looked out at the expanse of water that continued far beyond our panoramic view. To our left, we had an unobstructed view of the Sydney Harbor Bridge that led from Circular Quay to North Sydney. Slightly to our right was the Opera House. Perched on water's edge, its white tiles shimmered in the morning sun. Ferries and tour boats inched in and out of their slips almost directly below us and several sailboats taking full advantage of the breeze were navigating under full sail. Even though I had seen the

Harbor countless times from countless angles, it still took my breath away. As I watched my father try to absorb the full impact of his first encounter with one of the most magnificent sights on earth, I remembered my own initial experience and felt a trace of envy. But as I watched him frantically scan the horizon attempting to capture everything in his path, my envy disappeared and was replaced by a son's pride for a job well done.

"What do you think?"

"It's unbelievable."

"After you get some rest, we'll go check it out."

"Rest? Are you kidding? I want to go see it now."

"What do you want to see?"

"All of it, son. I want to see all of it."

**

I slid my chair under the shade of the umbrella and cringed from the screech of metal scraping concrete. As much as I loved the feel of the Australian sun, after a few hours, it can beat you to a pulp. I sat with both hands wrapped around my ice-cold third beer and welcomed the onset of the alcohol haze.

Across the table, my father was studying a tourist brochure. Our day had begun with a Harbor tour then continued with another boat trip, this one to the Zoo where we had spent three hours checking out the koalas, kangaroos and snakes that make Australia unique when it comes to native wildlife. After the ferry ride back, we walked the short distance from Circular Quay to the Botanical Gardens to examine some native fauna. Showing no signs of slowing down, my father had led me to the Opera House where he was informed that the outside of the structure contained 1,056,000 tiles. Ten minutes later, after I'd become convinced that he appeared intent on counting each one, I had what I considered to be a brainstorm. But my suggested pub tour of the Rocks was turning out to be more tour, less pub. I'd spent far too much time walking and not nearly enough drinking.

"After you finish that one," he said, draining the last of his beer. "Let's head back over to George Street. It says here that the Fortune of War has the oldest continuous liquor license in Sydney. Given how much they drink in this country, that's gotta be worth a look, huh?"

"Whatever you say, Dad."

"Jesus, Gene," he said, laughing. "You look a mess."

"My feet hurt."

"Poor baby," he said, leaning back in his chair. "So we hit the road north tomorrow?"

"Yeah. Unless there's something you haven't seen yet. Like maybe the sewer system."

He laughed and winked at me. "No, that can wait until we get back. I'm assuming that we'll be working here in Sydney once we start."

"It depends on what we end up doing." No match for the beer and sun, I yawned and checked my watch to assess my chances of getting a nap before dinner.

"Any ideas yet?"

"Nothing any good. How about you?"

"Nah," he said, shaking his head. "I'm still in tourist mode."

"Dad, we don't have to do anything you know. We can just stay tourists and it wouldn't bother me at all."

"No way, Gene. You promised. And you're not weaseling out now."

"I'm not trying to weasel out, Dad. I'm just saying we don't have to work if you don't feel up to it."

"Who's the one falling asleep on his feet?"

"It's jetlag."

"Bullshit. I think we should have one more," he said, waving to the waitress for two more beers. "It's my round."

He dug through his pocket and extracted a handful of multicolored bills. "I love this money."

"Shout, Dad," I said, suppressing another yawn. "Down here, it's not your round, it's your shout."

"Shout, huh? Okay, then it's my shout. I love this beer."

I shook my head. "Is there anything about this place you don't like?"

He considered the question. "The snakes at the zoo. I don't like the snakes." He smiled and nodded at a group of Japanese tourists walking past our table. "Maybe we could do something with groups like them."

"The language barrier would be a problem."

"Yeah. But I like the tourist angle."

"Not bad," I said. "Let's kick it around on the drive north and see if we come up with anything."

"I feel so alive." He smiled at the waitress approaching with fresh beers. "Thanks. Keep the change."

"Thanks, mate," she said, pleasantly surprised by the tip.

"What is this thing with mate?" he said. "Thanks, mate. No worries, mate. She'll be right, mate."

"Well, supposedly it comes from the original convict days when the living conditions were so tough, you really had to depend on your friends, you know, your mates. The total male bonding experience."

"That makes sense."

"But I think it's still used because it eliminates the problem of ever having to learn anybody's name."

My father laughed and took a long sip of beer. I watched him as he leaned back and took in his surroundings. A fresh breeze kicked up and he turned his head slightly to feel it against his cheek. He pulled his hat down and closed his eyes.

"That's right. I'd forgotten that this place was originally settled by convicts," he said. "No wonder I feel right at home."

Chapter Eighteen

Despite the development that had continued since my last visit, less than two hours north of Sydney the country began to offer up vast expanses as the urban noise dissipated. We headed to the Hunter Valley for a day of wine tasting, the temperature rising as we headed inland. We settled into a comfortable silence and the plush four wheel drive we had rented provided both of us with a panoramic perch. I glanced at my father and the smile that hadn't left his face since our arrival.

For our trip north, he had selected shorts and walking shoes complemented by a long sleeve work shirt and Australian bush hat. The outfit that could have easily degenerated into obvious tourist worked perfectly, and combined with the Australian accent he had perfected, he easily passed the native test.

I continued to watch him closely for any trace of illness. His weight seemed to have stabilized. The reddish blotchiness of his face had been transformed into a fresh tan by the Australian sun and I imagined that, to strangers, he would come across as an elderly man who simply took care of himself. My concerns about his health had been beaten back by his incredible energy level. At first, I had wondered if he was somehow faking his stamina. But since we'd spent virtually every hour in each other's company, I'd been forced to accept the fact that he was doing fine.

"Your mother would have loved this place."

I saw the sad smile on his face. He removed his sunglasses, wiped his eyes, and blew his nose. I frowned when he tossed the used tissue on the floor but settled for silent disapproval.

"How often do you think about her?"

"Only when I'm not thinking about something else," he said. "She was so glad you made it back before she...well, you know."

"Yeah." I cleared my throat. "Me too."

"Five years and I still miss the hell out of her."

"Yeah. Me too."

"Whew," he said, exhaling emotion. "Jesus. Just look at the two of us. You know what she would say if she were here right now?"

"Yeah." A grin appeared out of nowhere. "I'd rather be loved right now than longed for later."

"She certainly knew how to turn a phrase." Then his wistfulness turned dark. "You know, sometimes I worry that it was living with me that cut her life short."

"Jesus, Dad," I said, gripping the wheel tighter. "How can you even say that?"

"Think about it. All the stress during that period I was away. You were young and for three years she had to do it all by herself. Living with the stigma of being married to a convict. Then later on, she develops heart problems. It makes perfect sense to me."

"But when you got out, you went clean. And from that point on, she was completely happy."

"Yeah," he said. "She was happy."

"If anybody was miserable, it was you."

"Yeah." He put his sunglasses back on. "Well, you try working as a commercial fisherman for twenty years."

"Dad," I said, laughing. "That is not going to happen."

He laughed along and shook his head. "My son, the football prognosticator."

"What a rush that was."

"I know," he said. "I can't wait."

"You really miss it, don't you?"

"A net full of salmon might pay the rent, but it doesn't do much for the adrenaline. At least not for me. Some guys would get a stiffy at the sight of a forty pound fish but I got to the point where I couldn't even eat it. But it's what kept your mother and me together so I can't complain too much."

"That must have been a tough choice," I said. "You know, having to pick between the two loves of your life."

"Not at all. Nothing compared to her," he said, shaking his head. "The love of a great woman, Gene. That's what it's all about. Maybe you should try it sometime."

"Maybe."

I accelerated to seventy five and the barren landscape sped by. I followed the long, straight highway as my thoughts crisscrossed between the two women of importance in my life. Both women, now gone for different reasons, were linked by a shared belief that life should be lived with both eyes facing forward, not with one in the rear view mirror.

Chapter Nineteen

"It's like we've gone back in time to the Sixties." My father adjusted his hat, checked it in the side view mirror and followed me across the street. "What did you say the name of this place was?"

"Mullumbimby."

Several patrons from the crowded pub chatted noisily above the blare of the band playing inside. The windows were open and the pub had become fully integrated into the surrounding environment, not merely a separate place of business. And on this hot Saturday afternoon, the business was beer and music. And weed.

Several people, inside and out separated only by a three foot high windowsill, were casually passing joints and beers back and forth. I watched my father's reaction with interest. I had avoided discussing the area not wanting to taint his initial impression. I loved the area and considered this spot on the northern coast of New South Wales one of the most beautiful places on earth. Lush farmland worked its way through rolling hills that eventually led to vast stretches of magnificent beaches. And warm ocean water that welcomed and enticed you to stay forever. My father worked his way towards one of joints and, as soon as I heard him say, "Okay, but only for medicinal purposes," I headed for the bar.

The band announced a short break and the room seemed to utter a collective sigh of relief in the hope of catching their breath. I sipped my beer and scanned the room for Manny. A few minutes later my father approached with an even bigger smile than the one he'd been sporting since our plane first landed.

"I can't remember the last time I smoked weed," he said, laughing. He ordered beers for new friends and waved across the pub as the waitress carried the heavy tray in their direction.

"Good spot, huh?"

"This is heaven. Why did you ever leave this place?" He got caught on the memory. "Shit. I'm sorry, Gene." He looked down at the floor. "You came home to say goodbye to your mom. I forgot."

"That's okay, Dad." I remembered the phone call when he'd given me the news. "Forget it." I draped an arm around his shoulder. "What's important is that we're here now."

"Now here's a pack of trouble. I thought we ran you out of this country."

"Well, I'm back." I embraced my old friend. "And this time, I've brought help. Manny, how the hell are you?"

"I'm good, mate." He shook me vigorously by the shoulders. "Really good. He turned to my father and gave him the once over. "And you must be the one to blame for bringing this reprobate into the world."

"Call me Jerry." My father grinned and returned the vigorous handshake. "I've heard a lot about you, Manny. None of it good."

Manny winked at me. "He's gonna fit right in here."

"He already is." I nodded in the direction of the cloud of smoke. "Since when do they allow weed in public?"

"Ah, they don't." Manny said, dismissing the question. "But the cops usually won't bother you as long as you keep it away from the kids or try to sell it on the street. Shit, the stuff grows faster up here than you can smoke it. It's the only growth industry in town. Damn, it's good to see you." Physically he hadn't changed but crow's feet etched the corners of his eyes and, despite his smile, he seemed concerned.

"How's Millie?"

"Mate, she's fatter than the two pigs we're getting ready to slaughter. You won't believe it when you see her."

"Millie? Fat? She's the most health conscious person I know." I looked at my father. "She used to run about seven miles a day."

"Well, she ain't running now. I can't even get near her she's so big." He paused. "And in case you're afraid to ask, she's looking forward to seeing you."

"Are you sure?"

"What's this about?" my father said.

"Oh, Millie and I have had a few problems in the past," I said. "She thinks I'm a bad influence."

"Now there's a shock." My father winked at Manny.

"Manny was working with me on a little thing I had going before I left. Millie didn't like it at all."

"Even though it did pay for the down payment on our place up the hill," Manny said.

My father inched closer to both of us and his voice fell to a whisper. "What was the play?"

"It was nothing," I said, preoccupied with the reception I would receive from Millie.

"It was beautiful." Manny's eyes sparkled. "We hooked up with these two Japanese guys and worked the scam on Japanese tourists looking to invest down here."

"Sounds interesting," my father said.

"It was too complicated," I said, not wanting to relive the events leading up to my mother's death. My father waited out my reluctance. I nodded and took a sip of beer. "Basically, it was an exchange rate play. The Japanese guys were financial and computer wizards. Manny and I set up shop as a couple of entrepreneurs looking for venture capital for a manufacturing start up."

"What were you supposed to be manufacturing?"

"Stuffed toys." Manny laughed loudly then lowered his voice. "All things Australian. Koalas, kangaroos, crocodiles, you name it."

"You're kidding?"

"No," Manny said. "The Japanese eat that shit up."

"But the play for Manny and I was to get twenty million bucks out of potential investors. And then the Japanese guys went to work."

"Those two were amazing," Manny said. "They bounced that twenty million across a dozen different currencies. I had no idea how much you could make by simply changing the color of the money."

"How much?"

"Over the course of a year, we cleared a little over a million. And that got split four ways. But the beauty of it was that all the investors got their money back along with a letter explaining that we had decided not to go ahead with the plant due to some legal questions about environmental impact."

"So it was pretty much legal since no one got hurt?" my father said.

"It was…marginal, Dad. But without a victim it would have been tough to prosecute." I turned to Manny. "Is Millie really okay with me being around for a while?"

"She said as long as you're not actively working a scam from inside her house or getting me involved, you're welcome to stay as long as you like." He cocked his head and smiled. "Are you?"

"Am I what?" I returned the grin.

"Working something?"

"No," I said. "Not yet."

My father took a long swallow of beer and belched. "But we are looking."

**

"You certainly knew what you were talking about when you said we'd need a four wheel drive," my father said, between bounces.

The road that led to Manny's house and farm was a four mile adventure in uphill ruggedness. The road was

96

comprised of a patchwork combination of hard packed dirt, stone, and the occasional slab of concrete. Near the top of the hill, the road veered left and soon we were surrounded by a mixture of overgrown banana plants and unpicked avocado trees.

"It looks like he's a little behind in his chores," my father said.

"This isn't like him at all. He's a really hard worker."

The road ended and dumped us out onto a large crushed stone and meticulously groomed circular driveway. The large one story wooden house overlooked the distant ocean. The well-tended yard stretched for about an acre and was punctuated with a selection of native trees and plants.

"This is more like Manny." We exited the jeep and walked towards the house.

"It's beautiful up here."

Off to our right was a small fenced area that contained two large black pigs. A woman with her back to us was squatting down and reaching through the fence feeding and petting both animals. She turned her head as she heard us approach, then stood and smiled.

"Gene," she said, walking towards us wiping her hands on a towel.

"Jesus, Millie," I said, watching her slowly waddle in our direction. "Manny said you had gotten fat but, of course, he neglected to tell us why."

"Don't worry," she said, rubbing her massive belly. "His day is coming. How are you?"

"I'm great, Millie," I said, accepting her tentative hug. "I'd like you to meet my Dad."

"Jerry. Nice to meet you, Millie. When are you due?"

"Seven weeks." She laughed. "Seven long weeks."

"What's up with the pigs?" I said. "They look pretty tame."

"They are." She glanced back at the pen. "We got them when they were babies. We've been raising them for the party. Of course, now I've gotten so attached to them, I don't know if I'll be able to go ahead and eat them."

"Party?"

"Didn't Manny tell you? About a year ago we learned we were finally going to be connected to the town power grid. And all the neighbors decided to have a big party to celebrate the lights coming on."

"Neighbors?" my father said, looking around the dense foliage with a confused look.

Millie laughed and tossed her long hair back. Her pregnancy had made her even more beautiful, and I knew that my father was already fascinated by her.

"Ten years ago, this entire hillside was one parcel. The owner subdivided into a dozen lots. We got the last one. Now there are twelve families living up here."

"And none of you have electricity?"

"No, just generators. But that's gonna change soon. So we're having a big party to celebrate and those two are the guests of honor." She glanced back at the pigs staring at us with their snouts poking through the fence. "Take a couple of unsuspecting creatures, fatten them up, and then lead them to slaughter for your own personal gain." She stared at me. "Sound familiar, Gene?"

"Touché," I said, forcing a laugh. "Don't worry, Millie. I'll be on my best behavior. But if you need help with the slaughter, don't be afraid to ask."

"I'll keep that in mind, Gene." She glanced back and forth between me and my father and softened. "Okay, we got that settled. Let's go inside. Manny's unpacking the wine you had shipped from the Hunter Valley. Just my luck that several cases of wine show up during the one time in my life I can't drink."

We followed her as she slowly walked towards the house. The sun was beginning to drop into the horizon and I felt a soft breeze kick up.

"Say, Millie. What's up with the farm?"

"He stopped working it two years ago," she said. "Eight acres is just not enough to make a living. He was working eighty hours a week for virtually no money so we both decided he should stop before it killed him."

"And you're not working now because of the baby."

"No," she said.

"How are you guys doing for money?"

"Not well."

Chapter Twenty

"Son, there's somebody I'd like you to meet."

I stood and shook hands with the elderly man my father had been chatting with the past hour.

"This is Willie Wilkerson."

"Nice to meet you, Willie," I said. "I'm Gene."

"G'day, Gene. Quite the old man you got here."

"Yeah, he's a beauty all right."

I immediately pegged him as someone who'd spent the vast majority of his life outside. He wore a singlet and shorts and his work boots were well past their prime. He wore a hat similar to my father's; but his was sweat stained and well-worn.

"Your old man here was telling me you might be looking for some property." Willie rolled a cigarette and lit it without fanfare as he studied me.

I glanced at my father who nodded. Game on. "Sure," I said, smiling. "We're always on the lookout for a good piece of property."

"Then we should talk."

My father's eyes shone with excitement. My head was cloudy from the weed I'd smoked earlier with Manny and working was the last thing I had anticipated doing today. But the signals I was receiving from my father left me no choice.

"What have you got?" I sat down and waited.

"My family has had these parcels for eons. I hate selling them off but my kids don't want it. Damn fools only want the money." Willie exhaled smoke then sipped his beer. "I've got two miles of beachfront up the road that runs back towards the highway."

"How far back?" I said.

"About a half mile. But it bumps up against the highway in a couple of spots so there's no problem with access."

"That's a lot of land," I said, nodding at my father.

"About two hundred hectares," Willie said.

"Five hundred acres." I let the number sink in. "What's the land like once you get back off the beach?"

"It's good," Willie said. "Some of it's a little sandy but it's mostly pasture."

"Okay."

"I've got two other parcels, but I don't know if you'd be interested in those."

"You never know, Willie."

"One's up the road a bit from the beach parcel. But I gotta tell you, it's pretty marshy. About the only thing that seems to grow there are tea trees."

"Tea tree," I said. "That sounds familiar."

"You're probably thinking of tea tree oil. The Aborigines swear by the stuff but I don't get it myself. I got lots of tea trees." Willie laughed.

"How big is that parcel?"

"Four hundred hectares. Or in a language you Yanks would understand, about a thousand acres." Willie laughed at his joke and rolled a cigarette. "I've had it looked at, but it would be a nightmare to clear and build on. But I do have another nice hundred hectare parcel just across the highway. There's nothing on it, but it sure is pretty when the flowers are in bloom."

"What's the zoning?" I said, now very interested in what Willie had to say.

"That's the good news," Willie said, accepting a fresh beer from my father. "About ten years ago, I was going to develop it myself and got it all zoned commercial. Plus, the beach parcel is also zoned residential."

"Why did you decide not to develop it yourself?" I fought the adrenaline surge pumping through my blood.

"I got sick," he said. "Bad ticker. I'm seventy five now and, if my kids showed any interest, maybe I'd still do it. But who needs the headache at my age? So I decided to sell it, get my affairs in order, and travel. I always wanted to go to Italy."

"Good for you, Willie," I said. "You'll love Italy. So, when can we take a look at this property?"

"All I'm doing at the moment is sitting on my ass drinking beer with you two. How 'bout right now?"

I looked at my father who was nodding his head. "Sure. Let's do it."

**

I stood at water's edge finding it impossible to believe that a piece of property this magnificent could still be undeveloped and available. I studied the surf. It was breaking several hundred feet offshore and surfers streamed back and forth across an endless supply of six footers. I scanned the stretch of beach in both directions then turned around and looked back at the hillside that began about a half mile behind the beach. The gentle slope of the hill formed a natural amphitheater and I knew the ocean view from the hilltop would be magnificent.

My father was chatting with Willie a few hundred feet down the beach. I focused my video camera and panned the beach and surrounding hillside.

My father approached barefoot, carrying his sandals. He glanced back to make sure Willie was out of earshot. "Do you believe this?"

"It's magnificent," I said, watching a pod of dolphins put the surfers to shame.

"It's the kind of place you never want to leave."

"Well, Dad, if we end up using this property, you can rest assured we won't be coming back. Except maybe in handcuffs."

"Yeah," he said. "But what a piece of land."

"Did you two talk any numbers yet?"

"No, I thought it would be better if you were there. You know, two against one."

"Don't let his 'aw shucks' approach fool you, Dad. Old Willie is pretty sharp."

"Yeah, but he wants out. I've been pimping southern Italy for the past half hour. He'd get on a plane today if he could. Have you got any ideas about what we might do with it yet?"

"A bunch," I said, nodding. "But we need to take a look at the other two parcels first."

"Why even bother?" my father said, spreading his arms at the expanse of beachfront.

"I'm thinking active versus passive money."

"You do that, son," my father said, laughing. "Here he comes."

Willie approached and removed his hat to wipe his brow. "So what do you think?"

"It's pretty special, Willie. I'll give you that," I said. "But I can't help but wonder why it hasn't already sold."

"Over the past ten years people were always looking to buy it. But that was during the time when I was still thinking about developing it. I guess people finally got tired of asking. I literally just decided to sell it the other day. Lucky for you, huh?"

"Maybe," I said, smiling. "Can we take a look at the other two parcels?"

"You think you might want all of it?"

"You never know."

We drove back up the road that led away from the beach and veered onto a dirt track. The beach disappeared and the landscape changed dramatically as the road became impassable. The four wheel drive lurched forward and I stopped at Willie's request.

"Gentlemen," Willie said, hopping out. "Allow me to introduce the tea tree."

When Willie told us that the tree was the only thing that grew on the land, he had misspoken. I knew that many types of plants would flourish in this soil but the tea trees were having none of it. They had taken up residence and obviously didn't like outsiders moving in.

"I had a geological survey done several years back," Willie said. "There are three underground streams that work their way through this area on their way to the ocean."

"That's a problem," I said, surveying the massive thicket of trees.

"Not for these trees." Willie laughed. "But the geologist said it would be impossible to build here."

"Because it would wash away from underneath," I said.

"Yup," he said. "So, for once, it looks like Mother Nature wins one. Just my luck she does it on my land."

"I've seen enough of this." I hopped back in the driver's seat.

I managed to turn around and head back to the main road. We made our way up to the highway, traveled about a mile, and turned away from the beach onto another dirt road. This parcel was overgrown with a magnificent collection of native plants and flowers. The acreage was dotted with the same type of orchid I had seen at Manny's.

"Do you want to walk it?" Willie said.

"No, it looks like snake country to me," my father said.

"There are definitely snakes out there," Willie said. "No doubt about that. But that's nothing that a couple of big bulldozers wouldn't fix."

"Sure," I said, dismissing the thought that I would ever bulldoze something this beautiful.

"I had a guy who wanted to go into partnership with me several years ago. He wanted to build condos. With that view, I bet they would have gone fast."

"I'm sure they would have," I said. "What happened?"

"Just couldn't convince myself to do it. Add a partner, quadruple your problems. Know what I mean?"

"Yes, I certainly do," I said, flashing back to Emily. "You're handling the sale by yourself?"

"You bet. Well, me and my lawyer anyway. Why should I pay some real estate agent a fat commission for something I can do myself?"

"Okay." I nodded and looked at Willie. "How much?"

"For all of it?"

"Maybe," I said. "But can you break it down for me by parcel?"

"Son," he said, smiling. "I can do that in my sleep."

"Let's talk." I leaned against the four wheel drive and stared at the old man.

Willie folded his arms and stood a few feet away. Perhaps he was formulating the asking price but I doubted it. Perhaps he was continuing to size me up to see if, in fact, I was a serious buyer. Perhaps he was already visioning himself on the Italian coast with an olive-skinned beauty. Whatever the reason, he stayed silent. I continued to lean against the vehicle and wait.

"Obviously, the beachfront is far and away the most valuable," he said, slowly putting his sales pitch in gear.

"Without a doubt," I said.

"Mind you, it's still possible to find undeveloped waterfront property in this country but it's getting harder, especially here on the North Coast."

"I agree, Willie. You're absolutely right."

"Plus, it's two miles long. That's quite a chunk and you could do a lot of different things with it."

"It's a magnificent piece of property."

"So, for the two hundred hectares that includes the two mile stretch of beachfront, I want a hundred fifty thousand per hectare."

Before I could stop myself, I whistled at what I considered a bargain price. "Thirty million."

105

"Now I know that sounds like a lot of money."

"Thirty million is a lot of money, Willie," I said, laughing. "In any language."

"It sure is, mate." The fact that I hadn't fallen over upon hearing the price encouraged him to continue. "Now the parcel across the highway does have the view and you could do some different things with that. Houses or maybe a little farming."

"Yes," I said, shrugging. "It might have some potential."

"For those hundred hectares, I'm asking sixty each."

"Another six million."

"Right," he said. "And that leaves the four hundred hectares filled with the tea treas. I'll let that go for twenty thousand a hectare. But apart from the privacy it would give you, I don't know what you'd do with it."

"Me either," I said, making a mental note to research the tea tree. "That's another eight million."

"You're pretty good with numbers, aren't you?" Willie said.

"Yeah, I get by." I grinned at him and rolled the numbers around in my head. All up, we're looking at a grand total of forty-four million. Sound about right?"

"That's it," he said, rolling a cigarette.

"I'm assuming there's some room for negotiation," my father said.

"Make me an offer."

"Could you excuse us for just a second, Willie? We need to talk this over." I strolled away from the vehicle, my father trailing close behind.

"Forty-four million dollars?" my father said, shaking his head. "It actually sounds reasonable, but what the hell do I know? What do you think?"

"I think we need to figure out a way to get this done." I stared out at the ocean. "Give me a minute."

"Gene, I gotta tell you," he said. "I'm way out of my league here."

"Don't worry about it, Dad," I said, trying to concentrate.

"But I hate to lay the whole thing on you."

"Shhh."

I spent the next several minutes walking in a slow circle deep in thought. Several possibilities ran back and forth through my mind. I felt the adrenaline surge and I let it wash over me, push me, guide me to the correct path. I turned to my father and looked directly into his eyes.

"How big do you want to go with this one?" I said.

"As big as we can. We both know the amount of work is the same no matter how much money's involved."

"Good." I put my arm around him as we walked back towards the vehicle. "Then let's go big."

Willie extinguished his cigarette as we approached. If he was eager to hear our counter offer he gave nothing away.

"Willie," I said. "We'd like to make an offer right here, right now. We love that piece of beachfront."

"What about the other two parcels?"

"Oh, we're going to make you an offer for all of it but we both know it's the beachfront that makes it work. But I imagine that your life would be easier if you could sell it all in one shot."

"Absolutely," Willie said.

"We'll take all of it. For forty million." I let the number hang in the air.

Willie tried it on for size. "Forty million."

"Forty million. But we have a couple of conditions."

Willie turned suspicious. "Such as?"

"The first one is that you tell no one who has bought your property. We have several ideas and don't want to run the risk of any publicity or local gossip getting in the way."

"That's fair," he said.

"The second is that we want up to six months before we close."

"Jesus Christ, Gene," he said, red flags waving everywhere. "Six months. That's ridiculous."

"Look Willie," I said. "I know that's a long time but we've got a lot of financing to put in place. Plus, most of it will be from international sources. I'm not saying we'll need that much time, but I can't run the risk of the deal falling apart over some arbitrary closing date."

"I don't know," he said. "You're asking me to put my plans on hold for another six months. At my age, I ain't got six months to spare."

"Tell me about it," my father said, laughing.

"Not at all, Willie," I said. "In exchange for the six months, we're willing to put five percent cash down now. That's two million dollars you'll have within a week. And it's nonrefundable. If for some reason the deal doesn't close, you keep the property but walk away with two million bucks of our money free and clear."

Willie beamed then whistled softly. "Gentlemen, we have a deal."

"Have your lawyer draw up the agreement and let us know when it's ready. I'll get the signed contract back to you along with a check for two million."

"Unbelievable," he said.

"Willie, if I were you, I'd book a ticket to Italy," my father said, slapping him on the back.

"Why don't we go celebrate with a cold one?"

"I could probably force one down," I said.

We climbed back in the vehicle and I looked at Willie as I drove towards the highway. "Willie, now that we have a deal, would you mind telling me how much your family originally paid for the land?"

"That's the kicker, mate. In 1931, my grandfather won the whole lot in a poker game."

Chapter Twenty One

"There you are." I pointed at the computer screen.

My father sat down holding two cups of coffee. After two beers, we'd left Willie at the pub and headed straight to an internet café in Byron Bay, a coastal town only a twenty minute drive from the property

"Is that it?" he said, sliding one of the coffees in my direction.

"That's it. The *Melaleuca alternifoli,* better known as the tea tree," I said, not taking my eyes off the screen. "It says here the tea tree grows best in swampy ground. You don't have to convince me."

"Me either," my father said, sipping his coffee. "And I'm not the easiest guy to convince. Who would have ever believed that a cup of coffee would cost four bucks?"

I laughed but kept reading. "The Aborigines have used tea tree oil for thousands of years for a variety of medicinal and other health related purposes. Today, tea tree oil, although a relative newcomer to the general marketplace, is beginning to establish itself in the booming industry of alternative medicines."

"Define booming." He leaned closer to the screen.

"There's a link here," I said. "Let's see what it says."

I sat back and waited for the page to load. I scanned the section that summarized the alternative medicine market and then closed my eyes and let the numbers sink in. I blinked then reread them.

"Jesus," I said, rubbing my forehead. "Can that be right? Worldwide sales for alternative medicines total sixty billion?" I looked away from the screen and took a sip of coffee. I slid the coffee a safe distance from the keyboard and resumed reading from the screen. "Conservative estimates project that this market will continue to grow fifteen percent annually for the predictable future," And by 2015, it's expected to grow to over a hundred billion.

Eighty percent of the world's population uses botanicals as their primary form of medicine."

I took another sip of coffee and stared at the screen.

"How come I've never even heard about this? Man, I've been asleep at the wheel." I read from the screen. "It says that the most successful tea tree companies now use mechanized harvesting and distilling since manual harvesting has proven cumbersome and cost prohibitive. We'll need to be able to explain our plans for harvesting."

"We could bulldoze a bunch of access roads no problem."

"Dad," I said. "We're not trying to build it, remember? We're just trying to convince everybody else that we are."

"Sorry," he said. "I forgot for a minute."

"The oil is found in the cells of the leaves. The foliage is cut by harvesting equipment, fed directly into a mobile vat, and then towed to the distillery." I sipped more coffee. "That sounds too easy. There has to be a catch somewhere."

I clicked through the next page that dealt with distillation. Suddenly, I was becoming a very big fan of the tea tree. "Vats are sealed, connected to a condenser, and steam is passed through the tea tree foliage. Distillation is normally complete within two hours."

"Two hours? That's it?"

"Yeah," I said. "And here's the kicker. The whole operation runs on steam. A portion of the leaf residue remaining after distillation is used as fuel for the steam boiler, and the rest is spread on harvested areas as mulch. There's no waste. It's completely recycled. The harvested area is replenished by the mulch. And there's more. It says the tea tree grows extremely fast and the harvested foliage is fully regenerated within two years. This thing has got to be the darling of environmentalists everywhere."

"It probably takes a ton of the shit just to squeeze out a few bottles," he said, apparently reading my mind.

"Probably," I said, clicking to a new page. "But there's only one way to find out." I rubbed my fingers against my thumbs while waiting for the new page to load. The initial rush of adrenaline continued to spread.

"I'm getting excited," he said, draping an arm across my shoulder.

"Me too, Dad. Me too. Holy shit," I whispered. "A four hundred hectare plantation produces an average of two hundred kilograms of oil per day."

"How much is that in a language I can understand?"

"A kilogram is a little over two pounds."

He nodded. "Did you say per day?"

"Per *day*."

"Do the math for me," he said, leaning back in his chair.

"Okay, we've got four hundred hectares so that's two hundred kilograms of oil per day." I stopped when I saw the look he was giving me. "Sorry. A thousand acres producing somewhere around four hundred and fifty pounds of oil per day. That comes to what?" I did the math in my head. "Just over a hundred sixty thousands pounds of tea tree oil annually."

"And we don't even have to start from scratch. It's just sitting there waiting to be harvested. Does it say how much a pound of that stuff sells for?"

"Think bigger, Dad," I said, clicking to a new page.

"I don't get it."

"Think value added."

"I don't even know what the hell that means," he said. "Speak English."

"Who do you think buys tea tree oil from the people who process it?"

"That's easy," he said. "The people who do the manufacturing."

"Precisely. And where is the real money made when it comes to retail products?"

"Large scale manufacturing."

"Very good," I said, pointing to the screen. "Take a look at some of the things they make with this stuff."

"Son of a bitch," he said scanning the list of products that ran from antiseptic creams to mouthwash, foot powders to sore muscle lotions, cleaning products to dog shampoo. "So we're going into the tea tree business."

"That's part of it," I said, entering a new search.

"What are you looking for now?"

"I want to take a look at the native flower market, especially for orchids," I said, reviewing the search results.

"Okay, but hurry up. I'm getting hungry," he said, examining his left forearm. "Well, would you take a look at this?"

I leaned over and inspected the area he was pointing at. "I don't see anything," I said, turning back to the screen.

"That's my point," he said. "Remember last night when I burned my arm on that candle?"

"Yeah."

"You'll never guess what Millie rubbed on it."

Chapter Twenty Two

I'd decided to drive back to Sydney to give myself quiet time to think and develop the strategy we would be using. I'd left my father on the North Coast with a lengthy and growing list of things to do. My excitement level had been on a roller coaster since the deal closing handshake with Willie. One minute I would be flushed with adrenaline as one more piece of the complex puzzle fell into place, the next I would pale as the reality of how much work, and potential danger, lay before us.

Defining the categories of activities requiring attention was straightforward, but compiling a master list of tasks for each had proven elusive. Even now, after several hours behind the wheel deep in thought, the final list was far from complete. Office space requirements gave way to signage. Business name segued into slogan. Advertising possibilities drove me back to budget. Potential sales presentations forced me to deal with technology.

Whenever a coherent thought popped into my head, I raised a handheld recorder to my mouth without taking my eyes off the road, stated the category and associated activity, then placed it back in my shirt pocket until the next idea presented itself. Even this early into the project, I knew that the information contained on the recording device would probably be enough evidence to lock me away for an extended period of time.

"Category; Target List," I said holding the recorder a few inches from my mouth. "Activity; Identify the thousand wealthiest people in the world for personalized campaigns. Category; Advertising. Activity; Develop copy for full page ads in business magazines. Activity; Obtain costs for such ads. Activity; Finalize selected magazines to be used for June editions. Category; Sales Presentations. Activity; Contract with local video company to shoot flyover of property."

I called my father.

"Still on the road?" my father said. He sounded like he'd just woken up. "Where are you?"

"I'm about three hours out of Sydney." I slowed as the traffic increased. "You been napping?"

"Yeah," he said. "I must be getting old."

"Jesus, Dad. You've been going full bore since we got here. Add in the booze, the weed, and the lack of sleep."

"I'm on vacation."

"Not anymore, you're not."

"I've been thinking about the type of office we should rent."

"And?"

"I think we should go for a tropical, yet traditional, image. Something that gives the impression of stability. Like we've been around a long time. Hang a wooden sign with an antique look and feel."

"And close to a pub," I said.

"In this country, everything is close to the pub. What do you think?"

"I like it."

"And I found us a nice house to rent near the beach in Byron Bay. I think you'll like it."

"How much?"

"Well, it wasn't cheap. But it sure wasn't forty million." I laughed as I accelerated.

"I'll get working on the office space first thing in the morning."

"That's great. If the bank loan goes as planned, I should be back in a couple of days. I'll drop the rental off and fly up. You want to rent a car and pick me up at the airport in Brisbane?"

"Sure. I've been wanting to check out the Gold Coast."

"Sounds good, Dad. I'll give you a call tomorrow."

"You got it. Goodnight, son. Oh, one more thing."

"What's that?"

"I love you."
"I love you too, Dad."

Chapter Twenty Three

I sank into the deep leather chair and looked around the office reminded that some vestiges of colonialism died hard. Especially in the banking industry. The artwork and elegant furnishings surrounded by walls of dark, polished wood conveyed the intended message: Yes, we've got lots of money. What makes you think we're going to lend any of it to you?

I was waiting to meet with my third and, hopefully, last executive. I fully understood their caution since my Australian corporation was new and I was an unknown. On paper, I was just one more American entrepreneur seeking out a new locale to strike it rich. That was true. I was. Although probably not in the manner they were expecting.

The door opened and an impeccably groomed man in his fifties entered the office and approached with a forced smile. I recognized the blue suit, but I imagined this man's motivations were somewhat different from my previous clients. This man didn't appear to be looking or longing for love. He was either hanging on against the pressure of the young and hungry corporate climbers, or merely counting the days until he could get out.

"Mr. Johnson," he said, extending his hand. "Sorry to keep you waiting. I'm Wilbur Pelligrew, Senior Vice President for commercial lending."

"Nice to meet you, sir." I stood and returned the handshake. "You're my third Vice President today." I caught his raised eyebrow. "But you're my first *senior* Vice President."

"Yes, I'm afraid there are a lot of us," he said, maintaining his smile. "But if all goes well, I am your last stop."

Finally. Someone who could make a decision. I sat down and watched as he flipped open the file already on his desk.

"I understand that you're buying some land on our beautiful North Coast," he said, perusing a stack of photos.

"As a matter of fact, I am." I nodded, my hands folded respectfully on my lap.

"And a beautiful piece of property it is." He glanced up at me.

"Thank you."

"Would it be possible for you to tell me exactly what your plans are for the land?"

"I'm sorry, Mr. Pelligrew," I said. "At this time, given the competitive advantage we feel the property provides, unfortunately, I must respectfully decline to share much information other than to say it involves a combination of residential and commercial activities."

He removed his glasses and blinked several times in rapid succession. "I see. Well then, let me ask a few, shall we say, less intrusive questions."

"That would be fine," I said.

"Are we talking about manufacturing?"

"Yes, sir."

"Heavy or light?"

"It would be most accurately described as light. But it will provide at least two hundred jobs when running at full capacity with zero environmental impact."

"No environmental impact?" he said, raising that damn eyebrow again. "Perhaps as an American you use a different definition of zero impact?"

Now he had pissed me off. At that moment, I decided I wasn't leaving this room without two million dollars of his bank's money.

"I think you'll discover, Mr. Pettigrew that my definition of zero is identical to yours. In fact, one of the hallmarks of my firm is refusing to get involved with any enterprise that causes damage to the environment."

"So light manufacturing it is." He scribbled a note on my loan application. "When do you expect to have your operation up and running?"

"Depending on the date we close on the property, twelve to eighteen months."

"Ambitious," he said. "But then that doesn't surprise me."

I almost bit through my tongue restraining myself from leaping across the desk to stuff the Oxford tie down the British twit's throat. But I decided there wouldn't be room for it given how far the stick was shoved up his ass.

"I agree. The business plan is ambitious, yet still realistic."

"But you're not able to share that with me."

"No. Sorry."

He flipped through the application for a second time just to make me wait. He reread the notes his underlings had prepared from my earlier meetings. He checked his watch. Straightened his tie. Flicked imaginary lint off his sleeve.

"Let me make sure I understand this completely. You're looking for a loan for two million dollars for what might be called earnest money in order to secure the property."

"Yes, it's five percent of the purchase price and I have six months to complete the financing."

"That seems fairly straightforward. May I ask why you simply don't use the funds in your account? With the additional funds you transferred in this morning, you certainly have more than enough funds to cover this transaction."

"Mr. Pelligrew, I'm sure I don't have to explain the importance of establishing good corporate credit in a new country to a person such as yourself."

"No," he said, dismissively. "You most certainly do not. How much collateral can we count on?"

"How much would you like?"

"Since this is your first transaction with us, I'm afraid that I need to request that you maintain an account balance of at least half the loan amount for the first three months. After that, I would be happy to review the situation."

"That's more than fair," I said. "I don't anticipate the need to use that account for several months."

"Are you considering using an Australian bank for the remaining portion of the land purchase? Or perhaps the construction phase?"

"I'm currently examining many financing options and, of course, traditional mechanisms are on the list. Do you think your bank might be interested?"

"Certainly," he said, standing up to end the meeting. "Especially if you would consider some level of equity participation on our part."

"Mr. Pelligrew," I said, forcing a smile of my own. "Unfortunately, at this point we are working exclusively with individual investors. But if an opportunity ever arises to include outside entities as equity partners, rest assured, you will be the first person I call."

"I would certainly appreciate and welcome the opportunity. Congratulations, Mr. Johnson. I will have the funds transferred sometime tomorrow morning."

"Thank you, sir." I stood and shook his hand. "I've really enjoyed this."

"Welcome to Australia," he said. "I hope you enjoy many profitable years with your ventures."

"We're certainly off to a good start," I said, following his lead towards the door. "If you don't mind my asking, why would a loan for a mere two million end up on your desk? I would think that a loan of that size would be delegated down to one of the other two gentlemen I met with earlier."

"Yes, most people do. But I like to stay personally involved with our valued commercial clients. The personal attention one receives from a person such as *myself* is a hallmark of our reputation for providing outstanding service."

He puffed up until it looked like he was about to explode.

"I can see that. And it certainly seems to be working for you."

I waved goodbye, my earlier suspicion confirmed.

This guy was hanging on for dear life.

Chapter Twenty Four

"Now promise me you'll look at the whole thing before you say anything."

My father was bouncing around like a three year old with a credit card at a candy store. I stared at him, as did several other onlookers, as we made our way from the parking lot to the industrial warehouse.

"Now I probably spent too much money but I think it's worth it. I hope you like it."

I noticed the sign first. It hung from a wrought iron bracket on the second floor that provided easy reading from the street. The sign was egg shaped and forest green with gold lettering. I stopped a few feet away and looked up.

The Syndicate
Like minded people doing like minded things

"That looks great, Dad," I said, genuinely impressed.

"Yeah, it's good," he said, leading me through the glass doors.

I stepped into a large foyer that opened onto an elegant reception area. The ceilings were high and the hardwood floors gleamed.

"The wood floors run through the whole place. I've got three new rugs being delivered tomorrow. C'mon, I'll show you the offices."

He led me through a large wooden door into a large open space with offices tucked behind glass.

"This is your office. Nice, huh?"

I glanced around the large furnished office. A new computer sat on the corner of the desk and appeared ready for business.

"You got the computers hooked up?"

"They finished this morning. Software's loaded. Internet ready. Just like you asked for."

"Good job, Dad. I wasn't expecting this for another week."

"I know," he said, pulling me out the office and down the hall to a conference room. "Think this will work for the presentations?"

"This is perfect," I said, looking around at the furnishings and electronics on display. "What about the projection screen?"

"Watch this." He pressed a button near the light switch. A large white screen slowly descended from the ceiling. "Well?"

"This is amazing."

"Yeah, and it's got that big money feel to it."

"It does," I said, laughing.

"Now for the best part."

He led me back towards the entrance to another wooden door that led to the top floor. At the top of the stairs I stepped into a large furnished apartment that had been outfitted right down to fresh flowers.

"Australian orchids," he said, smiling. "Nice touch, huh?"

"What's this for?"

"For us, of course."

"We already rented a house, Dad."

"I know. But it's nice to have it available for those nights we work late. Or need a place for an afternoon nap."

I wandered around the loft, nodding as I moved from one area to the next. "This is nice." The kitchen and living area were combined in one large open space and along the far back wall I saw the same wooden doors as downstairs.

"Bedrooms," he said, anticipating the question. "There are two. Both master suites."

"How did you find this place?"

"Two hotshot lawyers from Sydney opened an office here and needed a place to stay when they were in town so they converted this from a storage area to a loft. And then one of their wives discovered that it was actually being used for affairs other than those of a legal nature."

"Ouch."

"Yeah, I'm sure. She got this place as part of the divorce settlement and decided to keep it and rent it out."

"How much?"

"Fifteen thousand a month. Plus, I dropped another fifty on furniture and office stuff. Did I do good, son?"

"Do I get to pick my own bedroom?"

"No," he said, grinning. "But you're gonna love the one I gave you."

Chapter Twenty Five

"Why don't you take a break and actually sit down while you eat?"

I looked up from the blueprints I was reviewing while stuffing meatloaf into my mouth. I nodded and joined my father at the dining room table.

"This is great." I stuffed another large piece into my mouth. "Just like Mom used to make."

"Who do you think taught her?" He opened a bottle of Shiraz and poured two glasses.

"Really? You taught her how to cook?"

"Yeah." He shook his head at the memory and laughed. "She was pretty bad when we first got married. But she got good in a hurry."

I sipped my wine and stared out through the large windows overlooking the ocean.

"What?" my father said, nibbling his dinner.

"I was just wondering what she would think about what we're doing."

"She'd be pissed." He wiped his mouth. "And not pissed in the Australian way."

"Yeah, I imagine she would." I dismissed the thought and returned to the meatloaf. "The blueprints look good. Tomorrow, I need to get them to the guy building the scale model."

"That architect in Seattle turned those plans around in a hurry."

"Yeah, he's good. And he owed me a favor."

"How much?"

"Fifty thousand."

"This is getting expensive," he said. "Are you sure you want to spend the extra money on the air and hotel?"

"Yeah," I said, refilling my plate. "It does two things. It helps us sort out the real players since they have to provide some financial information on the application. And it gives the impression that there's a chance we might say no to them. Nothing drives rich people crazier than the thought someone might not let them into a very exclusive group. That someone might have the audacity to tell them to take a hike."

"I don't get it. You're going to spend all that money just to make some rich people think they're not worthy?"

"No, not quite," I said, putting down my fork. "If I asked them to come all the way down here on their own nickel, they'd immediately be on guard. But if we're willing to front them first class tickets, plus three days at a high end resort, they immediately begin to think they're dealing with, as you so eloquently phrased it, like minded people."

"If you ask me, the whole thing sounds like one of those timeshare deals."

"That's pretty close, Dad. An elaborate, high end version of it. Apart from the sharing part. I don't think most of these folks are big on sharing."

"You would have made a hell of a businessman, Gene," he said, starting to clean up.

"I am a hell of a businessman."

"You know what I mean."

"Yeah, I know what you mean. But this way is a lot more fun, huh?"

"I'm getting nervous."

"You should be," I said, laughing. "It's big."

"Too big for me," he whispered.

"You'll be fine, Dad."

"So how much will all this travel and accommodation cost?"

"Somewhere around twenty-five grand per couple. And I thought we'd start with fifty couples.

"And that comes to?"

"Around a million bucks."

"You're out of your mind," he said, carrying our plates to the sink.

"Yeah, maybe. But what does that make you?"

"A frightened old man?"

I sipped my wine and decided he was speaking, at a minimum, a half-truth. But any fear working its way into my system didn't stand a chance against the adrenaline-fueled excitement that was building daily.

"What was prison like?"

He turned off the water and dried his hands on a dish towel. "It's like being in hell without having any of your old friends around. I don't recommend it."

"Occupational hazard, Dad."

Chapter Twenty Six

"Good morning, Gene. Did you get some sleep?"

"The usual." I smiled at the young woman we'd hired as our receptionist. "About four hours." I picked up the large stack of mail sitting on her desk. "Is this all mine?"

"Yes, your Dad already has his." She answered the phone. "The Syndicate. How may I direct your call? Hold one moment, please." She looked up at me. "It's Qantas."

"Put it through to my father," I said, heading off to my office.

I poured a cup of coffee and examined the whiteboard that dominated one wall. The appointment schedule was quickly filling and, judging from the size of the morning's mail, I realized that our initial round would probably be finalized by the end of the day. And not a day too soon.

I was exhausted and knew I'd need a few days of doing nothing before our first appointment next Monday. I looked at the whiteboard and reviewed the list of items.

Final draft of business plan. Done.

Finalize travel arrangements. I would be speaking with my father on that in the next few minutes.

Finalize hospitality tours. Also on my list to discuss with my partner in crime.

Finalize scale model. Done and on display in the conference room.

The rest of the items were small and could be dealt with later. I sat down and began opening the applications I had received in the mail. I continued to be surprised at the willingness of some of the richest people on the planet to fill out an application. I had named it the Declaration of Participant Interest but, call it what you will, it was an application. Some of the names I received today were well-known, others unfamiliar. Regardless of their identity or what they did for a living, they all had two things in common. Each one had a net worth of at least five hundred million, and they were all flying to Australia to see me.

"That was Qantas," my father said, entering the office and sitting down on the couch.

"Problem?"

"No, they just called to thank us for our business. That many first class tickets definitely got their attention. How many came in today?"

"It looks like another seven or eight," I said, joining him on the couch.

"Jesus." He shook his head. "Another couple of days trying to work with their schedules. What a nightmare."

"I'm sure it is."

"Monday, huh?"

"Yeah," I said, biting my lip. "Monday."

"Have you decided how you want to handle the daily schedule?"

"I think so," I said, continuing to peruse the mail. "Let's do the initial two-hour session here in the mornings. Then we'll give them a tour of the property and drop them off for lunch at the resort. We'll save the afternoon for ourselves in case we need to follow up with any of the other investors. We'll keep nights open for dinner and drinks. We might not need it since I'm betting they'll want to be by themselves at some point to talk and make a decision. But you never know."

"Got it," he said. "Sounds good."

"And another thing, Dad. Take it easy with the booze. We need to stay sharp."

"The things I do for this company."

"I'll be damned. Look who wants to play," I said, handing him a signed application form.

"Holy shit," he said. "William Lawrence."

"None other," I said, a wicked smile breaking out.

"What?"

"Draft a letter and tell him we are no longer accepting applications at this time."

"Are you nuts? He's one of the richest people in the world. He's gotta be worth fifty billion."

"I know," I said. "But he's also the Ty Cobb of the computer industry. Everyone hates his guts. When word gets out that we turned him down, people will be lining up to get in."

"Whatever you say," he said, heading back towards his office. "Say, you still want to take the weekend off?"

"I sure do."

"Feel like heading over to see the baby?"

"I don't think so, Dad. When I say I want to do nothing, that's exactly what I mean."

"Okay," he said. "Then I think I'll drive up to Brisbane and spend a day at the track."

"Not until you finish up everything here," I said.

"Yes, boss."

Chapter Twenty Seven

Doc slid his chair further under the umbrella and watched Merlin work. Oblivious to everything except the computer screen in front of him, Merlin's fingers machine-gunned the keyboard then stopped as the page reloaded.

"Here we go. I knew it was out there somewhere." Merlin glanced around the rooftop garden and, satisfied with the privacy, quickly drew two lines and snorted them back. He sipped vodka, rattled his ice, and sipped again. He exhaled loudly and settled back in his chair as he turned the computer screen towards Doc.

"There are half a dozen programs running. What am I supposed to be looking for?"

"You're a smart guy. You'll figure it out." Merlin said. "Start with the Qantas reservation system."

Doc maximized the screen and began scrolling through the information. Moments later, he stopped and looked at his diminutive friend. "All I'm seeing is a list of people flying Qantas over the next month."

"And you call yourself a spy?"

"Ex-spy. Look, Merlin, Hedaya and Rose will be joining us for lunch in a couple of minutes. Why don't I just acknowledge your superior intellectual powers so we can get on with this?"

"Now was that so hard?" Merlin sniffed then drained the rest of his drink. He cocked his head. "What did you say?"

"Nothing."

"Sort the upcoming reservations for next month by travel status then by payer information."

Doc tapped the keyboard and squinted at the screen. "Okay, now I can see who is flying first class but…shit. That's interesting."

"Yes, it is. And it gets better."

"Why would one entity be paying for that many tickets?"

"Why indeed?" Merlin waved at the waiter for another cocktail.

"If all the tickets were for the same day it might make sense. Like if a corporation was paying for a junket or a big meeting. But these tickets are all for different days spread out over several weeks."

"Very good. Your neurons are finally starting to fire."

"Fuck you, Merlin. You get up on the wrong side of bed again?"

"Who's got time for sleep?" He nodded thanks to the waiter and sipped his fresh drink.

Doc refocused on the screen. "Okay, we have the credit card number that was used to pay for all the tickets. Now we need to find out who owns the card."

"You're gonna need a different screen, aren't you?"

Doc glared at Merlin then clicked through the other open windows until he found the one he needed. "The card is registered to a company called The Syndicate. Sydney address. Name on the account is a Mr. Fred Johnson. Does that name ring a bell with you?"

"It does now. But it took a while. I had to back into it."

Doc waited in vain for more information. "Merlin, cut the crap, okay?"

"You're no fun at all." Merlin moved his chair next to Doc and took control of the keyboard. "Here's a photo of the Sydney address listed on the credit card application."

"It's a vacant lot. Where did you get the photo? Google Earth?"

Merlin rolled his eyes. "Google Earth? Really, Doc? Let's just say drones can be used for more than delivering missiles and leave it at that."

"Samuels?"

"Who else? As much as I hate the prick, he does come in handy from time to time. As soon as I saw it was a vacant lot, I knew something was going on."

"So who's this Mr. Johnson?"

"It's our guy's father."

"Hmmm. Interesting. Fake name. I'm guessing fake passport, too."

Merlin clicked on another minimized window and an image of a smiling old man appeared on the screen. "And here's the passport photo of our guy, Gene."

"They both look pretty happy."

"They should. They haven't got caught yet." Merlin clicked another window.

"What am I looking at?" Doc said, squinting against the glare.

"The Syndicate's corporate paperwork. It was registered as an Australian corporation in late January."

"Right before the Superbowl."

"Very good. And guess where the registration process originated."

"Vegas?"

"Give the man a cigar. I confirmed it was them when I figured out they'd flew to Sydney out of Vancouver."

"I'm guessing he got spooked while he was here and decided to go with a fake identity."

"Yeah, that's my guess too. Between that idiot Gentry and his girlfriend Grace, I'm not surprised he figured out the Feebs were watching him. Plus, who knows what information she gives out when she's horizontal."

"He and Grace were going at it?"

"Yeah. Didn't I mention that?"

"No. I would have remembered. Man, she gets around. So what's he up to in Sydney?"

"He's actually set up shop on the north coast of New South Wales in Byron Bay. Take a look."

Doc looked at the video playing on the screen. "Wow. What a beautiful piece of property."

"He bought it three months ago for forty million. Well, he gave the owner two million as a down payment. But it's basically his as long as he manages to come up with the other thirty-eight."

Doc watched the rest of the video play out. When it finished he sat back in his chair deep in thought. "So he's working a land scam?"

"Yeah. And he's trying to land some very big fish. Take another look at the Qantas reservations."

Doc clicked the window and scanned the list of names. "I recognize some of them. Safe to say they're all incredibly rich?"

"As long as billionaire meets your definition of rich."

"So what's the play?"

"That is still unknown, but I have a feeling we'll figure it out very soon." Merlin opened another window and a spreadsheet appeared on the screen. "This one was really hard to hack."

"Merlin, this is where I usually ask you how on earth you managed to get your hands on it and you just roll your eyes at me. This time, I'm not asking."

"No, go ahead and ask."

Doc stared at Merlin then nodded.

"Thought you'd never ask. I'm pretty proud of this one. I used the same technique I've been using with Hedaya's email account. I sent out a bogus inquiry to The Syndicate's email account and got an automated response back. Once I had an email from them, I was eventually able to work my way into our guy's personal email. And as soon as I got into that, I was able to get at any attachments he had on his emails. At some point he emailed this spreadsheet to his old man, and I was able to grab it. It's the master list of all the people they're targeting. Several hundred of the richest people in the world. See anyone you know?"

"Bill Lawrence from Prophecy. That makes sense. He's gotta be worth close to a hundred billion these days."

"He actually told our old boss to take a hike."

133

Doc laughed. "I'm sure Bill loved that. He hates to be told no."

"Actually it was a pretty smart move. Everybody hates having that asshole around."

Doc laughed again and resumed scanning the list. "Hedaya?"

"Yeah. How about that?"

"But Hedaya hasn't mentioned anything."

"He hasn't gotten his invitation yet. It says here that it was just express mailed yesterday. It's should arrive today."

"And you're thinking that, acting as Hedaya's personal emissaries, we should fly down there to check things out?"

"Yes, and I think we should bring along someone else on that list."

Doc scanned the list again. "Summerman? He made the list?"

"He did indeed."

"I knew he sold a lot of records but I had no idea he was worth that much."

"It's not just from record sales. He's made a lot of his money since he's been…well, able to take advantage of his situation. His invitation went out a couple of weeks ago, but he just crossed over so he probably hasn't seen it yet."

"First class on Qantas to Brisbane doesn't sound too bad."

"Screw that," Merlin said, drawing out two lines. "I'm thinking that Summerman's Gulfstream is a much better option."

The private elevator to the rooftop garden opened and an enormous beast made a mad dash for the pool. It leapt from the edge and landed with a huge splash spraying water over Doc and Merlin. The dog surfaced, barked loudly, and swam in small circles before climbing out. It padded over to the table and Doc was able to close the computer just before the massive animal shook. Both men were drenched by the time it was over, and the dog put its front paws on Doc's shoulders and wagged its tail.

"Hi, Murray. Nice to see you, too." Doc laughed and rubbed the dog's head. The dog licked Doc's face then turned its attention to Merlin. Merlin, no match for the dog's size, succumbed to the affection.

"Jesus, Murray. Go easy. Hi, folks."

Doc stood and shook the outstretched hand. "Nice to see you, Summerman. You just get in?"

"About an hour ago. Hedaya and I were just catching up."

Hedaya laughed. "If you can call handing over a suitcase full of cash catching up. Hey, Doc."

Doc nodded at Hedaya who turned to watch Murray smother Merlin with affection.

"Give the little prick everything you've got, Murray." Hedaya sat down and waved at the waiter. He tossed a large unopened envelope on the table.

"Murray, enough," Summerman said. "Why don't you go do a few laps and burn off some of that energy?"

The dog cocked its head then headed back towards the pool.

"Sorry about that, guys. He's always a bit wound up the first few days after we cross over."

"Not a problem," Doc said. "He looks great."

"Yeah, he is." Summerman beamed at the dog now churning the length of the pool.

Hedaya nodded at Merlin.

"Hello, Hedaya," Merlin said, nodding at the envelope. "What's that?"

"I don't know. It was just delivered this morning."

Merlin smiled and sipped his drink.

"That looks familiar, Hedaya," Summerman said. He started digging through his shoulder bag. "I haven't even gotten around to opening my mail, but I think I have one

135

just like that. Yeah, here it is." He held up an identical envelope. "That's odd. Wonder what it is."

Merlin waved his empty glass at the waiter. "It's our ticket to Australia."

Chapter Twenty Eight

I stalled for time and waited for the adrenaline surge to subside. I flipped through the stack of papers in front of me. I sipped my water. I checked my watch, focused on my breathing and looked at the man and woman sitting across the table. I wasn't particularly worried about making them wait. They had just flown fourteen hours to meet with me and I was certain another fifteen seconds wouldn't bother them.

I returned the smile of Samuel Brewster, a fit, late-fifties billionaire from Texas, now semi-retired. His wife, Suzette, surgically enhanced, yet still elegant, sat quietly and sipped her coffee as she appraised me. Both had the well-deserved reputation for being pleasant but tough business people.

"I'd like to welcome you and thank you for taking time out of your schedule to meet with me," I said. "I decided not to have any of my staff here so I'll be working all the technology by myself. We'll see how that goes, huh?"

I received a polite chuckle.

"So, I'll probably be up and down throughout the meeting and I apologize up front if you find it a bit disconcerting."

"Not a problem, Gene," said the man who insisted on being called Sam.

"Thanks. Is the resort taking good care of you?"

"It's wonderful," Suzette said. "The spa is fabulous."

"Yes," Sam said. "I can't believe we've never been down here before. We kept talking about it, but never managed to find the time."

"It's a beautiful country."

"Friendly folks, too," Sam said. "It's getting harder and harder for Americans to be able to say that about other countries."

I nodded sympathetically and took another sip of water.

"I'd like to start by saying that what we are creating here is one of the most unique opportunities that has ever been offered anywhere. And I know that the two of you hear that same pitch all the time, probably more times than you care to remember. But I am going to be presenting a vision, backed by a remarkable business plan and strategy that will be unlike anything you've ever seen."

"That's a big statement, Gene," Sam said, staring at me. "I may still be a young fella', but I've seen a lot in my day."

"I was hoping you'd say that, Sam," I said, smiling. "I want you to challenge what I'm about to show you. In fact, given your reputation, I'd be disappointed if you didn't."

"Fair enough," he said. "Give me your best shot."

I lowered the projection screen then started the video. A title card appeared on the black screen.

"Like-minded people doing like-minded things," Sam said, reading from the screen. "That's good."

"We like it, too." The black screen was replaced by a dramatic aerial shot of the property. The shot opened on the ocean with the property off in the distance and grew more impressive as the plane approached shore. I heard two soft gasps from across the table and nodded my head slightly pleased by their initial reaction.

"The upper north coast of New South Wales," I said. "Two hours south of Brisbane and just outside of Byron Bay. One of the most beautiful places you will ever see. And it's twenty minutes from where you're sitting."

"And you own it," Suzette said, leaning forward in her chair.

"Unfortunately," I said, laughing. "Not all of it. Just two miles of beachfront plus an additional two thousand acres."

The aerial shot continued past the beach and the highway. Soon a massive field of wildflowers came into view. The camera zoomed in and the screen filled with magnificent colors.

"Australian wildflowers. Orchids are the primary flower. But the land is also home to a variety of natural plants rapidly establishing themselves in the alternative medicine sector. The Syndicate will be actively pursuing the domestic and international flower markets as well as the alternative medicine industry."

"What's the estimated yield?"

"Conservatively, we anticipate an annual yield in the neighborhood of ten to twenty thousand per acre."

"Not bad," Sam said, nodding.

The airplane turned and the image of dense foliage appeared.

"What the hell is that?" Sam said, blinking at the screen.

"That is the *Melaleuca alternifoli*, otherwise known as the tea tree."

"Never heard of it," he said, shaking his head.

"Well, Sam," I said. "You will leave here today with a packet of information that will tell you more about the tea tree than you'll probably ever want to know. But you're going to love the tea tree, Sam."

The video cut to a close up of one of the trees.

"The oil extracted from the tea tree leaves is one of those freaks of nature. It grows best in swampy areas and it just so happens that a thousand acres The Syndicate owns is fed by three underground streams that have made the land pretty useless." I beamed at them. "Except for growing tea trees. We will be extracting the oil and then manufacturing a variety of medicinal and health products within eighteen months."

"How much oil can you take out annually?"

"Close to two hundred thousand pounds," I said.

"One shot deal, or does it grow back?"

"Sam, this stuff grows faster than a crowd at a car crash. Every single day, we'll be extracting over four hundred pounds of the oil, distilling it a mere two hours using a completely recyclable and environmentally friendly process, and then using it in two dozen products."

"There's a market for this stuff?" He turned towards his wife who shrugged.

"Over eighty percent of the world's population uses botanicals as their primary source of medical care, and the alternative medicine industry is currently sixty billion and growing at fifteen percent annually."

"Sixty billion?" He shook his head. "I've never even heard of it. The only thing my doctor talks about is blood pressure medicine and cutting down on red meat."

"You can see why we're pretty excited about what we've got here."

"What are the numbers for the manufacturing operation?"

"Again, we've chosen to stay conservative with the numbers but, at year five, we're projecting a net profit close to hundred million."

"Okay. You've got my attention. What about you, dear?"

"Oh, don't worry, Sam," Suzette said. "I'm listening."

"So you're looking for a business partner to fund this thing?"

"Oh, my no," I said. "I'm sorry if I gave you that impression." I beamed at both of them. "I asked you here to extend an invitation for you and Suzette to join our community."

"Community? What community?"

"This one." I removed the dark blue cloth covering the scale model. It sparkled from the lights above the conference room table. They stood in unison and approached the model to examine it more closely. I watched and waited for them to absorb what they were looking at. They stared at each other and waited for me to continue.

"A very special community of fifty families. Forty houses perched directly on two miles of personal beachfront and three acres. The other ten houses will be constructed on the hillside, each one on six acres, for those preferring not to be directly on the beach. I think you'll agree that the ocean view from that hillside will be magnificent. We have five different models of homes to choose from, each plan with a traditional Australian look ranging from ten to twelve thousand square feet. Of course, each community member will have total control regarding their own residence's amenities and furnishing.

"What's this thing in the middle?" Suzette said, pointing at the structure that sat on the beach dividing the houses into sets of twenty on either side.

"That is a one hundred room hotel with four gourmet restaurants, a small shopping area for guests and residents, and other associated amenities one would expect to find in a five star hotel."

"A hundred rooms" Isn't that pretty small?" she said.

"Yes, it is. But only by choice," I said. "We've included the hotel not necessarily for monetary reasons, although we do anticipate turning a decent profit. The hotel is being built for two reasons. First, we plan on using the staff to also take care of our community members. As you know, a hotel employs a wide variety of service personnel. Housekeepers. Landscape gardeners. Not to mention our master chefs. They will be deployed to assist community members in any way they're needed. Second, we thought the hotel would provide a place for community members to entertain friends. And in case you ever have family members visiting you don't want staying in your house, we think they will be more than satisfied staying in a five star resort."

My last statement struck a chord with both of them and they laughed. In unison they said, "Aunt Shirley."

"And tucked behind the hotel is a golf course so magnificent and private, it will rival Augusta National. The total membership will be the fifty families making up the community.

"And hotel guests?" Suzette said.

"Of course," I said, smiling broadly at her. "At ten grand a night, the least we can do is let them play a round of golf."

"That's funny," Sam said. He got up from chair and began circling the conference room table to study the scale model from all angles.

"As a community member you will own two percent of The Syndicate. As a limited partner you will not have, nor should you want, any day to day decision making in the business operations. We're creating this community as a place for you to relax and enjoy life. Running the operations will be the responsibility of the General Partner."

"And that would be you," Sam said.

"Yes," I said, nodding. "I am one of the fifty members and have assumed General Partner responsibilities for an initial period of five years. After that, I can be renewed or removed based on the vote of the Board of Directors that will be comprised of eight members selected from the community."

"Only fifty," Sam said. "Bear with me while I talk this through. I get a beachfront house on three acres, access to a five star resort, and a lifetime membership at an exclusive golf course."

"Plus your share of the profits. Using year five as an example, we anticipate writing checks to each community member somewhere in the neighborhood of two million dollars. That annual annuity, plus your equity in the community, combined with the quality of life we are offering is what gives our proposal its uniqueness."

Sam sat down deep in thought. "Two million's fine. In fact for what we'd get, it's excellent. But how much debt will we be carrying?"

"Debt? There's no debt," I said. "As you'll see later from the business plan, it's fully funded from the start. I hate debt. Especially large amounts that can drag down startups."

"I won't argue with you there," he said, scrunching up his face.

"Don't do that thing with your face, dear," Suzette said. "You'll get wrinkles."

"Yes, dear," he said. "What's this thing going to cost?"

"One billion in U.S. dollars."

"Twenty million," he said. "Twenty million from fifty people. That's what you're looking for."

"Yes, Sam. Twenty million."

"You are one smart son of a bitch, Gene," Sam said, staring at the scale model. I hoped he was picking out the lot for his dream house.

The door burst open and all three of us, startled, jumped back.

"I've been looking for you, Gene. Don't think I don't know what you're up to here."

"How did you get in here?" I said.

"Don't worry about that," he said, slamming a fist on the conference table.

Sam and Suzette stepped back from the table staring in disbelief. I came around the table and stood a few feet away trying to remain calm.

"What can I do for you, Willie?"

"Tea tree oil? Exotic flowers? Beachfront houses? A couple of hundred million a year in profit? What do you think I want?"

"Actually, Willie, I have no idea. Didn't you tell me you had no interest in developing the property on your own?"

"Yeah," he said, lowering his voice a notch.

143

"And didn't I give you fair market value for the land?"

"Yeah."

"Then what on earth is the problem?"

"I want in. That's what the problem is. I can't believe that you would drink beer with me, buy my land and then not invite me to join your little club. I want a share. I want one of the fifty slots."

"Hang on a second, Willie. Sit down. Help yourself to some coffee."

I helped him fill a cup and waited until he was sitting and unable to take his eyes off the scale model. I approached Sam and Suzette with an apologetic grimace.

"Sorry about this," I whispered. "He means well. But I think he's been very lonely since his wife died."

"Poor guy," Suzette said.

"Tell you what," I said, glancing back at the old man sipping his coffee. "Take a copy of the business plan with you. It's got all the numbers, plus some other information that will provide more details. And then I'll come by the resort tonight and we can discuss it over dinner. Okay?"

They looked at each other, then at Willie and nodded.

"That's great," I said, escorting them to the door. "I sincerely apologize for the interruption. I'll see you tonight."

I walked them out to the reception area where Sally, red-faced with embarrassment, was sitting behind her desk. I shook their hands then held the door open and watched them walk to their car chattering back and forth the entire time. I closed the door and headed back towards the conference room.

"Gene, I'm so sorry," Sally said. "He just burst in."

"That's okay, Sally. Don't worry about it. Why don't you take an early lunch? There's not much going on right now."

"Okay," she said, heading for the door. "I'll be back in an hour."

"Perfect."

I walked into the conference room and sat down across from the old man.

"Would you like another cup of coffee?"

"No," he said. "Three's my limit."

I watched as he removed his hat, then his wig, then the scraggly beard. He wiped his face with a towel and beamed at me.

"Okay?"

"Dad, you were magnificent."

Chapter Twenty Nine

I swallowed the mouthful of grilled Barramundi I'd been savoring, took a sip of wine, and wiped my mouth. I wasn't quite ready to answer the question. "I'm sorry, Sam," I said, leaning forward with my elbows on the table. "It's a little loud in here. I didn't hear your question."

"What were you doing before you started this project?" he said.

"Oh," I said, nodding. "I was doing some different things. Mostly real estate. But they were all basically means to an end. My real goal was to put together enough working capital to get this one off the ground."

"I know what you mean," he said. "I started out selling cars. Hated every minute of it. But I hated the oil industry even more. So for the first five years it was Cadillac city. Remember those days, Suzette?"

"Only when you remind me, dear," she said, laughing. "Gene, this fish is wonderful. And who would have thought that a chilled Pinot would go so well with it?"

"I know," I said, refilling her glass. "It's perfect."

"How's your buffalo, dear?" she said, staring down at the massive slab of meat Sam was rapidly working his way through.

"Great," he said, sipping his beer. "It's like beef with just a touch of venison thrown in. Want a bite?"

"No," she said, frowning at the chunk of flesh sitting in a pool of blood.

"Did you get that guy Willie sorted out?" Sam said.

"Eventually," I said, shaking my head. "Poor guy. He's really lonely. Now that he's got more money than he knows what to do with, he's got no one to do it with. I suggested that he should do some traveling. Visit the States. Maybe go to Europe."

"So you turned down his request to join The Syndicate?" Suzette said.

I took the ease at which she used the name as a good sign and nodded sympathetically. "I'm afraid so. He's a very nice man but I'm afraid, and I hope this doesn't sound…uppity, he's just not the kind of individual we're looking for."

They nodded in silent agreement and resumed eating. I looked across the crowded restaurant and spotted my father watching our table from the bar. I tugged my earlobe and sat back in my chair and waited.

"G'day, mate," my father said, approaching the table. "It's good to see you, Gene."

"Hi, Bobbie." I stood and shook hands. "How are you?"

"Great," he said. "Just great."

"Bobbie," I said. "I'd like you to meet Sam and Suzette Brewster from Texas. Sam and Suzette this is Bobbie Samuelson."

"Pleasure to meet you," my father said, shaking hands with both before turning back to me.

"Nice to meet you," Sam said, sizing my father up.

"Bobbie's in cattle out in Western Australia," I said.

"Yeah. But not for much longer huh, Gene?" He turned back to Sam and Suzette. "I think it's about time I started living with two-legged creatures if you know what I mean."

All three of us laughed along with the jovial Australian.

"Say, Gene," my father said, lowering his voice. "I was wondering if it would be possible to get a second slot." He glanced at Sam and Suzette. "Son in law," he said, shaking his head. "I figure if I'm going to have to support him, the least I can do is set him up in something with a guaranteed return."

"A second slot?" I frowned. "I don't know, Bobbie. We've got a lot of people on the waiting list as it is."

"Come on, Gene," my father said. "I know I joke around about him, but he's a good kid. I'll personally vouch for him." He reached into the pocket of his shirt and held up a

147

folded piece of paper. "I've got a check for the four million down payment right here."

"Let's not do this here, Bobbie. Tell you what, stop by the office tomorrow afternoon and we'll see what we can do."

"Deal," he said, beaming. "Well, I need to get going. Nice meeting you folks."

"Nice meeting you too, Bobbie," Sam said.

He waved and strolled out of the restaurant. I picked up my wineglass and waited.

"He seems nice," Suzette said.

"An amazing man," I said. "Very successful. And he loves to play golf. Apparently, he and his wife like to team up and play other couples for big money."

"Is that right?" Suzette said, looking at her husband.

"Well, then you tell him he's met his match. Suzette and I have been known to get pretty deep into the pockets of a lot of couples back at our club in Texas."

"You don't say?" I said. But he had, as had his own surprised club pro when prompted by my question on the phone last week.

"I'd like to discuss the numbers a bit," Sam said, finishing his beer.

"Absolutely, Sam."

"I noticed that you've set aside fifty million for working capital. Do you think that's going to be enough?"

"Yes," I said, nodding. "Since the tea tree can be harvested immediately, we believe we'll have more than enough cash coming in. The fifty million is there only if we need it. And since The Syndicate will be debt free from inception, we'll have no problem borrowing if we need to. But our plan is to avoid debt whenever possible."

"Any plans to ever take this public?"

"That's not even being considered at the moment. Going public would certainly bring in additional money, but The Syndicate is about more than money. Our community

148

members already have more money than they know what to do with. This is about creating a quality of life unmatched anywhere in the world. It's about having a place to go where you don't have to worry about anything. Your safety. Your neighbors. Or your investment. A place to relax with other people who truly understand what it means to live the life you've earned the right to live. A community you are proud...no, honored to call your own. Because in the end, Sam, Suzette, it comes down to family. To community. To a sense of belonging. To peace of mind. We're creating something very special here. A place of-"

I paused and waited.

"Like-minded people doing like-minded things?"

"Exactly. Yes. Thank you, Suzette. That's precisely what I'm talking about."

"What do we need to do now?" Sam said, holding his wife's hand on top of the table.

"I'll need twenty percent down to secure your membership and you'll have ninety days to pay the balance. And if you and Suzette change your mind during that time, your deposit will be refunded in full including any accrued interest," I said, finally allowing myself to bathe in the pool of adrenaline threatening to drown me.

Sam looked at his wife who nodded then savored the final sip of her Pinot. He reached inside his coat pocket and removed his checkbook.

"Make it out to The Syndicate?" he said, pen in hand.

"That would be fine, Sam."

"There you go," he said, handing me a check for four million dollars. "When do you need to know which lot and housing plan we've selected?"

"Anytime in the next few weeks would be fine, Sam." I folded the check and slipped into my shirt pocket.

"That corner lot on the southern end of the beach wouldn't still be available would it?"

"As a matter of fact, Suzette, it is. I had a feeling you liked that one. That's why I've already penciled your name on it."

**

I drove home from the restaurant following a familiar route but oblivious to my surroundings. But I was fully aware of the check resting against my chest. On the front steps, I stared at all the zeroes then slid the folded check back into my pocket.

"Well," my father said, looking up from the cricket match on television. "How did it go?"

"They're still deciding." I helped myself to a glass of wine and sat down next to him and put my feet up. He turned the volume down.

"Can't make up their mind, huh?" he said. "Funny, they seemed ready to go."

"Yeah," I said. "They just can't decide which type of house they want to build."

I grinned while continuing to stare at the screen.

"You little son of a bitch," He turned off the TV. "They did it?"

"They certainly did, Dad." I handed him the check.

He held it up, hands trembling, and stared in disbelief. "Four million bucks."

"It's a nice number," I said, trying to catch my breath.

"That's a profit of…what?"

"Well, we've got well over a million sunk in this thing so far, and I've got to make another payment on the loan for the two million next week. We don't want any red flags coming up at the bank. But we're up close to two and a half million."

"And I used to think that five grand was a good month."

I sipped my wine. "We just got lucky they were the first ones. They're looking for a place to retire to that's got weather, water, and golf."

"They'll find it eventually." He laughed and handed me the check.

"Yeah, I guess so."

"What's the matter?"

"I don't know," I said, shaking my head. "They're just such nice people."

"Is that a conscience I hear?"

"Maybe."

"Well, look at it this way, Gene," he said. "You haven't actually done anything illegal. Not yet anyway. Right now, you're just another businessman working on a deal."

"That's going to end when our six months run out." I glanced at the check one more time.

"Then that gives you plenty of time to get used to the idea of accepting big fat checks from people who have way too much and won't miss it."

"Maybe you're right." I turned the television back on. "Who's wining the cricket?"

"Australia's killing them. The Poms were all out for a hundred seventy-one. This young kid from Brisbane took seven wickets for thirty eight. Now's he batting not out for ninety-one and on the verge of his first century. The last couple of overs, the Brits switched from their pace guys and brought on a couple of spinners. Now they're working his outside leg to see if they can get him to edge one to the slips."

"Dad?" I said, still amazed by how quickly he had grasped the game.

"What's that?" he said, not taking his eyes off the screen.

"Are you sure you're not part Australian?"

151

Chapter Thirty

I leaned back in my chair and put my feet up on the desk staring at the stack of unopened mail. Choosing to ignore it for the moment, I closed my eyes hoping that at least a few minutes of long overdue sleep would arrive. I opened my eyes at the sound of my office door opening.

"Hey," my father said, standing in the doorway.

"What's up?" I removed my feet from the desk and yawned at him.

"I was just wondering what to do tonight. It's the first night off we've had in weeks."

"Why don't you go to the track? I think they're running tonight."

"I was thinking about seeing a movie." He grabbed the stack of mail from the desk and headed towards the couch.

"Not me," I said. "I'm staying home."

"You should get out more," he said, quickly flipping through the envelopes. "Here's another confirmation for the next round of fifty."

"How many does that make?" I reached behind the desk and grabbed two beers from the small fridge.

"Thanks," he said. "We've got about a dozen confirmed. But it's been picking back up the past few days. We'll need to decide soon if we're going to go ahead with another round."

"Yeah, I know," I said, wanting to talk about anything else.

"We can stop anytime you like, Gene."

"No, not yet, Dad." I looked up at the white board that confirmed less than two months remained before our six month agreement with Willie ran out. "We need to play it out as far as we can. But I have decided that this is my last one. And since we're going to have to spend the rest of our lives in hiding, we might as well get as much out of this as we can."

"Yeah," he whispered. "That makes sense."

"What? Is something wrong?"

"No, I just hate to see it end," he said, returning to the stack of mail. "Here's a letter from that woman in Hong Kong."

"Yeah, she said she might have some more questions. I thought she said she'd fax them."

He examined the contents of the envelope. "Well, she'd have a tough time faxing this." He began reading from the letter. "I am writing to request an additional two community members in The Syndicate. One membership is for my parents while the other is for my sister who is a senior partner in our family's clothing manufacturing company here in Hong Kong. I hope you are able to accommodate my request since I truly believe that they will become valued and respected members of the community. I will be forwarding additional background information and personal references in the very near future. Enclosed please find a check for the outstanding balance. It was wonderful meeting you…blah, blah, blah, very truly yours."

He blinked at the certified check, then handed me the piece of paper worth fifty six million dollars. I dropped the check on the desktop and stared at it.

"Fifty six million," I whispered. "Fuck me." I tried to catch my breath. I ran through the results of our first forty eight appointments. With the additional two slots the woman from Hong Kong had taken, we had now sold a total of nineteen memberships. Five other individuals had already paid in full and, when the fifty-six million was added in, The Syndicate's bank account had vaulted across the two hundred million dollar mark.

"Two hundred and four million? Can that possibly be right?"

"Uh, huh," I said, bewildered by the number.

"When you said we'd go big, you weren't kidding."

"I guess I wasn't." I stared off into space. "I think I need to take a walk." I stood, legs shaking, and headed towards the door.

"Oh, by the way," my father said, opening another envelope. "We've got a replacement tomorrow. The guy from Vancouver cancelled and I worked someone in from our list who just happened to be in Australia. He's a New Yorker. Is that okay?"

"Yeah, that's fine, Dad. Just leave the file in the conference room and I'll look at it the morning after I get back from the bank."

"Okay," he said. "And Gene?"

"Yeah?" I stared, wild-eyed, at a poster-sized photo of the property hanging on the wall.

"I need to say something I haven't said to you in a long time," he said, beaming.

"I know. I love you too, Dad."

"Nah, not that. But I appreciate the sentiment. What I was going to say was, on your way to the bank, be very careful crossing the street."

**

"Hello? Earth to Gene."

"What's that? Did you say something, Dad?"

"Only four times," he said, standing behind the counter that separated the kitchen and living room. "I asked if you wanted some dinner. I made lasagna. And I could whip up a salad if you like."

"That sounds fine," I said, continuing to stare out the window.

"Gene?"

"Yes?" I said, turning towards him. "I thought you were going to the movies."

"No, I'm too tired." He pointed at the stools that lined the counter. "Sit down and talk to me."

I sat and watched him pour two glasses of wine. He stood behind the counter and stared at me. I sipped my wine and stared back.

"What?" I said, breaking eye contact.

"You look like shit."

"Well, thank you very much for the insight, Dr. Freud."

"Don't snap at me, young man. Remember who you're talking to."

I grabbed a handful of aspirin and washed them down with a sip of wine. I looked out the window.

"The lifetime trump card."

"What?"

"The father role you can slip into every time you get pissed off at me. You'd think by now it wouldn't affect me."

"That's part of the deal of being a parent," he said "No matter how old you get, I've already been there. Sometimes it comes in handy."

"I guess," I said, glancing at the front page of the newspaper sitting unread on the counter.

"Wanna tell me what's bothering you?" He sat down on the stool next to me.

"I don't know what's bothering me," I said. "And that is what's really bothering me."

"I hope you're not looking for sympathy because a guy sitting on two hundred million ain't gonna get much."

"No, that's not it. I've always had these…ebbs and flows before, but I always came out of the down periods. But for the past few weeks, I've just continued to sink. And now I'm just empty."

"Joyless?"

"Yeah."

"No sense of purpose?"

"Yeah," I said. "How did you know?"

"PSD."

"Translation, please."

"Post Scam Depression," he said. "At least that's what I call it. You've decided that this is your last one, right?"

"Yeah, I'm definitely done," I said.

"And now your body has started going into withdrawal."

"Really, Dad? Withdrawal?"

"Absolutely," he said. "Let me ask you something. What was it that always brought you out of your down periods before?"

I pondered the question over a sip of wine. He waited, his wineglass sitting in front of him untouched.

"The next job," I said.

"Precisely. And now that you've told yourself there won't be a next one, it's only logical that you'd start asking yourself some pretty serious questions."

I waited for him to continue.

"My first two years after I quit were horrible." He laughed at the memory. "I was so depressed that I half expected your mother to tell me to start up again."

"I never knew that."

"You were twelve," he said. "You weren't supposed to know."

"Twelve." The memory registered. "That was the first time I ever stole anything."

"Yeah, I know," he said. "And ever since that first pack of gum, you always needed to increase the score just a little bit didn't you? Had to get the juices flowing."

"Yeah. I sure did."

"Look at your last three jobs. You did the dating service that made you a million bucks. Then the betting scam in Vegas went off without a hitch. And now this thing here has gone through the roof. The only way to top this one would be to take over a small country. The last one. Sad words for guys in our business, Gene. Sad words, indeed. But you need to keep one thought in mind for the next several months."

"What's that?"

"You were the one who made the decision. Instinctively, you knew it was time to stop. And you knew it even before the two hundred million started rolling in. That's good, Gene. I'm glad you're getting out because, eventually, you would get caught. The convict tradition of this place notwithstanding, given the numbers involved and the people you're screwing with, you'd go away for a very long time."

"What about you?"

"Me? I'm just an old man on the periphery here. What are they going to do to me?"

"Well, since we're going to end up in a place where they can't get us, nothing's going to happen to you."

"No, Gene," he said, shaking his head. "When this is done, I'm going home."

"What are you talking about? You know you can't go home."

"I know no such thing. That's exactly what I'm going to do."

"But that would mean that-"

"It means we say goodbye here." He placed a hand on my shoulder. "At least for a while. I can always come for a visit after you get settled."

I swiveled ninety degrees in his direction. "I can't let you do that."

He raised an eyebrow, then relaxed and smiled. "Look at it this way. You brought me down here and it's been incredible. Just having the opportunity to be a part of this thing has been a great experience. It gave me the chance to relive a part of my life I thought was gone forever. It's the best gift I've ever received."

"Don't sell yourself short, Dad. You're a big part of it."

"No," he said, picking up his glass. "It's all you, Gene. It's brilliant. And you're going to get away with it. My suggestion is that we finish these last few appointments and wrap it up. Forget about doing another round. After I head home, you go find yourself a nice native girl to settle down with and spoil rotten."

"Why are you doing this?"

"I'm old. And I'm your father. That means I can do anything I want."

Chapter Thirty One

The Cape Byron Lighthouse stands on the most easterly point of the Australian mainland and every fifteen seconds flashes a beam of light that can be seen thirty miles away. I wasn't expecting its illumination to shed any light on my current situation, but I figured it couldn't hurt.

How many times had I taken this walk along the trail perched high above the rocky shore below? Retraced the same steps, repeated the same thoughts and asked myself the same questions? Regardless, I knew my visits were soon coming to an end and I found myself savoring the experience and hoping the memory could be preserved.

Soon I would be saying goodbye to this place forever. In a few weeks, I'd be disappearing with over two hundred million of some very important people's money. Individually, each one could make my life a living hell. If they combined forces and tracked me down, I didn't stand a chance.

I sat down on the edge of the walking trail and leaned back against the fence. I closed my eyes and counted hundred dollar bills and woke as the sun was about to disappear. I drifted off again and dreamt of a tiger trotting down the walking trail in my direction.

Pinned against the fence by two massive paws, I slowly opened my eyes just as the beast started licking my face.

"Murray, take it easy."

"Yeah, we need him alive."

Three men laughed as they continued towards me. I slowly lifted an arm and began rubbing the animal's head. It appeared friendly and I certainly wanted to keep it that way. I wriggled free and stood as the three men approached. I recognized one of them immediately and looked down at the dog.

"So, you're the famous, Murray," I said, stroking the dog's thick fur.

159

"Hello, Gene."

I stared at the man who'd spoken my name.

"Do I know you?"

"Not yet. I'm Doc. This is Merlin. And this is-"

"Summerman Lawless," I said, extending my hand. "Nice to meet you. I'm a big fan. Or at least I was. I mean...I heard about the boating accident. You were lucky to survive."

"Yeah, I'm a lucky guy." He knelt and placed a hand on the dog's back. The dog immediately sat down at his feet.

I looked at the other two men. The tiny one was staring out at the ocean. The one called Doc stared at me.

"How do you know my name?"

"It was on the application form you sent, Hedaya."

"Sure. The casino owner from Vegas. Is he here? I hadn't heard back from him and was wondering if he was interested."

"No, he didn't make the trip," Doc said. "Merlin and I are here on his behalf. We're his...what are we, Merlin?"

"His associates," Merlin said, still staring out at the ocean. "Man, it is beautiful here."

"Well, if you think this is nice just wait until you seen the property."

"Save the sales pitch, Gene," Doc said.

"What?"

"I said save it."

The man continued to stare at me and I caught myself taking a step backwards.

"My office is closed for the day, but I'm sure I'll be able to schedule an appointment for you in a couple of days."

"What do you think, Merlin? Feel like waiting a couple of days?"

The tiny man turned away from the ocean and shook his head. "No. What I'd really like to do is find a pub and get a drink."

"That's not a problem," I said. "Lots of those around. I recommend the Beach Hotel. You can't miss it. Just head back in town and it's on the main drag overlooking the beach."

"Sounds good," Doc said. "Why don't you take us there?"

I coughed nervously and glanced out to sea, then looked at my watch. "I hate to say no, but I have to meet someone for dinner."

"I'm sure your father will understand," Doc said. "And isn't this the night he usually goes to the track in Brisbane?"

I felt my face drain of all color and I leaned back against the fence. "Who the hell are you?"

Doc looked at Merlin, who shrugged his shoulders.

"We're just some people shopping around for a man with your talents, Gene. And we might just end up saving your sorry ass." He knelt and began rubbing the massive dog's head. "Now how about that drink?"

**

Summerman closed the menu and looked up at the waiter. "Let's see. Four of your coldest lagers and a Guinness for my furry friend here."

"He looks like a tiger," the waiter said.

"He gets that all the time."

"Is he friendly?"

"Only when he doesn't have to wait too long for his Guinness." Summerman reached down to stroke the dog's head. "Please put it in a bowl. He struggles with bottles."

"No opposable thumb, right?"

Summerman smiled. "That must be it. Oh, and bring us some calamari."

"Wait," Merlin said. "Is the calamari raw or fried?"

"It's fried, sir. Is that okay?"

161

"I guess we'll see, won't we? But it's certainly going to be better than raw."

The waiter glanced around the table. "Will there be anything else?"

"Bring us the appetizer platter as well," Doc said.

"Good choice. Will that be all?"

The dog woofed once from under the table.

"Hold your horses, Murray. I was just getting to it. And bring him your biggest steak cooked rare."

"Just the steak or do you want the full dinner?"

"What comes with it?"

"Baked potato and sautéed spinach."

The dog growled...deep, long and steady. The waiter took a step back from the table.

"No spinach. He hates spinach. Just bring two potatoes, thanks."

"Yes, sir." The waiter backed away keeping one eye on the dog.

Summerman looked out over the magnificent beach. "You were right, Gene. This is incredible."

Fighting fatigue, I rubbed my eyes. "Look, guys. I have no idea what is going on here so let's start with this. Are you here to see the property or not?"

The three men glanced at each other before Summerman spoke.

"I'm sure it's a great opportunity but I doubt I'd ever have the time to enjoy it."

"I'd like to see it," Doc said. "But I have no interest in investing in your...what are we calling it, Merlin?"

"Scam."

My stomach churned.

"Yes, that's it. Scam. And a very good one it is, Gene."

"How much have you collected so far?" Merlin said, wiping his nose with a tissue. "Last time I looked, it was over a hundred fifty million. But that was a few days ago."

"What are you? FBI? Aren't you a little out of your jurisdiction down here? Who sent you? Gentry?"

Merlin snorted. "FBI? Gee, you sure know how to hurt a guy's feelings, Gene."

"I don't know why you're bugging me. I haven't done anything illegal." Even to me it sounded weak and hollow.

"It's an interesting argument," Doc said. "Depending on how it plays out, illegal might be hard to prove. But at a minimum, I think we can all agree that it's...what's the word I'm looking for, Merlin?"

"Marginal."

"Yes. That's it. Marginal."

"Just like the football betting scam you pulled in Vegas. Marginal." Merlin smiled at me from across the table. "And I must compliment you on that one, Gene. That was very well done."

"Thanks." I silently cursed myself. "I mean, I have no idea what you're talking about."

"But the dating scam is something else altogether," Merlin said. "Given the level of fraud, that one could put you away for a very long time."

"Maybe," I said. "How do you know about-"

"Plus the fact that it crossed state lines makes it Federal."

"Well, sure. That goes without saying," Merlin said.

"And if the Feebs could get your as yet unidentified partner in crime to cut a deal and turn state's evidence, that would be a big problem for you."

I found my backbone. "How much practice did it take you two to work out your spiel? Or am I just in the presence of genius?"

"Well, I can't speak for Doc. But Summerman is pretty smart. And I'm off the charts when it comes to IQ."

"Leave me out of this one," Summerman said. "I'm only here for the beer." He glanced at our approaching waiter carrying a tray. "Right on cue."

"Here you go, gentlemen. Four beers and a Guinness for your furry friend. Should I pour his?"

"Please. But pour it slowly. He gets cranky if he has to wait for the foam to settle."

"Thanks for the safety tip." The waiter slowly poured it into a bowl and placed it on the ground.

Murray licked the waiter's hand, then glanced up at Summerman.

"Good boy. Go ahead."

The dog began furiously lapping at the bowl.

"Will there be anything else at the moment?"

Summerman glanced down. "He's pretty thirsty. You might as well bring him another."

The waiter laughed and strolled off.

I took the first sip of my beer. It helped, but not nearly enough. I took a second and drained half.

"Gene. I thought that was you, mate."

I glanced up and saw Manny approaching the table.

"Hey, Manny."

"Where you been hiding, mate? Haven't seen you in weeks."

"Just working."

Manny nodded then stared down at the dog. "Bloody hell, that is one big dog." He glanced around the table. "Hey, wait a minute. I recognize him. He's Murray. And you're the rock star, Summerman Lawless, right?"

"You caught me, Manny. Nice to meet you."

"Son of a bitch. How do you know this bloody reprobate?"

"We're just getting to know each other. This is Doc. And the gentleman picking imaginary insects out of his hair is Merlin."

"You can't be too careful. This country has more things that can kill you than you can count." Merlin glanced up. "Nice to meet you, Manny."

Manny smiled and turned back to me. "You're still coming to the party, right?"

"Oh, that's right," I said. "The turning on the lights party. Saturday, right?"

"Saturday it is. And if you three are going to be around, you're more than welcome to come. And make sure to bring this guy." Manny knelt down and rubbed Murray's head. "What a good boy you are."

"Thanks for the offer, Manny," I said, "but I'm sure these guys have other things to take care."

Doc glanced at Merlin, then Summerman. "I'm free. How about you two?"

"I wouldn't miss it," Merlin said.

I forced a smile. "Okay, I guess that's settled. What time should we be there?"

"The party won't get rolling until around eight. But if you guys want to come early and help dress the pigs, you're more than welcome."

"Dress the pigs?" Merlin said.

"Yeah," Manny said.

"And what type of attire will they actually be sporting?"

"If everything goes to plan, nothing more than a very dark tan." Manny laughed. "I gotta run, mate. I told Millie I'd give her a break tonight from the babysitting. Nice meeting you. See you Saturday."

I waved goodbye then gulped down the rest of my beer. It was starting to look like the two pigs weren't the only ones about to get slaughtered.

Chapter Thirty Two

I flew in and out of the shower, dried my hair and dressed in record time. The clock next to my bed read seven minutes after nine and I cursed myself all the way to the office. I opened the front door expecting my nine o'clock to be in the reception area. But the room was empty except for Sally who looked up as I walked in.

"Good morning, Gene. I hope you don't mind, but I took your nine o'clock back to the conference room. He kept hitting on me and it made me nervous."

"He what?" I tried to recall the man's name then remembered he had been a last minute replacement. "Did he touch you? Ask you out? What?"

"He kept making hints about some of the things he'd like to do to me. He's a creep, Gene. If you don't mind, let me know when you're done so I can make sure I'm not here when you bring him out."

"Okay," I said. "I'm sorry, Sally."

"Don't worry about me. I can handle myself." She picked up the phone. "Ugh. What a way to start the day."

I walked to my office wondering who was waiting for me in the conference room. Sally didn't rattle easily and I could only imagine the behavior it had taken to provoke her response. I poured coffee and searched for the appointment file. I remembered telling my father to leave the file in the conference room. I walked across the hall and found his office empty. A quick search of his desk came up empty so I took another sip of coffee and decided to just wing it.

I slowly opened the conference room and peered in. The man was sitting with his back to me talking on his phone. The file sat unopened next to the scale model and I knew it was impossible to get to it without him seeing me. I closed the door and coughed softly causing him to end his call. He looked over his shoulder then stood and smiled at me.

My mouth dropped, but I eventually managed a small smile as I stared back at the familiar face.

"I'll be a son of a bitch," he said, laughing. "Is that you, Gene?"

"James? It is you," I said, shaking his hand. "I wasn't sure."

"Well, you probably didn't recognize the name. Since I sold the company, I've started using the initials exclusively. And I moved my office to New York. What the hell are you doing here? I thought by now you'd have your own talk show on true love."

"Slight change of plans, James," I said, opening the file.

"J.B.," he said.

"Yes. J.B. Sorry about that."

"This is amazing," he said, nodding at the scale model. "Couldn't help sneaking a peek."

I quickly flipped through the file and noticed her name was absent. Unable to spend the time deciding whether it was deliberate or merely an oversight, I handed him a thick folder. "J.B., could you excuse me for just one moment. I'm sorry to keep you waiting but this morning is getting crazier by the minute. In the meantime, why don't you start looking this over?"

"Not a problem, Gene," he said, studying the scale model. "This looks incredible."

"I'll be right back." I left the conference room and found my father in his office.

"Dad, did you just get here?"

"Yeah." He sat down behind his desk. "I don't go on for another hour."

"We got a problem. Potentially a very big one." I started pacing in front of his desk.

"Okay. What's up?"

"Our nine o'clock is one of the guys I scammed with the dating service. Actually, he's the one who's engaged to my former partner."

167

"Is she here?"

"I'm not sure." I paused, and then glared at him. "What the fuck does it matter if she's here or not? He knows who I am."

"It's just that from the way you described her, she sounds nice. I'd like to meet her."

"Jesus Christ, Dad," I said, forcing myself into a whisper. "If I go back in there and try to come across as some multi-millionaire putting together this deal, we're done."

"Then don't do that," he said. "Sit down, Gene. Take a minute."

I sat down on the couch wondering if she was here. How did she look? How was she feeling? What would she say? What would she do? I forced myself to focus on the immediate problem. My father waited in silence.

"Okay. Here's the play. I work for you. You're the CEO of The Syndicate. If it comes up, we just happened to meet while I was down here on vacation. Use your Australian accent. Tell him you're originally from Brisbane. Give me five minutes then come in with some excuse to pull me out of the meeting. Okay?"

"No worries, mate," he said, smiling. "Relax Gene. Maybe she's not even here."

"Yeah, maybe not." I rubbed my hands through my hair.

"Look at you," he said. "I need to meet this woman."

**

"Sorry about that, J.B."

"This is amazing, Gene," he said, flipping through the materials I had given him. "The Syndicate. Good name. Sounds like something straight out of a Grisham novel."

I laughed and drummed my fingers on the tabletop. "So, I guess congratulations are in order on both counts, J.B."

"How's that?" he said, glancing up.

168

"Well, first on selling your company and I heard you got engaged."

"Thanks," he said, nodding. "I guess I should be thanking you. For the second thing anyway."

"I'm not sure if I remember her. I made so many arrangements, they tend to blur."

"Five two, redhead with green eyes. At least she was. Now she's cut off all her hair and gone blonde. Not nearly as hot," he said, turning the page.

"I remember her. Emily, right?"

"That's the one."

"So when's the big date?" I said, drumming the table a little harder.

"Sometime next month." He closed the file. "We're supposed to be down here on a pre-wedding honeymoon. My schedule is brutal for the next six months so we decided to fit it in now."

"That sounds nice," I said. "Will she be joining us this morning?"

"If she ever gets out of bed, I imagine she will. All she's done the last few months in bed is sleep. If she keeps this up, by the time the wedding day rolls around, she'll be fucking useless. Say, these numbers look really good. Any plans to take this thing public? If you do, I've got a great guy I can recommend."

"No," I said, my initial impression of the man reconfirmed. "Not at this time."

"How many slots have you got left?"

"Only a couple I'm afraid. They're getting snapped up pretty fast."

"I can see why. Who's designing the golf course? You're going to need a name guy but you probably already know that."

"We're in final selection at the moment," I said. "And all three are name guys."

"Good." He pushed the folder away. "So, tell me, Gene. How did you end up down here? I would have thought your dating service had some legs. Hey, that's pretty funny. Had some legs. Get it?"

"Yeah, that's a good one, J.B." I managed a small laugh. "I was just looking for something a little different and fell into this one. Unfortunately, unlike you and the others buying in, I'm still a working stiff."

"Oh, well," he said, bored with me. "Maybe one day you'll get there." He turned at the sound of the door opening.

"Mr. Whitley," my father said. "I'm Charles Sheets. But all my mates call me Chucko."

"Nice to meet you, Charles," he said, shaking hands.

"Is your suite at the resort up to your standards?"

"Yeah, it's nice. But these days they all seem pretty much the same."

"I see. Yes. Well, I hope Gene is taking good care of you."

"We're just getting started but it looks promising. I do have a ton of questions though."

"Of course." He sat down at the table. "As the head of The Syndicate, I'll be more than happy to answer any questions you might have. Coffee?"

"Please. Cream, no sugar."

"Gene, be a good lad and get us some coffee will you?"

"My pleasure…Chucko."

I did a slow burn as I headed for my office and dialed the resort. I waited for the receptionist to connect me and then waited longer as the phone rang off the hook. I poured the coffee and reentered the conference room where my father was deep into a story about an imagined deep sea fishing adventure. He stopped in mid-sentence and looked at me.

"Finally." He took a sip of coffee. "A bit too much sugar. How's yours, J.B.?"

"It's okay. So what happened then?"

"Well, I'd had this marlin on the line forever. And he must have weighed eight hundred pounds."

The door to the conference room opened and I was the first to see her. Tired and worn down. But still exuding strength and beauty. Her face dropped in stunned silence, but she recovered, smiled and leaned against the door. The other two men sensed her presence and turned.

"Nice of you to finally show up," J.B. said. "Come on in, dear. Recognize anybody?"

"Is that you, Gene?" she said, strolling across the room and sitting down next to her fiancé. I took the absence of a kiss as a positive.

"Emily," I said. "So nice to see you. Congratulations. I always had a feeling you two would hit it off."

"You certainly are very good at what you do, Gene," she said, beaming. Her eyes continued to dart back and forth around the table. "But you're obviously doing something different now. What are you doing?"

"He's pushing a land deal," J.B. said. "I'll fill you in later. So Charles, you've got this marlin almost up to the boat-"

"I'm sorry to interrupt, gentlemen," I said. "But Tokyo needs to move up our conference call. And we need some time to go over the numbers. Okay, Chucko?"

"Oh, of course," my father said. "Damn time zones. I never know what day it is anymore."

"But I still have a lot of questions," J.B. said.

"Perhaps you could jot them down and fax them over," I said, trying not to stare at her.

"Nonsense, Gene," my father said. "That's not how we do business here at The Syndicate."

"No, of course not," I said, biting my bottom lip.

My father leaned across the table and whispered to both of them. "He's a good worker. Just a little misdirected at times. Tell you what. Why don't we get together for dinner and we'll take all the time we need to answer your questions?"

"Okay," J.B. said. "Just let us know where and when."

"The restaurant at the resort is very good. Let's say around eight."

The couple stood and Emily glanced in my direction one last time. J.B. shook both our hands while continuing to stare at the scale model.

My father pressed the intercom. "Sally, could you come back to the conference room?"

A tentative Sally entered and remained by the door.

"Sally, would you be so kind to escort our guests out? Also, could you call the resort to see if they can accommodate four at eight o'clock? You know that nice table outside we like?"

"Yes, sir," she said, holding the door open. She maintained a watchful eye as J.B, trailing Emily, winked at her. After they left, she looked at me and wrinkled her face in disgust. She closed the door behind her.

"Dinner? Did you have to do that, Dad?"

"Why not? He doesn't suspect a thing."

"That's not what I'm talking about and you know it. Do you promise to behave yourself?"

"Gene, I'm shocked you would even have to ask."

"Okay, Chucko." I said nudged him towards the door. "Time to get back to work."

I had no idea why I said it. I was done for the day.

Chapter Thirty Three

I tried walking in a small circle staring up at the suspended lighting. I tried standing still, hands thrust deep in pockets. I tried rubbing my forehead, fingers combing my hair. I read, and reread, every tourist brochure, pamphlet, business card, and sign I could get my eyes on. I walked outside to the edge of the pool and stared up at the clear evening sky.

I heard her approach before I saw her. When our eyes met, she waved and smiled. She was wearing the black cocktail dress that was my favorite, but I was drawn to the ring that would have been more at home on a chandelier. Instinctively, she shifted the shawl she was carrying to her left arm and the ring disappeared.

"You look beautiful," I said, touching her arm.

She let my arm linger longer than it should and kissed me softly on the cheek. Out of habit, my hand drifted south and beneath the silk my fingertips sensed firmness. She smiled at the move but took a small step to one side. My hand drifted away and landed back at my side.

"We both look horrible and you know it," she said.

"Speak for yourself." I helped her drape the shawl over her shoulders.

"We should get going."

"Sure." Determined to squeeze every possible moment out of the evening, I took her arm and slowly led us in the direction of the restaurant. "They said they'd meet us there."

"Who's the Australian?"

"My father."

"Really? A family operation? Well, he's very good. He had me fooled."

"I think he was switched at birth."

She laughed, but took her arm back. "What have you gotten yourself into this time, Gene?"

"Well, actually it started out as favor to my Dad. And then it just exploded."

"How big is it?"

"Two hundred million and counting," I said. "But if it makes any difference, it's my last one."

She stopped walking. "Two hundred million?"

"A few months ago, you would have thought that was a lot of money."

"Don't start."

"Does it?"

"Does it what?"

"Make a difference."

She wrapped the shawl tighter and stared down at her feet. "Maybe. You were right about him. He's a total prick."

"I know."

"But how?"

"What can I say? He fit the profile."

"But I completely missed it," she said, shaking her head. "How did that happen?"

"You didn't miss it. You tried to ignore it. He offered an alternative you thought you could live with. Or maybe it was temporary insanity."

She chuckled but her head stayed down. "It sure doesn't feel temporary at the moment. I'm just another possession. One more thing he can trot out and show his friends. Well, his colleagues anyway. I don't think he has any real friends."

"The trophy wife."

"Some trophy. The way I'm feeling lately, maybe third place in a bowling league."

It was my turn to laugh and it reminded me of Sunday.

"But the perks are amazing," she said. "I understand why people get sucked in. We're going to the White House for dinner."

"I hear they count the silverware so be careful."

"Does it make me a bad person?" she said, squeezing my hand.

"Stealing silverware?"

She punched my arm. "Asshole. I was referring to the fact that I'm still going ahead with the wedding even though I hate the bastard."

"If you're looking for clarification on the question of right and wrong, I think you're probably talking to the wrong guy."

"No advice then?"

"You could always run away with me."

"And spend the rest of my life hiding from the people looking for their two hundred million? Sorry, Gene. Life's too short."

"It can be pretty long if you're miserable."

"Maybe. But I imagine it's a lot longer inside prison."

"I'm not going to prison."

"Wherever you eventually end up, no matter how exotic, it's still going to be a prison, Gene. And you don't need me to tell you that."

"No, I don't." I stopped in front of the restaurant. "Here we are."

"This looks nice," she said, pushing back one side of her hair. "What do you recommend?"

"The flounder."

**

"Order me a steak." J.B. tossed his menu aside.

"Are you talking to me?" Emily said.

"Who else would I be talking to?"

"Well, since you didn't even bother to glance in my direction, I thought I should check."

"That time of the month, dear?"

"What?" Emily shook her head. "Pig," she whispered.

"It's just that it's getting impossible to tell the difference these days…dear." He stared at her. "Yes, I'd like a steak. You know the way I like it. Tasty, tender, and very rare. Just like you used to be." He winked at the table and stood up using both hands to support himself. "I've gotta see a man about a tea tree." He roared at his own joke and staggered off towards the men's room.

"How many pubs did you hit on the way over here?"

"Only two," my father said, apparently still sober. "But it was enough. Take a look at this." He started to reach into his shirt pocket then stopped and looked at Emily.

"It's okay, Dad," I said. "She knows."

He nodded and pulled a check out of his pocket. "Add another four million to the kitty." He paused and shook his head. "I am so sorry. Where are my manners? Emily, we haven't even been properly introduced. I am delighted to finally meet you." He took her hand and kissed it.

"It's nice to meet you, Mr. Wagner."

"What's this mister crap? Call me, Chucko." He laughed at his joke. Maybe he wasn't quite as sober as I thought.

"Chucko it is."

"I don't mean to be sticking my nose where it doesn't belong."

"Yes, he does," I said.

"But what on earth are you doing with him?"

"Dad, stop."

"It's okay." Emily said. "Sometimes I'm not really sure. But I'm pretty sure it has something to do with security."

"You mean money, don't you?"

"Sure. That's part of it," she said, taking the first sip of her martini. She savored it then looked at me. "It's all downhill from here. Right, Gene?"

"You too? Don't tell me you believe that bullshit line of his about initial moments?"

"There's a lot of truth to it," she said.

"Emily, you need to drink more wine," he said, holding up his glass. "You really don't mind that we just scammed your fiancé out of four million bucks?"

"It makes no difference to me," she said. "Besides, as he is always quick to remind me, it's his money. But he has agreed to bring me along to the White House."

"Be careful, I hear they count the silverware."

"What did I miss?" J.B said, sliding into his chair. "It sounds like you're having way too much fun."

"I was just telling them another fishing story. About one that didn't get away," he said, effortlessly slipping back into character. "Your bride to be is lovely, J.B."

"Yeah, she's a real keeper," he said, scanning the restaurant. "Is there a waiter anywhere in our future? I'm starved."

My father caught the waiter's eye. He approached, reviewed the specials, and departed with our orders. J. B. spread both elbows out on the table and looked at my father.

"So you're thinking is that I can have the house built within twelve months?"

"No worries, J.B."

"That's great, Chucko," he said, downing half his martini. "No, make that *beauty, mate*. Hey, that's pretty good." He nodded at the table impressed by his impression.

"What are we talking about, dear?" Emily said.

"Nothing really," he said, not looking at her. "I just got in on a deal with Chucko on a little vacation place. Trust me, you'll love it."

"I hate the sun. Remember?"

"Then I guess you'll just have to stay indoors," he said, finally turning in her direction. "Or in New York."

"That can be arranged," she said, just loud enough to be heard around the table.

"Gene, do you remember the two other women you hooked me up with?"

177

"Barely." I smiled at Emily who proceeded to kick one of my ankles.

"They were great," he said. "Especially that black haired beauty. She was something. Now what was her name?"

"I really don't remember," I said, desperate for a change of topic.

"Medium height, jet black eyes, hair down to her ass. And what an ass. Damn. What was her name? It's right on the tip of my tongue."

"Suzanne," Emily said.

"Suzanne. That's it." Confused, he paused and looked at Emily. "How do you know her name?"

"You told me. That's how," she said, recovering immediately. She returned to her martini and glanced at me over the rim through raised eyebrows.

"I don't remember but I guess I must have."

"So when are you two heading out?" I said.

"I'm off to Hong Kong in the morning for a week of meetings," he said, finishing his martini. He turned to Emily. "Have you decided what you're going to do yet?"

"Oh, I think I'll stay here for a few days and do some sightseeing and shopping, then head back to New York."

"Can't say I blame you," J.B. said. "I hate Hong Kong."

"You should look up Rose Wong while you're there," my father said. "She's purchased three memberships for her and her family."

I rubbed my forehead at my father's mistake. I looked at Emily who knew instinctively what had happened. To his credit, my father caught himself and attempted a casual retreat.

"Of course, you're both extremely busy people," my father said, picking up the wine list.

"I'm sure we'll have lots of time to get acquainted," J.B. said. "That's enough business for now," he said, reaching for the wine list. "What looks good?"

My father handed him the wine list and tried to ignore the look I was giving him. He sat back in the booth and exhaled loudly. J.B. flipped the pages back and forth. He frowned and looked up from the list.

"There's nothing here from the Napa Valley," J.B. said. "What restaurant worth its salt doesn't serve Napa wines?"

"You're in Australia," Emily said, making no attempt to conceal her contempt. "Try one of the Penfolds."

He glanced at her and grunted. For the next ten minutes we sat in silence watching him try to make a decision.

Chapter Thirty Four

"This is the most beautiful place I've ever seen."

I stretched out next to her on the sand and studied her as she took in her surroundings. The day was so perfect, it should have been Sunday. Eventually, she caught me staring.

She cocked her head. "What?"

"You're still the most beautiful thing I've ever seen."

"Don't start." She turned back to the ocean and watched the surf.

I crawled to my knees and brushed sand away. I inched closer and kissed her. She tentatively returned the kiss then gently pushed me away.

"I can see why people are signing up," she said. "This place would be incredible."

"Yeah. Gene's Imaginary World."

"Good name for it."

"Right over there is the imaginary hotel. On both sides are the imaginary beach houses. Up behind the hill sits the imaginary manufacturing facility. Welcome to my world."

"I've seen your world, Gene." She ran her toes through the sand. "That's the problem."

"Yeah, I know. Feel like a swim?"

"No suit." She smiled. "And there is no way I'm getting naked. Got it?"

"Loud and clear," I said. "It was worth a shot."

"Thanks for bringing me here. This is what I always imagined Australia was like. It's special."

"I'm going to miss it."

"Any ideas yet about where you're going?"

"South America. Or maybe somewhere in the Caribbean. I used to think it would easy to disappear. Now I'm not so sure."

"It's still easy to disappear…as long as nobody is looking for you."

I considered the idea and wondered just how hard they would come looking for me. Very hard I decided. I locked that thought away for another day.

"What about you?"

"The other night at dinner was the clincher." She wrapped both arms around her knees. "I can't marry him."

"That's good news," I said. "I mean for you."

"Yeah. But now what?"

"That seems to be the question of the day."

"You'll be fine, Gene. You always land on your feet."

"I just hope it's not into quicksand." I stretched back out on the sand. "South America doesn't interest you?"

"Not in the least," she said, tucking her head against my shoulder. "But I have to admit that the two hundred million has got my attention."

Chapter Thirty Five

"So I'm afraid that's my sad tale of woe." Emily laughed and held baby Jessica against her shoulder.

"The billionaire that got away," Millie said, sitting at the kitchen table in front of an unfolded stack of clean diapers. "You don't seem too heartbroken." She folded a diaper and reached for another. "Actually, you seem relieved."

"Yes," Emily said, wiping a liquid of indeterminate color from the baby's face. "He's awful. Ask Gene."

"Don't ask me," I said, from the living room where I was helping Manny fold diapers. "I'm not the one who almost married him."

"Those two have certainly hit it off," Manny whispered. "They're thick as thieves." He corrected himself. "No, that would be you and her wouldn't it?"

"Just fold your diapers," I said, glancing back towards the kitchen.

"She's a good one. Any chance you two might hook back up?"

"Well, one can hope," I said, shaking my head. "But she won't spend the rest of her life in hiding. And I can't blame her."

"Why did you have to steal so much money?"

"That certainly wasn't the plan," I said, folding the last diaper. I picked up the stack and placed it in a nearby chair. "But it was like being in Vegas on a hot streak. I just got on a roll."

"Yeah," he said, leaning in closer. "But what's the feeling really like when the stakes are that high?"

"Remember how we felt when we got our final checks from our Japanese partners?"

"Sure," he said. "I'll never forget that feeling."

"Well, multiply it by a thousand. But even that doesn't do it justice. You haven't told Millie anything have you?"

Manny shook his head as he carried the diapers to a closet. He grabbed two beers from the refrigerator, and kissed Millie on the cheek before sitting back down on the couch. "What are you going to do?" he said, handing me a beer.

"I gotta get out of here."

"Just like that? Jesus, mate, you just got back."

"My six month contract with Willie runs out soon. By then, I'll be somewhere in South America. I'm putting my Dad on a plane home and I have no idea where Emily's going. Probably back to New York I imagine. Say, I forgot to ask you. What's Willie up to anyway?"

"The day after he got your check he was gone. He went to Italy. He kept telling us down at the pub he's was gonna do it but we never believed him."

"Good for him," I said. "How do you think he'll take the blow of his deal falling through?"

"I wouldn't worry too much, mate. As long as he gets his property back, the two million you gave him should soften the blow."

"I'm gonna miss you, mate," I said, raising my beer in salute.

"You don't think you'll be able to slip back in for the occasional visit?"

"I doubt it," I said. "It would be pretty risky. Plus, it could put you and Millie in a tough spot."

"And what are you two conspiring about?" Millie said, approaching with the baby. She sat down in a chair and gently placed the baby on her knee facing the couch.

"I was just telling your husband how lucky he was that Jessica looks so much like her mother," I said.

"I'm sure you were," Millie said, managing a small smile.

Emily sat down on the couch next to me and patted my knee. "Is your Dad still sleeping?"

"Yeah, he's been napping all afternoon. I guess I worked him too hard."

"He doesn't look good, Gene," Millie said, gently running a hand through the baby's rapidly emerging hair.

"What are you talking about?"

"Well, for starters," she said. "He's lost about fifteen pounds since the last time you were here."

"No," I said, shaking my head. "Not possible."

"Yes, Gene. And the coughing."

"He's always had that cough," I said, protesting, but silently wondering if I had missed a change in his health.

"One of our neighbors is a doctor," she said. "Dr. Williams. I could call him."

"He's good, Gene," Manny said. "He delivered Jessica."

"I don't think it's necessary," I said, concern working its way into my system. "But I will ask him how he's feeling when he gets up from his nap."

"Thanks," Millie said. "That would make me feel better."

"Yeah," I said, staring off in the distance. "Me too."

Chapter Thirty Six

"Be careful," my father said, perched safely behind the fence. "Those tusks could rip your guts out."

"Thanks for the safety tip, Dad. I'll try to keep that in mind." I was already cognizant of the five inch incisors protruding from the head of the two hundred pound male.

Both pigs had already figured out this situation was different from their normal feeding time. Huddled, they backed into a corner and made it clear they were in no mood to be moved.

Manny called everyone together. My father leaned over from his side of the fence as we listened to Manny's instructions. I kept a close eye on the agitated male who was eyeing the hunting knife in Manny's hand.

"Okay, guys," Manny said, leaning over like a quarterback. "We'll need to separate them. Then we'll take care of the female first."

"Why her first?" I said.

"Because she doesn't have tusks and I don't have a fucking clue how we're going to handle the male," Manny said.

I appreciated the honesty but felt his Rockne speech needed some work.

"Why don't you just shoot them?" Merlin said.

Murray woofed his displeasure with that suggestion.

Manny glanced down at the dog, then at Summerman. "Is he okay out here?"

"He's fine," Summerman said. "He just isn't a fan of what we're about to do."

"How the hell does he know what we're about to do?" Manny glanced back and forth between the dog and Summerman. "And how do you know what he is and isn't a fan of?"

"Call it an educated guess."

Manny nodded. "Okay." He turned to Merlin. "To answer your question, I'm a terrible shot. I'd probably end up wounding them and Millie has already warned me not to let them suffer."

"They can die, but not suffer?" Merlin said.

"Funny how that works, huh?"

"Doc's a good shot."

"Leave me out of this, Merlin," Doc said. "I'm on vacation."

"I can't believe I'm even here," Merlin said, waving his arms. "What is up with these flies?"

"Welcome to Australia," Manny said. "Okay, as I was saying, we need to separate them."

"The male is definitely going to be a problem," my father said. "Those two have bonded and the thing to watch out for is his reaction when you take his girlfriend out. Who knows what he might do when he hears her scream."

Outside the fence, Murray woofed and pawed the dirt.

"How do you know she's going to scream?" Merlin said.

"We're gonna cut her throat," Manny said. "What do you expect her to do? Sing?"

"I was just asking," Merlin said.

"Okay," Manny said. "Doc and I will take care of the female. Gene, you and Merlin keep the male occupied and away from us until we finish with her. Keep a close eye on him."

"That won't be a problem," Merlin said, mesmerized by the large tusks.

"Summerman, stay outside the fence and keep Murray out of the way. But you'll also need to keep an eye on the gate. It's the one part of the fence that's a little shaky. If he gets too worked up, it probably won't hold him."

"And if the male charges, we just run like hell, right?" Merlin said.

"No, the best way to handle them is to confront them."
Manny crouched into a linebacker pose. "Like this. Stand
your ground and he'll avoid physical contact."

"Are you sure?"

"Well," Manny said, "that's what One Eye Bill down the
road tells me."

"One eye?" Merlin said.

"Long story," Manny said.

"All the good ones are," Doc said, wiping his hands on
his pants. "Have you ever been run over by a pig before,
Manny?"

"No, can't say that I have."

"Well, there's a first time for everything," Summerman
said, laughing.

"There you go," Manny said, laughing as he stood.
"Let's do this. We need to get these guys dressed and
roasted."

Murray barked loudly and the pigs huddled closer
together.

"Murray, knock it off," Summerman said.

The dog stopped barking, but continued to whine and
paw the dirt.

Manny took the lead and slowly approached the pigs.
The male took a few tentative steps towards him then
stopped and looked back at his mate who was fixated on
the knife Manny was holding. The male snorted and shook
his head.

"Cheeky little bugger, aren't ya?" Manny said. He
glanced back at Gene and Merlin. "You guys coming?"

"Is that rhetorical or do I actually get a choice?" Merlin
said, peering out from behind Gene.

"Be careful, Manny," Doc said, staring at the male.
"Don't get too close. He looks pretty tough."

"Yeah, well he'll soften up after about eight hours
rotating over a hot fire," Manny said.

At the mention of hot fire, the male lunged forward. Manny assumed the linebacker crouch as the pig rushed towards him. At the last second, the male veered barely avoiding contact. Even though Manny's theory had held, I didn't get the confidence boost I'd been hoping for. I watched Manny and Doc approach the female but kept one eye on the male who was snorting and running around in a small circle.

"Merlin, come here," Manny said, directing traffic with the knife. "Doc and I will keep him busy while you drop the rope around her neck."

"Are you out of your fucking mind?"

"C'mon, mate. Time's a wasting. Just drop it around her neck and hold on. She's pretty docile, but strong as hell."

On his third try, Merlin flipped the noose over the female's head and immediately the pig darted off. Ten feet of slack disappeared and Merlin was jerked forward and then dragged, face down, through the dirt.

"Merlin, let go of the rope." Doc watched Merlin bounce twice, then slide past in a cloud of dust.

Merlin released the rope and the cranky female snorted at him from the far end of the pen. The male took two steps toward Merlin then rejoined his mate.

"Motherfucker." Merlin climbed to his feet and began dusting himself off. "Don't you people have a butcher in this town?"

"Butcher? Where's the sport in that?" Manny said, staring at the pigs.

"This is going very well," my father said, laughing from behind the fence.

"Yeah," Manny said. "This isn't going to work."

"Jesus, she's strong," Merlin said.

"Wait till you get your hands on the male," Doc said.

"Like that's going to happen," Merlin said. He examined himself for cuts and bruises.

"Okay," Manny said. "Slight change of plans. Doc and I will get them separated. Merlin, you get ready to help us as soon as he moves away from her. Gene, you'll need to take care of the male by yourself. Just keep him occupied while the three of us deal with her."

Murray barked incessantly, his front paws up on the top of the fence.

"Murray, please," Summerman said. "We've got enough animal problems at the moment."

All four men crept towards the pigs. The male snorted and shook his head, tusks shining bright white in the late morning sun. The female made a dash for freedom but Doc was able to grab the rope still looped around her neck. She struggled, but found Doc more of a match. Manny also grabbed the rope and both men eventually wrestled the pig to the ground. Manny removed the knife from its sheath and inched closer.

The male, watching from a distance, decided to take a more active approach. He dashed towards his squealing mate and I stepped into its path. The male lowered his head and sped up. I assumed the linebacker crouch and held my breath. The pig launched itself into the air and, instead of a tusk in the thigh, and I caught two pig's feet right in the chest. Air left my body and I collapsed in the dirt. The male continued forward, then stopped and looked back at my writhing body.

Doc dashed over and placed himself between me and the male. Murray began barking furiously and wouldn't stop. On the ground, my head spun as I struggled in vain to take a breath.

"You okay?" Doc glanced down at me, then back at the male.

"I...think...so."

Doc helped me to my feet and I limped towards the gate suddenly craving meatloaf.

The female squealed as she struggled to her feet. Manny lost his grip and lunged at her with the knife. The male snorted, dashed at Manny and plunged a tusk into his left buttock. Manny screamed and dropped the knife. Merlin dashed the last fifty feet and dove over the fence. Doc grabbed Manny and dragged him away to safety. The pigs huddled in the corner, pawed dirt, and snorted in victory.

I walked through the open gate and dropped to the ground.

"Well done, son. Now you know why I never went into farming. You okay?"

"Yeah, I'll be fine."

Murray approached and nuzzled my shoulder. I sat up and managed to rub his head.

"Well, that went well," Manny said, stepping through the gate. He leaned against the fence and tried to determine the seriousness of his wound.

Doc knelt and cut away a section of Manny's jeans. He examined the wound. "You're gonna need stitches, but it doesn't look too bad."

"Hurts like hell," Manny said.

"Let's get him up to the house," Doc said. "Gene, are you okay?"

"Yeah, I'll be fine. Just bruised."

"How about you, Merlin?"

"Fuck you, Doc."

Doc laughed and looked around at the others. "He's fine. I loved your face plant."

"I hate repeating myself," Merlin said, "but this time I'll make an exception. Fuck you."

Chapter Thirty Seven

I woke from a short nap where I dreamt a cloven-hoofed devil was dancing on my chest to techno. I opened my eyes and saw Murray staring at me. He gently draped a paw on my shoulder. Apparently, no one had bothered to tell him he was no longer a puppy.

"Hey, Murray," I said, stroking his head. I looked down at the purple bruise on my chest and got out of bed and checked my breathing. I pressed my fingers against my chest and was convinced it was only bruised. I got dressed, grabbed an envelope from my bag, and headed to the kitchen.

The house was buzzing with activity. Several people I didn't recognize were coming in and out of the house carrying out a variety of tasks under Millie's direction. Emily and Summerman were sitting on the living room floor trying to untangle a long string of lights. My father was sitting on the couch supervising and sipping a beer.

"Hey, it's Pig Boy," my father said.

"Funny, Dad." I said. "What did I miss?"

"Well, let's see. These folks are getting ready for the party. Summerman and Emily are making a mess of that string of lights. And Manny headed into town with Doc and Merlin for stiches and the main course."

"Main course?"

"Pigs. Of the already dressed variety."

"So the slaughter plans have been abandoned?"

"Well, it would be a little hard to pull off without the guests of honor." My father laughed and looked at Murray.

"Indeed." Summerman scowled at the dog. "Isn't it, Murray?"

The dog woofed softly and stretched out on the floor.

"You lost me," I said.

"My little friend here," Summerman said, "thought it would be a good idea to open the gate and let our dinner escape."

"Really?" I looked at the dog then back at Summerman. "He opened the gate?"

"Ask him yourself," Summerman said, untangling a portion of the light strand.

"Murray? Did you let the pigs out?"

The dog raised its head and thumped his tail on the floor.

"And a good boy he is," Millie said, entering the living room. "I never liked the idea in the first place."

"So they just took off?"

"Apparently," Millie said, bending over to pet the dog. "He must be pretty smart if he could figure out how to open that gate."

Summerman glared at Murray. "Yeah, he has his moments."

"So they're in town buying pigs?"

"Yeah," Millie said. "As soon as my genius husband gets his ass sown back together. And the pigs better be already dead."

"Say, Millie, can I have a word with you?"

"Sure. Follow me. I've got a bag of potatoes that need to be peeled with your name on them."

"Great." I shuffled my feet as I followed her into the kitchen.

"How are you feeling?" she said, handing me a potato peeler.

"I'll be fine." I pulled the envelope from my pocket. "I was going to do this later but I guess there's no need to wait. This is for you and Manny. And the baby."

"What is it?" She opened the envelope and examined the check. "Gene, what do you think you're doing?"

"It's a gift, Millie. That's all. Manny told me about your money problems. Don't worry, it's from a personal account and the people I got it from never even missed it."

"Jesus," she said. "Just when I've finally rationalized how we got the money to buy this place, you come around offering more."

"You'll just have to trust me when I tell you that you can spend this money with a clear conscience."

"But this is a lot of money." She continued to stare at the check.

"It didn't cost me a nickel." I smiled at her. "Take it."

"Every time I come up with a reason to hate you, you go and pull some shit like this," she said, laughing through the tears rolling down her cheeks.

"You'd do the same for me." I started peeling a potato.

"Don't bet on it. Thank you, Gene. You have no idea how much this means."

"Forget it."

"Actually, a lot of things are starting to make sense."

"What things?"

"About you. Why you're the way you are. She nodded in the direction of my father.

"This should be good."

"I always wondered where you got your…tendencies. And now I think I've figured it out."

"Have you now?"

"Yes," she said, holding my stare. "You got it from him."

"Got what?"

"The gene," she said. "The larrikin gene."

"The larrikin gene? You're not going scientific on me are you, Millie?"

"You know what a larrikin is?"

"Sure. A gadfly. Someone comfortable living slightly off center. Or in my case, someone who has no trouble bending the rules to get an advantage."

"Yeah. That'll do. It's a much more pleasant definition than con artist."

"Con artist?"

"Absolutely."

"Fraud?"

"Probably."

"Criminal?"

"For your sake, I hope not. What have you been up to, Gene?"

"Actually, I'm here because I wanted to see you and Manny."

"I'll buy that," she said. "Then let me rephrase it. Why are you back in Australia?"

"Originally, I was planning on a vacation. I'd been working non-stop for a couple of years and needed a break."

"A break from what?"

"Do you really want to know?"

"No," she said, shaking her head.

"I thought it would be nice to bring my dad along. He's never been here."

"That's was sweet of you. Continue."

I laughed. "Tenacious aren't you? Manny married a handful."

"Yes," she said. "And it was very lucky for him that he did."

"Touché. Well, my Dad has a criminal past but he quit a long time ago. Because my Mom forced him to. But he always missed it. Since she died, his own larrikin tendencies have been reactivated."

"Okay, I guess I can live with that," she said. "What about Emily?"

"What about her?"

"Any long term plans on the horizon?"

"I don't think that's going to happen. I think I screwed that chance up."

"Same old Gene."
"Yeah. I'm afraid so."

Chapter Thirty Eight

Manny eased himself onto the blanket and sighed.

"How's your ass?"

"Bloody hurts. But nothing that a few more beers won't fix."

I glanced around at the group of partygoers. "This is quite the collection, mate."

Manny laughed as he scanned the guests scattered around the lawn. "You got that right." His eyes lingered on Doc and Merlin hunkered down, chatting quietly on the front porch. "So what's the deal with those two? They're thick as thieves."

"I'm not sure yet. But they're definitely not here to buy property." I picked at a blade of grass. "And they know a lot."

"About what?"

"About most of the shit I've been up to the past several years."

Manny stiffened. "Including our currency scam? Jesus, mate, I've put that way behind me. Are you telling me those guys might start digging that up?"

"Relax. You've got nothing to worry about. I don't think they're here to mess with me. It's strange...they haven't said anything yet, but I think they want me to work with them."

"Doing what?"

"Haven't got a clue." I tossed a handful of grass into the air and watched it drift away.

It was early afternoon and dinner wouldn't be served until the pigs, purchased earlier from the local butcher and now slowly rotating over hot coals, finished cooking sometime around eight. Children of all ages scurried across the lawn as the adults laughed and chatted between hits of weed and cans of cold beer. Murray was the primary center of attention.

"Amazing dog." Manny handed me a lit joint. "Have you met everybody?"

I nodded and took a long drag.

"Thanks again for the check, mate. I can't believe how generous you are."

"Forget it," I said, through a mouthful of smoke. "I won't even notice it's gone."

"Still, it's a lot of money."

"Nothing like you could have made working with us."

"Yeah, work with you again and spend the rest of my life as a eunuch. Thanks, mate, but no."

I extinguished the joint in the grass and spotted a flower growing near my chair. "Orchid, right?"

"Yeah," Manny said. "They're everywhere. Christ, I still can't believe the way things grow up here. Remember that rubber plant that Millie had in her flat in Sydney?"

"That little thing she had in the front room?"

"Yeah. Well, take at a look at now." He pointed to the far side of the lawn.

"I don't see it. Is it near that tree?"

"That's it." Manny said. "The bloody thing must grow six feet a year."

I stared up at the tree that must have been fifty feet tall.

"Well, would you look at that?"

I followed his line of sight and saw two pig heads poking through the back section of the fence. They were fixated on the other members of their species rotating slowly above the fire.

"The bastards have returned to the scene of the crime," I said.

"That's strange," Manny said. "But they've never been out of the pen before. Probably don't have a clue how to fend for themselves in the bush."

**

197

"This guy is amazing. I thought you said he played rock and roll." Manny, hammered, tossed his empty beer can aside and grabbed a fresh one from a cooler.

"He does. But it sounds like he can play anything."

"He and that dog are certainly joined at the hip."

We continued to watch Summerman work his way through a jazz improvisation with Murray draped over his feet under the piano.

"I'm starving. When are those pigs going to be done?" I said.

"How would I know?" Merlin said. "I was barely able to make it out of the butcher shop without losing my breakfast. Disgusting way to make a living."

"I can't wait to get a big chunk of crackle." Manny said.

"Crackle?" Merlin said.

"Yeah. The skin gets all crackly when you roast it. Crackle. You'll love it."

"Not gonna happen," Merlin said. "I've already broken every personal hygiene rule today, and I have a strict policy against eating footballs."

"You're loss, mate. Man, I wish that thermometer would pop. I'm bloody starved."

"Those pop up thermometers are pretty unreliable," I said.

"Well, it's the only one we got."

"Looks like our two friends are still hanging around," my father said.

Manny watched the two pigs still peering through the fence at the rotating objects. "They haven't taken their eyes off the spit for hours. Think they understand it could have been them?"

"I sure hope the little bastard realizes he could be next," I said, massaging my chest.

Doc, taking a break from tending the fire, staggered up to grab a fresh beer. "Manny, it looks like they still have a ways to go yet. What do you think about kicking up the fire?"

"Whatever you say. You're the pit master." Manny stretched out on the grass.

"Pitmaster? I've had a dozen beers," Doc said. "At the moment, I'm not even master of my own bladder."

Manny yawned. "Whatever."

"Back to work," Doc said, swaying.

"I better go with you to make sure you don't fall in the fire," Merlin said.

"Whatever," Doc said. "You're the pit master."

Doc staggered off and proceeded to dump a large bag of charcoal onto the fire. He studied the fire then dumped a second bag. Merlin pulled him back from the fire and I felt the temperature rise.

"Can't wait for the crackle," Manny said, fighting off sleep.

"Just look at this," my father said, surveying the party.

"What?" I said, trying to follow his eyes.

"All of it. The sense of community."

"Like-minded people doing like-minded things?"

"Yeah," my father said. "It's too bad it'll never happen."

"Maybe."

A slow hiss started. It sounded like a steam valve releasing pressure. Over the next several seconds, it continued to grow louder.

"What the hell is that?" my father said.

"No idea." I listened closely to the hissing that now dominated the party.

"That was your job." Doc waved his arms in the air as he yelled at Merlin.

"I did my job. You told me to score the pigs and that's exactly what I did. Remember? I was the one who went into that germ infested shop and paid for them."

"Not score as in procure. You idiot," Doc said. "Score as is in pierce."

"Pierce? What the hell are you talking about?"

"Whenever you roast a pig, you always pierce the skin to let the fat drip out," Doc said, struggling to be heard over the hissing.

"How the hell was I supposed to know that? I always get my pig pre-packaged."

"You're an idiot."

"Fuck you, Doc."

The hissing rose to factory level. People stood, mesmerized by the sound the rotating pigs were making. The two pigs observing through the fence started squealing. Summerman stopped playing and Murray sat with his head cocked. Doc and Merlin glared at each other as they stepped back from the fire.

And then the pigs exploded.

Two giant fireballs were now rotating above the pulsing charcoal. Chunks of crackle burst into the twilight and floated back to earth like burning potato chips.

The male pig squealed loudly, stared at his mate and both disappeared in the direction of the setting sun. I didn't expect to see them back anytime in the near future.

The guests scrambled and stared at each other through their beer-weed-fueled haze. Doc dashed off, returned with a hose and eventually succeeded in putting out the pigs.

"I think it's done," my father said, nibbling a piece of pork that had dropped on his arm. "Delicious."

"We lost the crackle," I said.

Manny propped himself up on his elbows. "We lost the crackle?"

"Yeah," I said. "Sorry, mate."

But the pigs, what was left of them, were delicious.

Chapter Thirty Nine

We were sitting on the verandah that wrapped the house and overlooked the distant ocean. I studied my father sitting next to me. He was thinner but continued to have the energy level of a much younger man. His afternoon nap, now a regular part of his daily routine, had rejuvenated him and he'd been the life of the party throughout dinner. He'd bounced baby Jessica on his knee, flirted with Emily and Millie, and used every opportunity to take good-natured jibes at me and Manny. He seemed to be the picture of health, but I still felt compelled to ask. "Dad? Are you feeling okay?"

"Are you kidding? I feel great. How could anybody not be great in this place?"

"What I mean is…how are you feeling? You know?"

"Gene, I'm fine. I've never been better."

"You look like you've lost more weight."

"I carried around an extra thirty pounds for years. I finally lose it and now you want to give me a hard time."

I sipped wine and sat back in my chair.

"Manny," my father said. "As soon as Jessica is able to handle the flight, you and Millie need to come for a visit."

"I'd like that," Manny said. "Give us a year or so."

"And I'll have several cases of wine from the Hunter Valley waiting for you. That was a good day wasn't it, Gene?"

"Yes, it sure was," I said, remembering the trip that now seemed like a lifetime ago.

"I need to go check on the baby," Millie said.

"Oh, let me do it," my father said. "I need to hit the loo."

Millie smiled at him and sat back down. My father headed inside very much a man at peace with the world.

I looked at Millie. "He says he feels fine,"

"He certainly has more energy than I do."

"He should," I said. "He takes a three hour nap every afternoon. When's the last time you got three hours of uninterrupted sleep?"

"I don't even remember," she said, rocking in her chair. "And I'm blaming you, Romeo."

Manny jolted out of his catnap. "What did I do?"

"At least he's getting some," I said.

"Getting some?" Emily said. "Gee, what woman in her right mind could refuse an offer like that?"

"It wasn't an offer," I said. "Just a simple statement of fact."

"That's good." she said, laughing. "Because I'd hate to have to shoot you down again."

My father returned with a fresh bottle of wine. He refilled all the glasses and sat down.

"She's fine," he said to Millie. "Sound asleep."

"Thanks," Millie said.

My father took a sip of wine that went down the wrong way. He started coughing and it turned violent. I handed him a handful of tissues and waited for him to stop.

"Jesus," he said, between coughs. "At my age…you'd think I would know…how to drink a glass of wine."

Finally, the coughing stopped and he wiped his mouth and put the wad of tissues in his pocket. "Whew. You better cut me off."

I noticed residue on the corner of his mouth. "Dad, you missed a couple of drops of wine."

"That's not wine, Gene," Millie said, jumping to her feet. "That's blood."

**

Every possible reason as to why I was the worst son on earth ran through my head as I sat on the verandah waiting for the doctor to finishing examining my father. I tried to identify what clues I had missed. Had I been that callous,

202

so self-absorbed with my own schemes to see the evidence directly in front of me? For an individual touting himself as an expert at understanding human behavior, I had failed miserably with the one person I cared about most.

Or had he been that skillful at hiding the truth from me?

Emily stepped onto the verandah. "What are you doing out here by yourself?"

"Just sitting here hating myself."

"I see," she said, sitting down next to me. "Well, I wouldn't be too hard on yourself."

"I'm afraid the cancer's come back."

"You're going to take him home, aren't you?"

"Yeah. Summerman has offered to fly us back in his Gulfstream."

"Good friend to have."

"I don't think I'd actually call him a friend."

"Who are those guys with him? They make me nervous."

"I'm not exactly sure yet." I stared off into the distance.

"Is there anything I can handle for you here that might...?"

"Keep me out of jail?"

"Something like that."

"No," I said. "That's too much to ask. And it could get pretty hairy before it's all done. But I've still got some time before people start asking the tough questions."

"Are you sure?"

"I'll be fine. What about you? What are you going to do?"

"I'm not sure. I just got off the phone with you know who."

"And?"

She laughed. "And he's having his maid in New York pack my stuff for storage. I guess billionaires don't like being told no."

"So where are you going to go?"

She slowly rocked back and forth. "Actually, I was thinking about sticking around here for a while."

"To do what?"

"I was thinking about the possibility of running The Syndicate until you were able to get back."

"What?"

"Why not?"

"I thought you were done working the dark side."

"I am." She stared off into the distance. "I'm thinking we should actually build the thing."

"Build what?"

She slid her chair closer. "All of it. I've read the business plan. I know it could work. We just need to keep going."

"You're out of your mind."

"We're good on so many levels, Gene. All we need to do is go legit. Just think about it. No fraud. Nobody trying to track you down. No more looking over your shoulder. We could do this."

I considered the possibilities as a different ache worked its way into my chest. "I miss our Sundays."

"Me too."

The doctor stepped onto the verandah, and I stood as he approached. "How is he doing?"

"Given his condition, he's doing fine. But he's ready to go home. And he needs to see his oncologist immediately. I gave him a shot to help him sleep, but you need to get him on the first plane out of here.

"Thanks for coming over, Doc. I know it's late."

"It's quite all right," he said. "I was already up and dressed."

"At one in the morning?"

"Yes, I have two new visitors at my place who seem hell bent on getting into my garden."

"Really? Who?"

"Two very confused pigs."

**

I slowly opened the bedroom door. "Dad?"

"Yes," he whispered. His eyes were closed and he was on his back tucked under the covers.

I leaned over the bed and studied him. "Dad?"

"The money's on the table," he whispered. "Did you remember I ordered double pepperoni?"

"You shithead." I flicked a finger against his arm.

"Ow. Oh, it's you." He opened one eye. "I thought you were the pizza guy."

"You're such a bastard." I pulled a chair close to the bed and sat down. "We're flying home this afternoon."

"That's fine by me," he said, sitting up. "I think I've had enough vacation. Wait a minute. We?"

"Yes. I'm going with you."

"That wasn't part of the plan."

"The plan's changed, Dad."

"But what about…everything else?"

"I've got some time to figure things out. And Emily has some ideas I'm considering."

"Emily? You think that's an option?"

"Maybe. But I've got some time before the agreement with Willie runs out. And I could probably buy another three months if I had to."

"That's plenty of time."

"Is there something you want to tell me, Dad?"

"Yeah, it's probably time for me to come clean," he said, looking up at me like a chastised child. "I guess you deserve to hear it."

"You're worried the cancer's back?"

"Something like that," he said, avoiding eye contact. "Actually, it never left."

"What are you talking about?"

"It never left," he said. "I lied to you."

205

"You lied? About cancer?" I shook my head. "What about your doctor?"

"He lied, too." He smiled and shrugged his shoulders. "But only after I threatened to stop seeing him altogether."

"Why on earth would you do that?"

"If I hadn't, would you have brought me along?"

"Maybe."

"Would you have let me work on this thing with you?"

"No."

"There's your answer. But you would have been on my case about my drinking, staying up late, eating the wrong foods. In that way, you are just like your mother."

"Yes, I would have," I said. "But only for your own good."

"For what?" he said, sitting up in bed. "Just to see if I could stretch six months into seven? The hell with that. I've lived more in past few months than I have since your mother died."

"You've got six months?"

"Had," he said. "I had six months, Gene. But it's okay. I've been taking my medicine and seeing the doc who lives down the road every couple weeks."

"Really? How the hell did you pull that off?"

"Hey," he said, sitting up. "Remember who you're talking to."

"But your energy level has been amazing. How did you sustain it?"

"That's a funny question coming from you. How do you think I did it?"

I considered the question then nodded. "Adrenaline."

"Best drug on earth," he said. "Hey, cheer up. We're not done yet. We'll go home, sort some stuff out, and reminisce about our adventure. It'll be great."

"I can't believe I didn't see it," I said, tearing up. "How did I miss it?"

206

"Remember who you're dealing with here." He handed me a box of tissues. "If I can fool a bunch of billionaires, I can certainly slip something past you."

"Dad-"

"No. Not today. We'll have lots of time for that. Go start saying your goodbyes."

"Okay." I gently brushed the side of his face.

"Go." He closed his eyes. "Oh, one more thing."

"Yeah?"

"Thanks."

"For what?"

"All of it."

**

I've always believed that if people knew they were about to do something for the last time, they would approach the task differently before beginning. If the task was treasured, one would proceed slowly, hoping to stop time and make it last forever. Like the first sip of a martini, it would be savored, wallowed in, absorbed through the skin, and then driven into the brain to become memory. I wondered how many times I'd sleepwalked through events not realizing it was the last time and lost them forever due to the simple fact I hadn't been paying attention.

"I think we should go for a swim," Emily said, slipping off her sandals.

I let the handful of sand I'd been holding drift through my fingers as I watched her unbutton the loose shirt that concealed what I had believed I'd never see again. She casually tossed the shirt in my direction then removed her shorts and panties.

"The sun feels great," she said, stretching her arms skyward. "Are you going to join me or not?"

Fighting every instinct, I vowed not to rush. I slowly stood and felt my toes grip the sand. I disrobed not once taking my eyes off her. The intensity of the sun had disappeared, but it still warmed my shoulders. She led me to the edge of the water then let go of my hand. I watched her initial tentative steps into the water before she plunged into the sea. She popped to the surface and tread water as she pushed her hair back with both hands through a tremendous smile. Coyly, she beckoned to me with one finger and I felt the warm water envelop me as I swam towards her.

I surfaced and threw my arms around her in one motion. I pulled her close and savored the kiss, salty, yet delicious. She gently stroked the side of my face then dove again. She circled and swam between my legs, pulling me down where we shared an underwater kiss lying on the bottom of the shallow water.

We swam further out and bodysurfed back to shore. I was reminded of the ocean's power when a wave rolled and bounced me off the bottom. I coughed saltwater and stretched back out on the sand. The sun went back to work, its efforts interrupted only by the waves that died near my waist.

She drifted towards me, propelled by a wave's last burst of energy and floated above me before sinking into my arms. Effortlessly, we slipped back into the familiarity of lover's past. We let the water take us and we drifted until I was sitting, her legs wrapped tightly around me, only our heads visible to the outside world. Beneath the water, our shared passion was rekindled and quickly intensified. Above the surface, we stared into each other's eyes and said a silent goodbye.

We walked slowly to our car, stopping once to take a final look at what we were leaving behind. When the sand disappeared, we put our shoes on and trudged up the dirt road. I drove slowly back to the house and it wasn't until I heard a church bell ring that I realized it was Sunday.

Chapter Forty

"You got everything, mate?" Manny tossed a suitcase into the back of the SUV and surveyed the immediate area.

I ran through the checklist in my head. "Yeah, I think that's it."

"What time you flying out?"

"As soon as we get to the airport over in Byron Bay," I said.

"Must be nice to have your own jet," he said. "Rock stars, huh?"

"Yeah, must be nice." I accepted his embrace and grimaced from the bear hug.

"Take good care of Millie and the baby."

"Will do. And we'll see you real soon."

I laughed. "Sure. See you soon." Both of us preferred the lie and left it there.

Millie approached carrying Jessica with my father and Emily trailing slightly behind.

"Gene, thanks again. For everything." Millie shifted the baby to her other arm and leaned in close. "I'm so sorry about your Dad."

"Okay, I'm not dead yet. Let's try and stay under control here, shall we?" My father shook Manny's hand and gave Emily a long hug. "We've had an amazing time. Let's not go and spoil it." He gently kissed Millie on the cheek. "Thanks for everything."

"You take care of yourself," Millie said, tears welling in her eyes.

"Come here." He pulled Emily into a tight hug. "I hope you two figure it all out."

"I guess we'll have to wait and see." Emily patted his shoulder and glanced at me. I shrugged and removed the car keys from my pocket.

"I've been saving the best for last." My father held the baby up in front of his face and a tiny hand grabbed his nose and held on. "You are something else."

Perhaps in that moment he witnessed everything life offered. Perhaps he felt reassured, or a touch of envy at the years in front of her. Perhaps, in her, he saw me and remembered himself at an earlier age. Whatever the reason, his façade shattered and he gave a teary wave and climbed into the passenger's seat.

"Call me when you get home," Emily said.

"I will," I said, fighting back another wave of emotion.

"We'll figure it out."

"I hope so."

I started the engine and closed the door. I slowly headed down the hill and waved through the rear view mirror. We drove in silence until we hit the main highway.

"Whew. That was tough," my father said, adjusting his bush hat and sunglasses.

"Yeah," I said, knowing all too well that the emotional goodbye on top of the hill was only a prelude of what was to come.

**

"I think you should pick one of these babies up," my father said, rubbing Murray's massive head.

I glanced around the cabin of the plane. "Sure, Dad. Next time I have forty million I don't know what to do with."

"One thing about big money, it certainly provides convenience."

Summerman walked up the aisle carrying a tray of drinks. He looked at my father. "If you'd like to take a nap, there's a very comfortable bed in the back. Murray, why don't you show him where it is? And try not to hog the covers."

The dog rose and wagged its tail. My father laughed and stood. "A nap sounds good." He followed Murray down the aisle into the bedroom and closed the door. Summerman sat down in my father's seat and glanced at Doc and Merlin who were sitting across from us.

"How do you want to do this?" Summerman said.

"Do what?" I said, glancing back and forth.

"I'll start," Doc said. "Gene, we have a proposition for you."

"Really, Doc? And all this time I thought you were just looking for a nice piece of beachfront property."

Summerman laughed. "If I thought you might actually build the damn thing, I might be interested in that lot on the southern end."

"Sorry, that one's already gone," I said, staring at the ocean below. "If you guys aren't cops, why are you screwing with me?"

"Screwing with you?" Doc said. "Is that what you think we're doing, Gene?"

"What would you call it?" I said.

"Well, for starters," Merlin said, "how about keeping you out of Federal prison?"

My hand trembled as I sipped my cocktail. "All I've done is collect some down payments on a real estate deal."

"Look, Gene, we don't care what you're up to. In fact, watching you and the way you pulled this thing off has convinced us even more that you're our guy."

"Your guy? To do what?"

Doc glanced back and forth between Summerman and Merlin. They both nodded. "To work with us. To join our posse."

"You have a posse? Isn't that nice. You got a fort and secret handshake?"

Summerman laughed and sipped his Guinness.

Doc smiled. "Merlin, I don't think he believes us."

"They never do." Merlin said. "Gene we're offering you the opportunity of a lifetime."

"Merlin, you need some new material. I've pretty much worn out that deal of a lifetime line the past few months."

Merlin shook his head and removed a glass vial from his pocket. "The hell with him. Let him rot in prison for all I care." He drew out two lines of coke and snorted them back.

I watched the coke disappear then spoke to Doc. "Tell me about this posse."

"We do…projects on behalf of various important people."

"Would I know these people?"

"Not unless you spend a lot of time in the bowels of government."

"So you do work for the government," I said.

"No. We're more like…what's the term, Merlin?"

Merlin sniffed and wiped his nose with a tissue. "Independent contractors."

"I see." I studied them carefully and looked for leverage. "How does one become an independent contractor for these important people?"

"As far as you're concerned, you just say yes," Merlin said. "Don't be an idiot."

"Merlin," Doc said, raising his hand for silence. "You aren't helping."

Merlin shrugged and took a sip of vodka.

"Gene, Merlin and I got into this when we left-"

"Got asked to leave," Merlin said.

"Okay, fine," Doc said, glaring at him. "When we got asked to leave the Company."

"CIA," I said. "I knew it."

"Ancient history," Doc said, "But we still do…projects for them. And other people with similar interests."

"Actually, we're really just getting started," Merlin said.

"Another start up." I returned Merlin's stare. "Just like my operation. I guess we're basically the same. Right?"

Merlin chuckled and drew out two more lines. "No. We conduct ourselves in a way that makes us professional entrepreneurs out to protect the world from the bad guys. You got caught. That makes you a criminal."

"I haven't been caught. In fact, I'm not sure I've actually done anything illegal."

"I see," Merlin said. "Doc, do you think Roger Gentry would share that sentiment?"

"I doubt it."

My eyes widened at the mention of Gentry's name. "You're telling the truth, right? About not working with him."

"Work with Gentry?" Merlin laughed. "You think we'd waste our time helping that idiot?"

"Actually, Gene," Doc said. "We're trying to help you deal with the problems Gentry is creating."

"I can handle Gentry."

"I told you, Doc," Merlin said. "This guy is hopeless. Let him go to prison and we'll keep looking for somebody else."

I turned towards Summerman. "So what's your deal, rock star? How did you get hooked up with these two? You ex-CIA as well?"

"God, no." Summerman glanced at Doc and Merlin who nodded for him to proceed. "Actually, the posse was my idea."

"Was it now?"

"Yes. I saw the opportunity and talked Doc and Merlin into joining. Now we're doing the same with you. At least we're trying to."

"You wanted a lot of money," Merlin said. "Here's your chance. And by the time we're done, it will dwarf the two hundred million you scammed down there."

"I didn't scam it." I drained my drink. "I'm actually thinking of building the thing."

Merlin laughed. "Sure you are."

"I don't think I like you."

"Get in line." Merlin stood and headed off to refresh his drink.

"Look, I appreciate the offer. But I think I'm going to stick with my plan to build the project in Oz."

"You're never going to build it, Gene," Doc said. "What do you think is going to happen to you after we land in Oregon?"

"What have you guys done?"

"We haven't done anything," Doc said, making room for Merlin to sit back down. "Let's just say that our Mr. Gentry is quite tenacious. Incompetent, yes. But nonetheless, tenacious. Your hometown is small and he'll know within a day that you're back."

"And he would very much like to speak with you about a little land deal you were involved with in Florida," Merlin said.

Bewildered, I blinked at all three men as I tried to find my bearings. "How do you know all this?"

"Join the posse and Merlin will tell you," Doc said.

"Stick around long enough and maybe he'll even show you how he does it," Summerman said.

"Not likely," Merlin said.

I shook my head and stared down at the distant ocean. "No, I'm going to stick with my plans. I'm going to take care of my father's situation and then deal with whatever Gentry is trying to hang me with."

Doc sighed. "Have it your way, Gene. But we'll be around just in case you change your mind."

"I won't be changing my mind. I'm going to build it."

"Well, if that's the case," Merlin said. "I hope you have a group of very patient investors."

Chapter Forty One

"That's all of it." I dropped the suitcase on the living room floor. "I don't get it. We leave with four bags and come back with seven."

"Presents," he said, heading off to check another section of the house. "Remind me tomorrow to unpack so I can give them to all me mates at the pub."

"You'll have to wait a day or two for that, Dad," I called. "Tomorrow you're going to the doctor, remember?"

He walked back into the living room and stood with both hands on hips trying to decide what to do next. "I remember." He stared off into space. "Well, nobody broke in. That's good news."

"Why don't you take a shower and try to get some sleep?"

"That sounds good. Feel like a glass of wine?"

"No. But I think I'll make coffee," I said, heading to the kitchen.

By the time it was brewing he was already out of the shower. I glanced at my watch, calculating that it was already midday tomorrow in Australia. I called and it went to voicemail. I set the phone down and stared at the gurgling coffeemaker.

I heard the coughing start. I'd developed a system for classifying the bouts of incessant hacking, and this one appeared mild so I poured coffee and headed outside to the verandah. Summer continued in coastal Oregon but the north wind whipped and kept the temperatures in the low seventies. I sat down in an Adirondack chair and sipped my coffee. Despite the luxurious travel we had enjoyed, jet lag attacked.

I wondered what she was doing at this moment. I needed to talk with her. For reassurance. To help me keep the faith. To tell me that everything, in the end, would be perfect. Or as close to perfection as we could make it.

215

Another wave of self-loathing washed over me but I was too tired to fight back. It pounded my brain and threatened to eat me away from the inside. I absorbed the punches and waited out the onslaught while gripping both arms of my chair. I tried summoning every positive memory I could find. Times when I'd done the right thing, times when I could look at the mirror and find a familiar face staring back. Apart from the check I'd given to Manny and Millie, I was falling short on good deeds of late. After several minutes of rare but real soul searching, I was left with the realization that over the past five years, I had performed only two truly selfless acts, and they both involved coming home to watch a parent die.

"Are you okay?" My father stood in the doorway sipping wine.

"Yeah, I'm fine," I said, loosening my grip on the chair.

"Nice night." He sat down next to me.

His hair was still damp from the shower and he was wearing the bathrobe and slippers I had given him for Christmas. He looked out over the ocean.

"I want to die here."

"Excuse me?"

"I want to die right here. On this porch. With this view."

"You're kidding?"

"Gene, my pending death is hardly a joking matter," he said, winking.

I choked back emotion and forced a smile.

"When the time comes, I want you to promise that you'll bring me out here. I'm going to go out sitting on my porch in the middle of a storm."

"Okay, Dad," I said. "But I don't think I can promise you a storm."

"Oh, it'll rain." He fixed his stare on a point off in the distance. "It'll rain."

**

216

"Gene, you can go in and see him now."

I looked up from the magazine I was reading for the third time and saw my father's doctor standing in front of me.

"How is he?" I stood and stretched.

"Considering he's had just about every test known to mankind performed on him today, I'd say he's doing pretty well."

"But how is he?" I searched his face for a glimmer of hope.

"He's the same as when you brought him in this morning, Gene. He's dying." The doctor gestured for me to sit down. He sat down next to me and cleared his throat. "Try to remember that he's accepted that fact. And you should both feel lucky you had the chance to do some things together before his time was up. Too many people never get that chance."

I nodded then looked at him. "You know, Doc. I was pretty pissed when I found out that the two of you had kept it from me. Especially after he told me you had agreed to let him go with me."

"That's what he wanted, Gene. At first, I didn't like it either. But then I asked myself what's the worst that could happen? Since the worst was going to happen regardless, I figured what the hell. As it turned out, the trip was probably the best thing for him. He spent most of his time living and not thinking about dying."

"I guess."

"I'd like to keep him here overnight. The last test took a lot out of him and he's pretty tired. Why don't you go have a quick chat with him and then head home? We'll release him in the morning."

"Okay," I said. "Thanks, Doc." I started walking down the hall then stopped. "One more thing. My father wants….he'd like…for it to happen at home."

"Yes, he told me. Go see his nurse and ask her about our Hospice program. They're amazing people and I highly recommend that you use them."

"Okay. Thanks, Doc."

I entered my father's room and noticed, for the first time, stark evidence that he was, in fact, dying. Despite all his time in the sun, he was pale and his face seemed to have disappeared into itself in the space of a few short hours.

"Hey you," he whispered. "I think I should have studied a bit more for these tests."

"You look great," I said. "But they want to keep you overnight so they can be sure you get some rest. I'll be back in the morning to get you."

"Okay," he said, closing his eyes.

"Can I get you anything before I go?"

"I'd love a cold glass of ginger ale," he said.

"You got it."

"Thanks, son," he said, drifting off to sleep.

I stood watching him and felt another wave of emotion build and overtake me. I forced myself to ride it out until it subsided. I wiped my eyes with my sleeve and tiptoed out of the room in search of ginger ale.

I located the cafeteria and found a row of vending machines. I began feeding quarters until I heard the dull thud of a soda can dropping.

"Gene?"

I turned and saw the FBI agent, as stunned as I was. "Roger."

"What are you doing here?"

"My Dad," I said, shrugging. "He's really sick."

"Mine too." Roger chewed on his lip. "Fucking booze."

"Mine's got cancer."

"Damn," he said. "How bad is it?"

"Terminal. He's probably got a month. Maybe less. What about your dad?"

"Couple of weeks at best. His liver's totally shot along with every brain cell he ever had. It's a mess."

"I'm sorry to hear that, Roger."

"Yeah, thanks," he said, stubbing one foot into the linoleum that produced a soft squeak. "I hear the two of you were up in Canada."

"Yeah," I said. "Kind of a farewell trip for us."

"Strange place to go in the winter," Roger said, apparently back on the clock.

"Not if you love hockey," I said, deflecting the question.

"Oh, that's right. Your Dad's always been a hockey nut. Did you see some games?"

"Oh, yeah." I made a mental note to review the progress of the current hockey season. "We started in Vancouver and worked our way east."

"I'd be worried about flying in that weather," he said, continuing his fishing expedition.

"Train," I said, knowing that a cash payment for train tickets would be untraceable. "It was beautiful. You ever travel by train?"

"No," he said. "Look, we need to get together for a beer. In fact, I'll be at The Barbarian tonight. I think it would be good for you to stop by. Probably do us both some good. Let's say, around eight."

I looked at him and pondered his last statement. Was it a request or a command? "Yeah, eight works. I'll see you then."

I returned to my father's room and peered in. He was lying on his back and I waited anxiously until I was certain he was breathing. I placed the can of ginger ale in an ice bucket, stole one last look and exited the hospital.

I squinted from the bright sunlight and put my sunglasses on. I squinted again when I saw a woman leaning against my car. As I approached, I shook my head at the sight of the familiar face that probably meant more bad news.

"Hi, Gene," she said, removing her weight from the side of the car. "You look good."

"Hi, Grace," I said, staring at my FBI waitress from Vegas. "I won't even try to guess what you're doing here."

She laughed and flipped back one side of her hair the wind was tormenting. Her new ring sparkled and I immediately recognized its significance.

"I need to talk to you."

I opened the driver's side door and motioned her towards the passenger side. We sat silently waiting for each other to speak. She looked good, but tired. It had only been months since our last encounter, but she seemed like a stranger from a distant past. I remembered her passion, her need for almost constant physical contact, but I couldn't recall the slightest degree of shared intimacy.

"Engaged?" I said, glancing at the ring.

"Yes," she said. "Two months ago. Actually, it was a bit of a surprise." She paused. "Not that he asked me. Surprising I said yes."

"Roger?"

"Yes. Did he tell you?"

"No," I said. "But unless you're looking for me, why else would you be here?"

"That makes sense," she said, not taking the bait.

"Congratulations. But I have to say it seems like an odd combination. He's so…"

"Straight?"

"That'll do," I said, laughing for the first time all day. "And you're so-"

"Bent?"

"I was going to say adventurous. But I guess that works," I said, remembering why I had felt such a strong initial attraction to her.

"Roger told me that he ran into you. I'm sorry to hear about your father."

"Thanks. It's hard." I started the car.

"He's taking it pretty hard himself," she said. "They haven't been close for years. But it's still not easy."

"No, it's not."

She shifted in her seat. I watched her try to get comfortable and waited.

"I have a huge favor to ask," she said. "And it's probably the worst time to be asking it."

"I see,"

"It's about what you and I did in Vegas," she said, unable to maintain eye contact.

"Sleep together?"

"I was going to say fuck each other's brains out. But I guess that works."

I laughed again. It might not have been the best medicine, but it was helping.

"I told him we didn't."

"Okay," I said.

"Is that going to be a problem for you?"

"No. Our secret is safe."

"Good." She stretched out her legs and relaxed into the seat. "When did you find out I worked for the FBI?"

"Does it matter?"

"Probably not," she said. "But was it before or after we hooked up?"

"Before."

"I screwed up. Again. I'm lucky to still have a job."

"Actually, it was Roger who blew your cover."

"What? How did he do that?"

"He made a casual remark last Christmas and I put it together from there."

"The bastard's been blaming me all this time."

"Blaming you for what?"

"For not getting more information out of you. And then he was convinced I got compromised by sleeping with you. What a crazy way to make a living."

"Why on earth did you agree to marry him?"

221

"He's been really good to me. In most ways." She stared out the window. "Plus, it's time. I've got two daughters who could use a father figure in their lives."

"I've been wondering," I said, unable to let the subject pass. "Does the Bureau actually encourage you to sleep with the people you're investigating?"

"We're told to use whatever methods necessary to collect information."

"I guess that leaves it pretty open."

"Yes. And that's the way the Bureau likes it. But it's created a problem for me."

"How so?"

She exhaled and gave me a coy smile. "Because I've started using that method a lot. And I really like it."

"You don't have to convince me, Grace."

"I wish somebody could convince Roger."

"So, you want me to tell him that we never slept together, right?"

"Yes. He told me you were getting together tonight and I know it's going to come up. He's obsessed by the thought of you and me together."

"Okay," I said. "I can do that. But I do have one question."

"Okay," she said.

"Are you asking me to do this for your upcoming marriage or for your career?"

She considered the question then looked at me. "Probably both."

I shook my head. "You're going to marry a man without passion and then try to fill the void with Bureau-sanctioned infidelity?"

"Pretty fucked up, huh?"

"Well, it's one way to go," I said. "Anything you want to tell me about my meeting tonight?"

"Sorry, Gene," she said. "I've already told you way too much."

"Okay," I said. "You take care of yourself. And good luck."

"Thanks," she said, opening the car door. "Maybe I'll see you again sometime."

"Yeah. The next time I need investigating, you'll be the first one I call."

"I'd like that," she said, climbing out.

"Hey, Grace. How did you know this was my car?"

"I work for the FBI, remember?"

Chapter Forty Two

I walked into The Barbarian at eight sharp and didn't recognize a single soul. I peered through the dim lighting waiting for my eyes to adjust and remembered that, long before I was old enough to work here, Roger and I had gotten caught by our fathers in a night of underage drinking. I walked past the pool table where I'd first met Emily and continued to the back of the room. He was sitting in a booth and it appeared he'd been there for some time. I sat down without ceremony.

"What'll you have?" he said, draining the last of his Miller Lite.

"Anything but that," I said, nodding at the bottle. "Heineken is fine."

"Heineken," he said, shaking his head in disgust. "Goddamn Germans. Would it kill you to drink an American beer?"

"Probably. Actually, it's from Holland. At least you got the right continent."

He scowled and grunted and gave our order to a passing waitress. He leaned back in the booth and turned smug.

"How many of those have you had?" I said.

"Who cares? Like father, like son, huh?"

I noticed the black half-circles under his eyes and total look of dishevelment. I noticed because I had seen the same thing in my mirror thirty minutes earlier.

"Remember when we used to play cops and robbers?"

"Sure," I said, smiling at the memory. "Every time you caught me, which wasn't often, you'd sentence me to life without parole."

"You always wanted to be the bad guy. What was that all about?"

"I always thought it was more fun as the one being chased. But maybe it was just like father, like son."

"Precisely." He slapped his hand on the table. "It's in the genes. Just like me with the booze. And here we are. The sons of our fathers still playing the same game."

"I'm not playing any game, Roger."

"Oh, but you were, Gene. You've been a very bad boy."

His statement hit more as confirmation rather than revelation.

"Very bad indeed," he said, moving his hands away from the table to provide room for our arriving drinks. He reached into his pocket, pulled out a ten, and waved the waitress away. "This one's on me."

"Thanks," I said, taking my first sip. Given the upcoming conversation, I doubted any of the ones that followed would be as good.

He dropped both elbows on the table and leaned forward. "You remember your old buddy from Florida?"

"I have a lot of friends in Florida," I said. Now fully aware of where the conversation was headed, I forced myself to remain patient until I learned how far down the track it went.

"Hector Villanueva? Surely you remember him."

"Sure, I know Hector. The last time I heard he was somewhere down in South America."

"Yes, he was. Until last month when he surfaced in Miami to attend the funeral for one of his uncles. We picked him up at the cemetery."

"Family," I said. "They'll get you every time."

"Amen to that, brother. Anyway, old Hector decided that our offer of cutting his sentence if he helped us out was just too good for him to turn down. And he named you, along with several others."

"I see." I focused on my breathing and waited.

"Funny. We were just in the process of figuring out the best way to track you down when you fell into my lap this afternoon."

"So what do we do now?"

"Well, that's a bit of a problem. I know you've hated my guts for quite a while now."

"That's not true, Roger." I shook my head. "We just drifted apart when we left school."

"Bullshit," he said. "It started way before that."

"Maybe," I said. "But the main problem was that our fathers were sworn enemies. That made it hard on both of us."

"Whatever," he said. "What I'm trying to say is that we have history. And I know what you're going through with your dad right now. I understand it because I'm dealing with the same shit."

"And?"

"If you give me your solemn promise not to run, I'll talk to the Bureau about holding off on your indictment until after your father has…well, you know."

He sat back and studied me closely. I assumed he was watching for signs covered in his training that might indicate the onset of dangerous behavior. But all I did was sit there and sip my beer.

"Who else around here knows about this?"

"Just me and Grace," he said, making short work of his fresh beer.

"Shit, that's right. I forgot. Congratulations."

"How did you know about that?"

"I ran into her outside the hospital today. She's a good woman."

"We'll deal with her next," he said. "What do you say, Gene? Do I have your word, or do I have to arrest you right here on the spot?"

"Can you promise me that my father won't find out?"

He thought for a moment, perhaps considering his own father's peace of mind. As I waited I realized that his answer would have no impact on my immediate plans.

"Yes," he said. "I think I can do that, Gene."

"Okay, we got a deal."

For some reason, he felt compelled to shake hands and I reached across the table to finalize our bizarre version of cops and robbers. He sat back, smiled, and snapped his fingers at the waitress for another round.

"Gene," he said, turning chummy. "I need to know what happened between you and Grace in Vegas. I'm talking about what happened physically."

"Not a thing," I said. "I don't sleep with the FBI."

"I see. So what did she do to blow her cover? Talk too much? Maybe leave her badge lying around?"

"No." I smiled, finally able to have a little fun of my own. "You did it last Christmas when the four of us ran into each other at the bar. We were talking about Vegas and you said that I was going to love staying at Mandalay Bay. The only person who knew that was Grace."

"Uh-oh. She's gonna be pissed if she finds that out."

"She already knows." I handed the waitress a ten and waved off her half-hearted attempt at making change. "We talked about it this afternoon."

"Damn," he said, already a third of the way through the beer. "I've been on her case for months about screwing that up. She's gonna have a field day."

"Maybe you could make it up to her by giving her a plum assignment working undercover? I think she'd like that."

"That's a great idea." His eyes narrowed again. "You two never hooked up?"

"No, I was just trying to figure out why the FBI was taking such an interest in me," I said. "And now I know."

"Now you know," he said, lifting himself out of the booth with both hands. He stood at the edge of the table and looked down. "I'm serious about this, Gene. If you split, it will only make it a lot worse for you when I track you down."

"I know," I said. "Should I have my lawyer stay in touch with you?"

"That won't be necessary. I know where you're going to be."

"Okay. Thanks, Roger."

"Funny," he said. "First time a criminal has ever thanked me." He reached into his pocket and tossed a twenty on the table. "Have a few more on me," he said, staggering towards the door.

I did.

**

"Is something bothering you, son?"

I stopped packing my father's bag. "No, I'm fine, Dad. I just had a few too many Heinekens last night."

"Lucky you," he said, buttoning his shirt. "Let's get the hell out of this place. It gives me the creeps."

I nodded and resumed filling the small overnight bag. I snapped it shut and watched him struggle with the last two buttons. He took a final look in the mirror, pulled on his hat and announced he was ready. As soon as the clerk handed him a copy of his paperwork, he was headed towards the exit.

"That's better," he said, stepping outside to a warm, windy day. "That place is like a morgue."

"What do you want to do today?" I said, tossing his bag into the trunk.

"I think I'd like to just sit on the porch." Waving me away, he climbed into the car. "I've got a new book I'm only hallway through and I'd hate to leave not knowing who the killer is." He winked and pointed at the ignition. As I was pulled out of the parking lot, I saw Roger arrive. I waved casually and received a head nod in return.

"His old man is in there," my father said.

"Yeah, I heard."

"The booze finally got him," he said, staring straight ahead. "You have to wonder how he might have turned out if he'd made some different choices."

"Yeah," I said. That particular question had definitely been making the rounds of late.

"Dad, how did you prepare yourself when Mom got sick?"

He focused on the road ahead. "Pretty much the same way you're handling it, I guess. At first, I tried to overcompensate and constantly hover around her. And that drove her nuts. Eventually, we just added her sickness to our daily routine. It just became a part of us. What is it? Are you worried that you're not handling yourself properly? Or handling me?"

"I don't know." I said, holding onto the wheel with both hands.

"You're doing fine, Gene. Have you given any thought to what you're going to do?"

"I'm working on it," I said.

"Don't let my situation stop you."

"Okay, Dad," I said, pulling into the driveway.

We walked inside and heard the phone ringing. I answered on the fourth ring.

"Hello," I said.

"Hi."

Her voice was so clear she might have been in the next room.

"Hey, how are you?"

"I'm good."

"Is that Emily?" my father said.

I nodded as he walked past me on his way to the porch.

"I want to talk to her before you hang up."

I nodded and refocused on the phone.

"I've tried calling a few times but got voicemail. You been busy?"

"Yeah," she said. "I'm dealing with a lot of things. But I did do a night of babysitting."

"How was that?"

"It was great. She's such a beautiful baby."

"Maybe you'll have one of your own soon."

She fell silent and I waited for her to change subjects.

"How's your Dad?"

"He's going downhill pretty fast. I think he used up everything he had left during the trip."

"I'd like to talk to say hello when we're done. How are you doing?"

"I've been better."

"So what's going on?"

"Actually," I said, suddenly concerned about the possibility of wiretaps. "There's been a development."

She immediately recognized the code word that indicated all business conversations were to be avoided.

"I see," she said. "Well, I can't wait to hear all about it."

"I should know more in a couple of days, so I'll tell you all about it the next time I call."

"How's the weather?" she said.

I smiled when I heard the question, the one used to identify the seriousness of the development. I looked outside at the cloudless sky and the trees swaying in the wind.

"It's okay," I said. "But I think we're in for a big storm later."

"I'm sorry to hear that," she whispered.

"Where are you right now?"

"I'm sitting in that big leather chair in the living room."

I closed my eyes and remembered the view. "Help yourself to the wine. There should still be a couple of cases in the closet off the garage."

"I already found it."

"Let me go get my Dad," I said. "I'll call you soon."

"Good."

"I love you."

"I love you, too. Be careful."

"I'll try." I set the phone down on the counter and walked outside. I nodded at my father who slowly stood and shuffled inside. I sat down knowing that a big storm was definitely headed in my direction.

Chapter Forty Three

"It's nice to see you, Gene." The elderly man extended his hand. "I can't even remember the last time I saw you."

"Hello, George," I said, shaking the lawyer's hand. "It's been a long time. How are you?"

"I'm great. Just great," he said, sitting down behind his desk. "I'm so sorry to hear about your Dad. He was always one of my favorite clients. At least he was until he got out of the business."

"Thanks. You were good to him. Or so he tells me. But he has no idea I'm here and I'd appreciate it if he didn't find out."

"Of course." He turned serious and waited.

"I have a bit of a problem."

"Gene, I really didn't think this was a social call," he said, laughing at his own joke. "How can I help you?"

"I have a problem with the FBI. It's something from a long time ago, but it's resurfaced."

"I see." He removed a fresh yellow legal pad from a desk drawer. "Before we go any further, let's clear up one question."

"Okay," I said.

"Are you guilty?"

"Yes."

"Okay. Why don't you tell me all about it?"

I reviewed the details of my role in the selling of already sold condominiums in Florida. He listened closely and jotted notes on his pad. I finished hitting all the major points then fell silent.

"This wouldn't have anything to do with Hector Villanueva would it?"

"How the hell did you know that?" I said, completely caught off guard.

"Lucky guess," he said, shrugging his shoulders. "Plus the timing is so close to his recent arrest. Hector has been a bit of a folk hero around my profession for some time now."

"Hector? Really?"

"Sure," he said, laughing. "Anybody who pulls off a scam like that and continues to snub his nose at the Bureau from his beach house is someone a lot of lawyers admire."

"Unbelievable."

"I imagine Hector thought that eventually the Bureau would just forget all about him. But what he didn't know was that one of the silent partners in those condo complexes was a state Senator from Florida who was getting some nice kickbacks for some rather generous legislation he pushed through. Politicians usually don't mind people getting screwed. Just as long as it's not one of their own. So you worked with Hector. From what I've heard, he thought he was untouchable."

"La invulnerabilidad de la invencible," I said, studying the large fish mounted behind his desk.

"What's that?"

"The invulnerability of the invincible. It was Hector's motto," I said. "I always thought it was redundant, but he liked the way it sounded in Spanish. So what do you think?"

"Well, this could get tricky. The Bureau was pretty embarrassed by the whole thing and I imagine they'd like to make an example out of some people. Have you ever been arrested before?"

"No."

"Good. That'll help. Plus, it was a long time ago. Could you demonstrate that you've stayed clean since then?"

"With some help, maybe."

"I see," he said leaning back in his chair. "Why haven't they picked you up yet?"

"I made a deal with Roger Gentry to turn myself in after my father's funeral," I said, surprised by how well one sentence captured my current situation.

233

"Gentry," he said. "Amazing how so many pricks end up carrying badges."

"He's okay," I said. "He's just doing what they pay him for."

"Yeah, maybe. But there's no reason for him to enjoy it as much as he does. So Hector sold you out?"

"That's what they tell me," I said.

"Fortunately," he said, scribbling furiously. "I've done quite a bit of work in Florida and know my way around pretty well."

I watched as he jotted down several names on his pad. He put down his pen and checked his watch.

"Where do we go from here?"

"Well, I'll make a few calls and then we wait until they indict you. Then we'll plead not guilty and get you out on bail. I'll build the best case I can about how you were duped as a young man by Hector and that you really didn't understand what was going on until it was too late. From there, we'll try to establish the fact that this was a one time indiscretion on your part. If I need to, I'll threaten to call the Senator to the stand and embarrass him in court."

"How long would that take?"

"Probably six months to a year depending on how hard the Bureau pushes to get the case heard."

"Damn," I said, feeling my life picking up downhill speed. "And if they find me guilty?"

"I'm sure we can negotiate probation for a first timer."

"What's that involve?" I was bewildered by my own ignorance of the details associated with actually getting caught.

"Probation? Well, at first, you'd have to present yourself to the authorities on a weekly basis and keep answering the same questions until they're convinced you're behaving yourself. After a while, we should be able to get that reduced to once a month, or at least every other week. And since it's the FBI, you'd have to get used to being followed, having your bank records monitored, maybe even having your phone tapped."

"How long would I be on probation?"

"Depending on the actual charges, I'd say three, maybe four years."

"Four years? No fucking way."

"It's the FBI, Gene. Not the sort of people you want to be in bed with."

I formulated a joke, but kept it to myself.

"What if I just pleaded guilty?"

"Why on earth would you do that?"

"I guess it's because lately I've been forced to realize how short life is."

"Because of your father?"

"That. And other things as well. If you add the trial time to the probation I could be looking at five years of my life. That's just too much time."

"But you won't have to go to prison, Gene. You need to take that into serious consideration."

"How long would the sentence be?"

"Well, if you voluntarily turn yourself in and demonstrate genuine remorse and then get lucky enough to catch the right judge, a year, maybe two."

"I can be completely done with this in a year?"

"Perhaps. But it's still a year in prison. Federal prison. Is that what you really want to do?"

"I'm going to need some time to think this over."

I drove home baffled by the irony that the more time I spent pondering how to change my life into one with meaning and purpose, my list of problems requiring resolution kept growing.

Chapter Forty Four

"He's asleep. And he should be out for a few hours."

I closed my book and motioned for her to join me on the porch. I'd been waiting for a chance to talk to her alone when she was off duty and could relax.

"How about a glass of wine?"

"That sounds great, Gene. But just a small one, please." She sat, removed her shoes and wiggled her toes as she looked out at the ocean. "It's beautiful out here."

I headed inside to grab another glass. I returned, filled both and eased back into my chair. "I've been meaning to ask you something."

She glanced at me over the top of her wineglass. She took a sip and waited.

"How do you deal with death so easily?"

"What makes you think it's easy?" She smiled and patted my arm. "Good wine."

"You seem so natural around it. It's killing me."

"That's because he's your father."

"Even he's handling it better than I am."

"Yes, he's amazing. But then, he's had six months to get ready."

"I just wish he would have told me sooner."

"Why?"

I sat in silence searching for a good reason. "To better prepare I guess. And have more time to say goodbye."

"You never get more time, Gene. You just get to use the time available in different ways. And from what he's told me, you two had a wonderful trip."

"It was great," I said, fighting back against the knot in my chest.

"And besides, goodbyes can be overrated."

I stared at her, confused by the remark and the casual manner she'd delivered it.

"I see it all the time. Family members who rarely take the time to call come riding in at the end like the cavalry just to make themselves feel better. What really matters is what happens day to day, year after year." She finished her wine, set her glass on the arm of the Adirondack chair and stood. "The intensity of the pain one feels is directly correlated to the amount of love they've given. From what I've seen, I can only imagine how much pain you're in."

I blew my nose and cleared my throat. "Sorry."

"You've got nothing to apologize for. But in the morning, we'll need to talk about when to start him on the morphine."

"Already?"

"Yes. I'm afraid so."

"Okay. Thanks for everything, Alice."

She smiled and waved me off. "Don't mention it. It's what I do."

**

I heard the bell and headed from the kitchen to my father's bedroom. I smiled down at his gaunt face and he managed a weak one in return.

"Can I have some water? My guts are on fire."

He managed a few sips through a straw and began coughing. I held him upright and used several tissues to capture the copious phlegm tinged with blood. I gently returned him to his pillow.

"Thanks." He wiped the side of his mouth with a hand and stared up at me. "I can't take much more of this, Gene."

"I know, Dad." I grasped his hand. "Just hang in there."

The phone started ringing and he waved me away.

"Are you sure you're okay?"

"Yeah," he said. "Go answer it."

I returned to the kitchen and picked up the phone. "Hello."

"Hi. It's me."

"Damn. I'm sorry, Emily. I forgot to call."

"It's okay. How's he doing?"

"It's close," I said.

"That's so sad," she whispered. "How are you?"

"In some ways better. Others worse. I miss you."

"I miss you, too."

Our long silence was broken by the sound of the bell.

"I'm going to need to run . He's ringing his bell."

"He's got a bell? That's nice."

"You didn't really expect him to go quietly, did you?"

"No." Eight thousand miles away, she laughed. "Call me as soon as you can. There's something I need to discuss with you. Something I need to get clarified."

"Will do. Bye."

I headed to my father's bedroom and glanced at the clock. It was almost nine and starting to get dark. I remembered that I had promised to call my lawyer and now knew it would have to wait until tomorrow. I had also neglected to write checks for a variety of bills that were due. I'd spent the entire day sitting by my father's bed reading aloud the final chapters of the book he'd been trying to finish. When I reached the last page we'd both laughed hard at the realization, for the first time in either of our lives, that the butler had, in fact, done it.

"What can I get you, Dad?"

"Wheel me out to the porch."

I spied the wheelchair my father detested but had been recently forced to accept. I looked back at him and he nodded. I wheeled it bedside.

"What do you want to wear?"

"Anything but these goddamned pajamas."

I lifted him up and helped him slide to the side of the bed, his once muscular legs dangling off the edge.

238

"Jeans and a sweater," he said, deciding. "And my bushman's hat."

I pulled the items from his closet and helped him undress. After working thick socks onto his feet, I gently pulled a pair of loose-fitting jeans over his legs. After adding a shirt and sweater, I placed the hat on his head. Before he sat down in the wheelchair, he turned to the mirror and took one last look at himself.

"Ladies, eat your heart out," he said, adjusting the hat.

Resting one arm on his back for support, I helped him settle in, grabbed a blanket from the bed, and wheeled him slowly through the house. I lifted him effortlessly out of the wheelchair into his rocker and draped the blanket across his legs.

"Take that damn thing back inside would you, Gene?" he said, nodding at the wheelchair.

I did as I was asked then sat beside him and held his hand. The sun was sinking and an ominous set of dark clouds appeared on the horizon.

"What did I tell you?" he said, smiling.

It did appear that his storm was approaching. The wind picked up and I heard the rumble that followed an intense lightning flash.

"Look at that," he said, eyes wide open. "It's so beautiful."

I watched the storm race towards shore as darkness drew near. Newspapers and magazines whipped past us and off the porch. I felt the first drops of windblown rain. Through it all, my father laughed and his eyes grew wild. Momentarily, the wind dropped as the storm came closer to shore.

"I need to thank you, son." He squeezed my hand.

"What for?"

"For this." He coughed and wheezed but found the strength to talk. "How many people know when they're

239

going to die, and then get the chance to do exactly what they want on their way out?"

Unable to speak, I gently returned his squeeze.

"Promise me you'll try to figure out what makes you happy."

"I promise," I said, grateful for the raindrops splashing my face.

"I love you."

"I love you, too."

The storm hammered the house and we held hands in silence, protected from the intense wind and rain that enveloped the house.

"Mary," he whispered.

I watched my father's stare drift towards the ocean and fixate on a distant point.

"Yes, it's me, dear. I'm on my way." He smiled and closed his eyes. "Is that…a tiger?"

"Dad?"

"Murray…is that you?" He cocked his head slightly to one side. "Summerman? What are you...?" He giggled. "Yes, I get it. Wow. Yes, I'm ready."

A huge bolt of lightning cracked directly in front of the porch. My father gave my hand a hard squeeze then I felt his grip drift away. He nodded his head once before letting it drop.

And then he was gone.

Chapter Forty Five

"Great party, Gene." Alice leaned against the counter and watched the crowd begin to dwindle.

"It sounded a little strange when he first mentioned it, but I think it worked."

"It was a great way to say goodbye." She raised her glass in toast. "To your dad."

"To my dad." We touched glasses. "I didn't know he had so many friends."

I looked at the urn on the mantelpiece knowing I had only one more piece of business to take care of.

"Have you decided what you're going to do?"

"I'm leaving," I said.

"Really? When?"

"Probably sometime tomorrow."

"Where are you headed?"

"In all likelihood, Florida." I put my glass down and waved goodbye to another guest. "How would you and your kids like to housesit?"

"What?"

"Housesit. Here. I have no idea when I'll be back and I don't think I'm ready to sell it. And I sure don't want to leave it empty."

She laughed. "I'd love to, but I don't think I could swing the rent."

"I said housesit. Not rent." I caught her raised eyebrow. "Look, you'd actually be doing me a favor."

"Gene," she said, shaking her head. "That's strictly against the rules. You can't do that."

"I already talked with your boss and told her that you had no idea of what we wanted to do. It was one of my father's last wishes."

"Gene, I don't know what to say."

"Just tell me that you'll take good care of the place and think about us once in a while."

In the middle of her bear hug, Roger and Grace approached. I shook both their hands and introduced them to Alice.

"Sorry, Gene. He was a good guy."

"Thanks, Roger. I heard about your dad. I'm sorry for your loss." Somewhere I knew my father was taking great delight in outlasting his former nemesis.

"He was something else that's for sure."

"I'm so sorry, Gene. About all of it."

"Thanks, Grace. Did you have a good time tonight?"

"Strangely enough, yes."

"Are you going to be around later?" Roger said.

I glanced at the urn on the mantelpiece. "Yeah, I've got one thing to do, but I'll be here."

"Okay, I'll see you then." He walked away towing Grace by the elbow.

"Friend of yours?" Alice said.

"No."

**

Carrying the urn, I stepped onto the beach and felt the moist, cool sand on my bare feet. Apart from Roger waiting on the porch, the house was empty. It was a little after two in the morning, and the fatigue I'd been fighting for the past several days had finally taken hold.

I walked down the beach and found an isolated stretch away from the nearby houses. I sat down, placed the urn between my legs, and looked out to sea.

"Okay, Dad. I guess this is it," I said, looking down at the urn. "I hope it's nice wherever you are and that you're out of pain. Alice is going to housesit just like you wanted, and everybody had a great time at the party." I started convulsing with emotion and felt the breeze stiffen. Taking that as my cue, I stood and put my back against the wind.

"You take care of yourself. And be sure to tell Mom I love her."

I carefully removed the top and shook the urn into the air. I watched ashes rise like a cloud then dissipate and disappear. I waited until the last trace of ash had been swallowed then walked back towards the house.

At the base of the bluff leading up to the house, I looked up the hill and saw Roger still waiting. I waved to let him know I was on my way and carefully climbed the rocky trail.

"You all set?"

"I'm all yours."

"Okay," he said, walking next to me as we headed towards the house. "Gene?"

"Yeah."

"You never told me how your trip to Australia went."

"Australia? What makes you think I was in Australia?"

"C'mon Gene. Your dad couldn't stop talking about the place."

"Yeah, I know," I said, remembering my futile and short lived attempt to restrain him. "But that doesn't mean we were in Australia."

"The wine? The hat?"

"They were just gifts."

"Of course."

"Would it matter?" I said, stopping at the top of the porch steps.

"Nah." He shook his head. "Whatever it was you were up to down there is somebody else's problem. Our case on you is officially closed."

"Thanks for telling me that, Roger. I appreciate it."

"I don't enjoy this as much as everybody thinks I do, Gene. I'm not the bad guy here."

"Of course not," I said, smiling. "That's my role, remember?"

He forced a small laugh. "At least it's not life without parole."

"Let's hope not," I said, heading into the house. "When's the wedding?"

"Next month. I hope. She goes back and forth on it." He closed the door. "Got any good tips for the wedding night?"

I paused, then grinned. "Maybe for once in your life you should try something different."

"What do you suggest?"

"Try being the bad guy. I think you'd enjoy it."

Chapter Forty Six

"Your Honor, I would like to again stress that my client willingly turned himself in, has shown a great deal of remorse, and this is the first and only time he has ever gotten in trouble."

My lawyer sat back in his chair, pleased with his performance. I looked around the judge's chamber grateful that this negotiation was being handled in private. Given the ease at which the prosecution and judge had agreed to determine my sentence behind closed doors, I assumed this was a normal process and quite different from the public tumult of television dramas.

"Don't you mean this is the first time he's got caught?" The judge eyed me with a combination of contempt and suspicion.

"Your Honor, I must respectfully protest that assumption," my lawyer said. "There is absolutely no evidence to suggest even a hint of previous malfeasance."

"Cut the crap, Counselor." The judge leaned back in his chair and folded his hands behind his head. "You say he's been clean for the past five years, but I see no record of employment. Or anything else that might convince me he's been a productive member of society. Would you care to explain yourself, Mr. Wagner?"

"I've done a variety of things, Your Honor," I said. "I've worked many places for cash. I've spent time overseas. My background and lifestyle might seem unusual but there's nothing extraordinary about it. And I think the facts before you bear that out."

The judge grunted and flipped through a set of bank statements.

"Do you mind telling me how a man such as yourself acquires a quarter of a million dollars?"

I smiled and silently thanked my accountant. He'd been instrumental in setting up my various companies and was extremely skilled at hiding money. The fact that I only had to explain a quarter million was a blessing.

"Not at all, Your Honor," I said. "Most of that initially was a gift from my father. From there, I was able to save a little, invest a little. You know how that works."

Behind me, I heard the sound of someone shifting in their seat. I glanced back at Roger who was listening to my lies but stayed silent. He nodded his head slightly, flashed a weak smile, and went back to being all FBI.

"And do you think that your financial statements could withstand the scrutiny of an IRS audit?"

"Absolutely, Your Honor," I said, again silently thanking my accountant.

"I see," he said, rummaging through his papers. "So what does the prosecution have to say about all this?"

The lawyer representing the Bureau cleared his throat and opened a file that was resting on his lap.

"Not all that much really, Your Honor," he said. "As you know, our main target Hector Villaneuva is already in custody."

"Believe me," the judge said, dismissing the comment with a wave of his hand. "I've heard all I need to hear about Hector. And I would love to know who the genius was that gave that cocksucker immunity before I got a chance to have a little chat with him."

Chagrined, the FBI lawyer began fiddling with his own set of papers.

The judge turned back to me. "How on earth did you get mixed up with someone like him?"

"He fooled me, Your Honor," I said. "But then it seems like he fooled a lot of people."

"The little bastard," the judge said. "He sold a goddamn condo I already owned right out from under me."

The FBI lawyer bit his lip and stared up at the ceiling.

"I'm still dealing with the goddamn fallout. The other so-called *owner* is trying to take *me* to court. It really frosts my cupcakes . Where is that little prick, Hector, anyway?"

"He's in protective custody, Your Honor."

"Lucky for him."

"Be that as it may, Your Honor, the Bureau has completed a rather intense investigation of Mr. Wagner, and it is our conclusion that his role in the aforementioned matter was relatively minor."

"Okay." The judge leaned forward and looked at my attorney. "I've been informed that your client doesn't want probation included as part of his sentence."

"That's correct."

"I find that to be a rather strange request. Very strange."

"I'm a strange guy," I said.

"Yes, I'm sure you are Mr. Wagner."

"That was my decision, Your Honor," I said. "It's my understanding that the probationary period could last several years. I would prefer to spend a year in prison and be done with it rather than have this hanging over my head."

The judge stared at me through narrowed eyes. "What did you say?"

"I said I rather spend a year in prison and get it over with."

The judge shifted in his seat and focused on my lawyer. "Counselor?"

"With respect, sir, we're asking for a one year sentence."

"What? He sold my condo right out from under me and you think he's going to get a year?"

"Actually, Your Honor," my lawyer said, color draining from his face. "Technically, my client wasn't the person who sold your condo. That person was Mr. Villaneuva."

"I see. Well then, let me ask you a question. Is Mr. Villaneuva sitting here at the moment?"

"No, Your Honor.

"Then, technically, it appears to me that your client is in a bit of trouble." The judge glared at me. "But if you're that concerned about avoiding probation, I'm willing to consider that option."

My lawyer beamed and grabbed my forearm. "Thank you, Your Honor."

"Three years," the judge said.

"What?"

"Three years. No probation."

"But, Your Honor, the prosecution has already agreed to one year."

"I don't give a shit what they agreed to. Three years federal prison. I'm thinking Marianna. I hear the food is quite good." The judge smiled and began stacking his papers.

"Your Honor, really." My lawyer's face flushed with anger.

"Would you like to try for five, Counselor?"

"No, Your Honor."

"Okay, then. Three years it is." The judge stuffed the papers into a folder then pushed it aside. "Enjoy your stay with the state of Florida, Mr. Wagner. And when you're done, I sincerely hope you'll find one of the other remaining forty-nine more to your liking."

"Yes, sir." I felt my stomach churn.

Outside the judge's chambers, I shook hands with my lawyer.

"I'm so sorry, Gene. I had no idea that was going to go down that way."

"Yeah. Me neither." I watched him leave, final check in hand, with a small wave of his hand.

"Okay, Gene," Gentry said, approaching. "Put your hands in front of you."

"Jesus, Roger." I shook my head but complied. "Isn't it a little late in the game to be handcuffing me?"

"Better late than never," he said, snapping a pair of handcuffs onto my wrists.

I looked down and started laughing. "Where on earth-"

"I found them in the garage a couple of weeks ago and thought you'd get a kick out of it.

I stared down at the bright green plastic handcuffs he had once taken great pride using on me at least three times a week. "They still work," I said, testing their strength. "That's funny."

He reached down and removed them and placed his hand gently on my shoulder. I walked next to him as we both climbed into the front seat of his car.

"Three years," he said. "Tough break."

"Yeah."

I was shaken but did feel fortunate in some ways. I had been able to give the gift of Australia to my father and rekindle some friendships and passion at the same time. I had also been given, in some strange way, a new outlook on life. I still had no clue where life would lead, but I was slowly beginning to discover a few answers. Most importantly, I had received one very special gift. A gift from my father. And it was a gift without wrapping or colored bows, given through example, and accepted almost unconsciously. It was the gift of living each day as if it were your last, yet still managing to accept with grace and dignity when it was time to leave.

Chapter Forty Seven

I stared across the table at the man in the bright orange suit. It could have been any man, any suit, but unfortunately, for him, it just happened to be this man, that suit. His mood, after three and a half days, didn't match the color that covered him head to toe. For that to be case, he'd need to be clad in black. I watched him warily as he leaned forward and checked his hair in the reflection cast by a metal dinner plate. He brushed stray hairs from his face, thrust his chest, and cast a long look around the room silently announcing both his presence and demand for others to keep their distance.

"What are you looking at?"

The whispered toughness drifted across the table. Despite my fear, I smiled. "Nothing," I said, shaking my head. "You just remind me of someone I used to know."

"You ain't ever met anybody like me."

I felt a trace of sympathy for the man in the orange suit. But then I almost always feel somewhat sorry for men like him. But I guess that's just me, still searching for my good side.

He would soon change tables, unable to endure the perceived invasion of his space, yet unwilling to endure the consequences that an additional act of violence would bring. His sole concern was the food that had brought him to this table at this precise moment. I knew that not only did he believe this, he would tell me so. Somewhere in the middle of the bowl of weak broth that passed for soup, he would turn his head towards me and either extend a finger, or jab one into my chest. Through a dark whisper he would ask what I was doing sitting at his table, looking at him, fucking up his day. Unprompted, he would announce his genuine dislike of all things human, and threaten me with the ominous silence violent career criminals have truly mastered. He was dark and sullen, deeply disturbed, and extremely dangerous. And nothing offered or provided could dent the stark reality of this world weary young man. Beyond salvation, he sought neither companions nor friendship. And I knew his only chance at making a positive contribution in this life was as a cautionary tale to others who travelled the same solitary path but still prayed for an alternative route.

I glanced across the table and watched him devour his food, his back almost touching the wall behind him. I wondered what latest round of poor decision making had precipitated his return since misguided men, driven by violence and a misplaced sense of their own destiny, make bad decisions all the time. Perhaps he was back because only when surrounded by the ramifications of his chosen profession did he feel less vulnerable. Perhaps, when surrounded by others of his own ilk, he felt more protected. I looked around the room at the disparate collection of criminals, the vast majority ignoring all behavior except their own. Perhaps the others on display to the man in the orange suit didn't notice they were being watched. Or care. Or even think about it. Mirrors offer self-reflection only to those searching for it.

Perhaps.

These days, I didn't have a mirror. Or need one.

"What are you writing?" he said, eyes narrowed, knife and fork in hand. "Is it about me?"

"No. It's kinda like a poem," I said, the lie sliding effortlessly off my tongue.

"A poem," he said. "Shit. Another fucking fairy boy. Now you've gone and put me off my lunch." He climbed to his feet. "You stay away from me fairy boy or you and I are gonna have a problem."

I watched him stomp off carrying his lunch tray to a table in the far corner of the room. There was no need to make myself a mental note. He was already at the top of my list of people to stay away from.

The first two months here have been tolerable and highly educational. I guess it's sometimes easier to visualize your goals when you're forced to look at the other side of the coin. The prison falls somewhere between a maximum security facility used to house our most violent and the country club atmosphere provided to white collar criminals whose violence against society, although often extreme, usually sheds no blood.

I put down my pen and took a bite of my sandwich. Meatloaf. Nothing like my mother used to make, but good enough to jog the memory. I closed my journal and reread the letter I'd received from Emily that provided a detailed report of The Syndicate's progress. Her first step had been to write a check for thirty-eight million to Willie for the property. He's left Australia for good and she's heard he bought a villa and fallen in love with an Italian widow.

She has already started work on the Tea Tree business. I still don't know exactly understand how she managed to get it running so quickly, but she tells me that it will start producing income in a couple months. I'm thinking about trying to negotiate a contract with the company that operates this prison as well as thirty others across the country. Incarceration is a growth industry and I learned a long time ago that you never know when a good business opportunity might present itself. A few of the houses are under construction, and we'll be breaking ground on the resort and golf course early next year.

Emily is beginning to drop hints about wanting a family. Whether or not she is serious, it gives me something to think about other than four walls and thirty-four more months. And if we do take that giant leap, I know I'll spend a great deal of time thinking about the question of nature versus nurture. As a father, I know that I will do everything in my power to provide. I just hope I'll be able to do it well. And from the right side of the street. I also hope that whatever gene has been haunting my family skips a generation.

Yet I know myself all too well. And I'm sure I'll find myself encouraging my kids to develop the ability to poke a little fun and occasionally test the boundaries. Even now, after everything that's happened, I know I'll be gently nurturing that little bit of larrikin lurking in us all.

Chapter Forty Eight

"Ready?"

"Yeah. Let's get this over with. I can't believe we're not gonna keep it. I worked my ass off finding it and now have to give it back."

"Try to think big picture."

"I am thinking big picture. I'm thinking about everything we could do with two hundred million. It's depressing."

"Then stop thinking about it." Doc knocked on the door and waited.

"Who is it?"

"Room service."

"That was fast."

The door opened and the woman's anticipation turned into surprise. Doc pushed the door open and he and Merlin stepped inside the suite and closed the door behind them.

"Hello, Emily." Doc glanced around and nodded at Merlin. "Make sure she's alone."

"Doc?" The woman pulled her bathrobe tight. "What the hell are you two doing here?"

Doc stared at her and waited until Merlin returned.

"She's alone," Merlin said, sitting down on the couch.

Doc gestured at a nearby chair. "Have a seat, Emily."

"You mind telling me what this is all about?" She glanced back and forth between the two men, nervousness beginning to emerge.

"It's about two hundred million bucks," Merlin said. "I'm hungry. What did you order anyway?"

"Breakfast," she said, bewildered.

"Eggs?" Merlin said.

"Yeah."

"How did you order them?"

"Over easy."

"Forget it. If I want a good dose of salmonella, I'll kiss a chicken." Merlin picked up the room service menu. "You hungry, Doc?"

"Later." Doc waited until Merlin put the menu down and refocused. "We need to chat, Emily."

"Okay. But I really don't have anything to say."

"It's one thing to try and walk away with the money. We can both understand that." Doc glanced at Merlin who nodded in agreement. "But to do that to Gene is inexcusable."

"And what did I do to him?"

"Lie. Give him false hope," Doc said.

"Not to mention stealing his two hundred million."

She pushed her hair behind her ears and turned defiant. "It's our two hundred million. I didn't steal it. And why the hell would you care what I do?"

"Because we need his help," Doc said, "And we need him focused. And...what's the word I'm looking for, Merlin?"

"Unencumbered."

"Yes, that's it. Unencumbered."

She rubbed her forehead, deep in thought. "Okay, can we back up for just a second?"

"Sure. Go ahead." Doc leaned back and lit a cigarette.

"Who are you? When I met you guys in Australia you were looking to invest in some land."

"Like I'm dumb enough to put twenty million of my hard earned money into some land scam." Merlin chuckled as he headed for the minibar.

"You don't have twenty million, Merlin," Doc said.

"I did a couple of hours ago until you made me give it back." Merlin poured vodka and orange juice over ice and returned to the couch.

"You guys FBI? Or government spooks?"

"No, nothing like that. That's ancient history." Doc smiled at her. "Like I said, we need Gene's help and he won't be very useful if a bunch of disgruntled rich people are turning over rocks to track him down."

"How did you find me? I just got here."

"Merlin's very good at what he does."

"Thank you, Doc." Merlin sipped his drink. "I just needed to think like a criminal who was comfortable stealing a couple hundred million and fucking over her partner in the process."

"I'm not fucking him over. I love Gene."

Doc laughed and shook his head. "Wow. You're good." He looked at Merlin. "We could use someone with her skillset."

"Yeah. It's too bad she's completely untrustworthy," Merlin said, draining his drink. He got up to make another. "Want one?"

Doc shook his head. "Merlin started with a list of countries with no extradition to the States."

From the bar area, Merlin stirred his drink. "And when you look at that list of countries, there's only a couple we thought were good options for you. I crossed out all the shitholes in Africa and the Middle East as well as any place where the weather wasn't great. And then it hit me. Indonesia. More specifically; Bali. A great place to get some sun, hunker down, and get a little peace and quiet."

"You can buy a lot of peace and quiet with two hundred million," Doc said.

Merlin nodded. "Especially in a place as corrupt as Indonesia."

"Well, sure. That goes without saying. We knew you'd get yourself a new passport before you left Australia. And as soon as Merlin pieced together the money trail and the name on the account, it was easy."

"It was the proverbial piece of cake," Merlin said. "Hmmm. Cake. We gonna be much longer here, Doc? I'm starving."

"We won't be long." He lit a fresh cigarette. "Once you got here, all you'd need to do was lay low for a few years. Get yourself another new identity, maybe a new face, and you'd be good to go. And from what we've learned, you're very good at changing who you are." Doc glanced at Merlin. "I think I hit a nerve." He looked back at Emily who was chewing softly on her bottom lip. "I must congratulate you on the dating scam. Most impressive."

Merlin nodded. "I agree. It was beautiful."

"You're too kind," Emily said. "You two think you're pretty smart, don't you?"

"I'd have to lose forty IQ points to be considered smart," Merlin said.

"I don't like you."

"Get in line."

"Too bad that pig didn't do some real damage."

"She is feisty, Merlin. We gotta give her that."

"Yeah, she's a real pistol. Emily, I almost hate to ask, but I'm wondering about something."

"Good for you. What do you want to know?"

"Where was his dick when you first floated the idea about going forward with The Syndicate?"

"Fuck you," Emily whispered.

"I bet you were riding him like you were coming down the backstretch at the Derby."

"Stop."

"A breathless whisper, mid-stroke, about how wonderful it would be if only there was a way it could go on forever. By the time you were done, I bet you even had him convinced it was his idea."

Emily exhaled and searched both men's eyes. "What if I just give the money back?"

"Too late for that, sweetheart," Merlin said. "It's already gone. And by next week, all of it will be back in the investor's accounts along with a letter from Gene explaining that the project has been cancelled due to some unforeseen circumstances."

"It's all gone?"

Merlin smiled. "Well, I did you leave you a dollar."

"What?"

"Inside joke." Merlin turned to Doc. "How much longer are we going to be here? I'm starving."

"We won't be long. I just have one more question." He gave Emily a hard stare. "How could you do that to him?"

"Do what?"

"Write him that letter. Make all those promises to him. What on earth is the matter with you?"

"Letter? What letter? How do you know about the letter? Shit." Her façade finally burst and tears rolled down her cheeks. "It was my way of giving him hope…to help him get through the next three years."

"Only to crush him later on?" Doc said.

"Maybe. But he would have been out of prison by then. I thought it would be easier for him to deal with it at that point."

"Back in society with some of the richest people on the planet looking for their two hundred million? You're a real fucking saint," Merlin said.

"And who knows? Maybe we could have gotten back together…figured out a way to make it work."

"Jesus," Doc said. "You're relentless."

Emily's eyes flared. "He's the one who made me what I am."

"Wow. Now there's an interesting take." Doc crushed out his cigarette. "No, Emily. He's just the sucker who gave you the platform to hone your craft."

"Are you saying none of this is his fault?"

"He's spending three years in Federal prison. I think we're way past wondering about his innocence."

She crossed her legs revealing way too much thigh. Merlin shook his head and sipped his drink. Doc enjoyed the view and waited.

"You sure there's nothing I can do to convince you to leave me with a little bit of the money?"

"Sorry, Emily," Doc said. "We don't work that way. Besides, Merlin's asexual, and if I don't have to work for it, it's never memorable."

She snorted and tightened her robe. "Your loss. So what happens to me?"

"Fortunately for you, nothing," Doc said. "As long as you agree to stay away from Gene, our interest in what happens to you is over." Doc stood and looked at Merlin. "You ready?"

"Absolutely." Merlin finished his drink and got up off the couch. "Enjoy the rest of your stay in Bali."

Doc and Merlin headed towards the door.

"Wait, how am I supposed to pay my bill? I don't have any money."

"It's already taken care of."

"What am I supposed to do for spending money?"

Doc shrugged. "I'm sure you'll think of something."

Chapter Forty Nine

I stepped into the bright sunlight and shielded my eyes. My first visitors in two months and I was intrigued, especially since they had arrived unannounced. I recognized the two men sitting at a picnic table and gave them a tentative wave. I sat down across from them. They both looked tired yet very aware of their surroundings.

"You guys have a habit of visiting people in prison?"

"We're only here out of necessity," Doc said.

"Really? And what exactly makes it necessary?"

"We have a proposal for you," Merlin said.

"Actually it's the same proposal we made on the plane," Doc said.

"I'm going to need a little clarification here."

Doc smiled. "You're going to fit right in."

"I beg your pardon?"

"Nothing. Never mind. We're here to offer you a way out of here."

"Are you now? You're a regular patron saint."

"Yeah. Something like that."

"Well, all I know is in thirty-four months I walk out of this place a free man. Can you beat that?"

"Our plan is to get you out of here today."

I laughed and picked at a loose orange thread.

"You're not interested in getting out?"

"Gee, I don't know, Doc. This place has so much going for it."

"I'm sure the residents are delightful," Merlin said.

"Here's the thing. I've got something big lined up and I'm not about to do anything to screw it up."

"No, you don't," Doc said.

"Excuse me?"

"You don't have anything lined up. She's gone. And so is your two hundred million."

I felt my stomach roil and tried to catch my breath. "What are you talking about?"

"You know exactly what I'm talking about. It was an amazing scheme. And if she hadn't panicked and shown her true colors, perhaps it could have worked as a legitimate operation. But now, I guess we'll never know."

"Emily's gone?"

"She's in Bali. Merlin and I just spent a lovely morning with her a couple days ago."

"That reminds me. I knew there was something I forgot to tell you," Merlin said. "She landed in Johannesburg yesterday.

"That was quick."

"She is resourceful. I'll give her that."

I listened to their rapid fire patter and shook my head. "What are you talking about? I just got a letter from her. A very detailed letter about how things were going down there."

"Yeah, we know. And we should have intercepted that letter before it got to you." Doc glanced at Merlin. "Remind me to tell Samuels about that guy's screw up at Fed Ex."

Merlin nodded as he wiped his nose with a tissue.

"She told us she was trying to offer you a glimmer of hope while you were in here," Doc said.

"Yeah, she said she didn't want you to worry…or some fucking crap like that."

"I think she wanted to buy herself as much time as possible to slip away and disappear, but Merlin disagrees."

"My take is that she saw the two hundred million and just couldn't resist running the ultimate con on the guy who taught her everything she knew. Think of it as one part tribute; three parts fuck you, thanks for playing."

I ran my hands through my hair and tried to make sense of what they were telling me. "I gave her access to everything. The contracts, the bank accounts…shit."

261

"We know," Doc said. "Two hundred million. For someone like her, I'm sure the temptation was irresistible."

I sat at the picnic table in stunned silence.

"But enough about her," Doc said. "We're here to offer you a job."

"A job?"

"Actually, think of it more as a career move with some fantastic growth opportunities."

"That's good, Merlin," Doc said. "I like that description."

"Thanks."

"Doing what?"

"At first, you'll be doing exactly what I tell you to do. But you'll be doing things you're already good at."

"Exactly," Merlin said. "Like scamming people by pretending to be someone you're not."

"Sure. And end up right back in here."

"No. We're actually very good at what we do," Doc said. "And I think you'll find that our operation, our posse, is almost officially sanctioned by some very senior people."

"*Almost* officially sanctioned?"

"Long story. If you like, we can get out of here and discuss it in detail over dinner."

"Just like that?"

"Just like that, Gene. I have a copy of your pardon right here."

He tossed a document on the table. I stared down at it.

"At first, the judge had a few problems pardoning you. But he signed off after we chatted and I'd reminded him of a few of his own...what's the word I'm looking for, Merlin?"

"Indiscretions."

"Yes. Indiscretions. That's it.

"She took off with all my money?"

"Yeah," Doc said. "But that's ancient history."

"Emily wouldn't do that to me."

"Face it, Gene," Doc said. "You gave her the opportunity to do it because you stopped thinking."

"With his head anyway," Merlin said.

"Well sure, that goes without saying."

"How could she do that to me?"

"Funny question coming from you," Merlin said.

"I still don't think I like you."

"What can I say?"

"Get in line?" Doc said, laughing.

"You're a real hoot, Doc," Merlin said.

Trying to recover and find solid ground, I asked the nagging question. "But why do you want me?"

Doc lit a cigarette and blew smoke out the corner of his mouth. "For the time being, let's just say you have a certain skill set we're in need of and leave it at that."

"What will I be doing?"

"For starters, you'll be serving as Sir Bentley Carruthers' personal assistant."

"The sneaker guy?"

"That's the one."

"Why on earth would I do that?"

"Because that's what I'm telling you to do."

"You're not wasting any time," Merlin said.

Doc looked at Merlin. "I think it's important to set the proper tone right from the start, don't you?"

Merlin laughed. "You're a real piece of work."

"What happened to his previous assistant?"

"He took...what did he take, Merlin?"

"Early retirement."

"That's a good way to put it," Doc said. "Early retirement. I need to remember that one."

"So I'm just going to walk out of here and start working for this sneaker guy?"

"Basically. We'll coach you through the interview process. Merlin's already finished your resume. You have a most impressive background." Doc laughed.

Merlin chuckled. "Great references, too."

"Oh, by the way," Doc said. "Sorry to hear about your father. I really liked him."

"He was a good guy," Merlin said.

"Yeah, he was." I caught a whiff of boiled cabbage coming from the kitchen. "So, I'm really free to go?"

"Well, you can stay here for dinner if you like. But Merlin and I are gonna check out this restaurant we saw down the road on our way in."

"I'm thinking surf and turf myself," Merlin said. "And you must have a long list of things you've been missing."

"Actually, I do have a sudden craving for good meatloaf."

"Meatloaf. I knew it." Merlin rolled his eyes at Doc. "He's a total Philistine."

"Play nice, Merlin. Okay, let's get you checked out and get the hell out of here. This place gives me the creeps."

I stood and stared at my two new business partners. "This is too fucking weird."

Doc smiled. "You haven't seen anything yet. By the way, you're not afraid of ghosts, are you?"

www.ingramcontent.com/pod-product-compliance
Lightning Source LLC
Chambersburg PA
CBHW060309260626

47160CB00007B/2550

* 9 7 8 0 9 8 4 9 6 7 5 9 9 *